THE
FT. LARNED
INCIDENT

THE TAY-BODAL NOVELS BY MARDI OAKLEY MEDAWAR

DEATH AT RAINY MOUNTAIN
THE WITCH OF THE PALO DURO
MURDER AT MEDICINE LODGE
THE FT. LARNED INCIDENT

ST. MARTIN'S MINOTAUR
NEW YORK

THE
FT. LARNED INCIDENT

MARDI OAKLEY MEDAWAR
II

Design by Nancy Resnick

Library of Congress Cataloging-in-Publication Data

Medawar, Mardi Oakley.
    The Ft. Larned incident / Mardi Oakley Medawar.—1st ed.
    p. cm.
    ISBN 0-312-20878-2
    1. Indians of North America—Oklahoma—Fiction.   2. Kiowa
Indians—Fiction.   3. Oklahoma—Fiction.   4. Healers—Fiction.
I. Title: Ft. Larned incident.   II. Title.

PS3563.E234 F77 2000
813'.54—dc21   00–025612

First Edition: August 2000

10   9   8   7   6   5   4   3   2   1

FOR DONALD GURNOE

OK, partner, here's another one to
keep your lips moving while you wait out winter
up there on the Red Cliff Rez.

ACKNOWLEDGMENTS

My special thanks to Keith Kahla and Cherry Weiner. And, of course, for always and ever, Gus Palmer Jr.

AUTHOR'S NOTE

Although this is a work of fiction, the names of a majority of the characters are real, and this work is based on the actual lives of these very real men. I have done this intentionally. On too many occasions their names have been misused, their extraordinary lives distorted. I am only a storyteller. As such it is not my responsibility to right a plethora of wrongs. But during the course of telling a story, I can give my people back their heroes. I can restore to these heroes . . . their names.

The Plains [in 1868] were covered with vast herds of buffalo—the number has been estimated at 3,000,000 head—and with such means of subsistence as this everywhere at hand, the 6,000 hostiles were wholly unhampered by any problem of food supply. The savages were rich too according to Indian standards, many a lodge owning from twenty to a hundred ponies; and consciousness of wealth and power, aided by former temporizing, had made them not only confident but defiant.

—Gen. P. H. Sheridan,
Personal Memoirs

THE
FT. LARNED
INCIDENT

ONE

At first I thought I'd been startled from sleep by the sound of my own snore. Then I began to remember the dream I'd been having. I couldn't remember all of it, just snatches of screaming people, hundreds of lodges burning. These snatches were so frightening that I lay in my bed with one hand on my chest feeling the stuttering thump of my heart. It found an even brisker pace when my muddled gaze focused on what appeared to be an intruder. The morning light was weak, dawn smudging itself against the dusty panes of my only window. I continued to stare at the silent, watchful trespasser as the gray light filtering in gradually began to brighten the interior of my little one-room house. Finally I realized that I had been holding my breath on account of my own overalls, shirt, and hat sagging off the wall peg.

Oddly enough this was not a relief, for outside the cabin there wasn't the normal morning birdsong, no final chirp of crickets. The quiet of this new day was overwhelming. And the silence triggered a long-buried memory. In an attempt to shake all of this off, I climbed out of bed and, dressed only in my nightshirt, puttered barefoot to the high chest of drawers standing to the left of my bed. Then, like the beginning of every morning, there I was, staring into the framed mirror hanging just above the bureau. The bad dream, the too-quiet of the morning, still held me in an almost strangling grip. Staring at my weary reflection, I knew this was not going to be just one more ordinary day.

A very long time ago, a very dear mystic-type friend tried hard to convince me that I shouldn't be afraid of the nudges one might receive from the other realm. He said that what a person ought to do is follow the direction the spirits point in. Well, that was all fine and good for him. He fully embraced the spiritual. My instinctive reaction has always been to run in the opposite direction. But now I'm too old. With old legs there is no more running. Silently cursing my long dead friend, I called out, "My best friend! What is it you want?"

There was no answer from a disembodied voice, only silence and dust motes dancing inside the rays of feeble sunlight streaking through the window. After a minute or two of that, and to relieve my eyes of my own reflection while I awaited his revelation, I began to touch, then lift, each item neatly placed on the cabinet top. A wooden boar-bristle brush, a pair of tweezers, a glass bottle of witch hazel, a glass bottle of Jergen's lotion. I love the smell of this lotion. I wear it every day. But only on my face so that I can smell it better. Setting the bottle down, I hesitantly lifted my eyes again to the reflection in the mirror. I tried to smile at the ugly old man there and he—with his craggy features, sagging jowls, deeply seamed wrinkles, bulbous nose, and hooded eyes, all of this framed by wild almost white hair—tried to smile back. I thought with a huff that if my long dead friend had nothing better to do in the beyond than to pester me about my ugliness, then his spirit must be extremely bored. I was about to turn away when a mist began to form over the mirror. Now, that caught my complete attention, and I peered again at the glass. The mist was not like the kind that comes whenever cold air meets warm. This mist was more like smoke. It moved. It swirled. And in the center of this movement, a face formed. A face covering over what I could see of my own. Both hands gripping the cabinet top, I watched transfixed as, gradually, I began to recognize the young man in the mirror. And I was so very glad to see him. So glad that I was nearing crazy with happy, as my wife used to say. That young man's specter slowly dominated the glass. I knew that I, the old man that I am, still existed, but what I prayed, and mightily, was that the young man now gazing steadily back at me would stay for as long as possible. So I dared not move, was afraid to take so much as a deeply drawn breath, terrified that doing so would be enough to break our fragile connection.

I had never been one to stare so longingly at that young face. I'd felt back then that the nose was too stubby and the mouth, ever pressed in a thoughtful way, too grim. Then there were the unusually pronounced cheekbones, the deep pits, caused by smallpox, heavily littering the cheeks. Exactly how a young man like that ever attracted a beautiful

3

highborn woman' like Crying Wind I'll never understand. I asked her about it once, and she'd said, "Probably because I wasn't looking at your face."

That made me laugh. Although I never stood any taller than five feet eight inches, my body was trim and firm. Crying Wind used to say that mine was the prettiest body a man could ever have. Her body, however, was phenomenal. I have never forgotten the first time I ever saw her legs. They had been wonderfully exposed because her skirt was pulled between them, the hem of the skirt tucked into the belt around a narrow waist as she stood in the shallows of a creek filling water containers. There had been a lot of other women standing in that creek and hordes of little children playing along its banks. Behind me, life in the camp was in its usual bustle. But when my eyes fastened on her, my attention tunneled. Suddenly there was only person in my universe.

Crying Wind.

We married two weeks later. For both of us, it was a second marriage. It was also a woefully unbalanced marriage for Crying Wind was beautiful and of our highest class, a born-to Onde, and I was of our nation's middle class. Crying Wind also brought a son into our marriage. He was about four years old then, hardly able to talk without garbling every word. He was cute and at the time extremely likeable, so I adopted him, naming him after me, his new name being Tay-bodal's Favorite Son. An odd name, really, when one considers that, widower though I was, I had no other children from whom to single him out as being my favorite. Then there was the fact that from almost the instant of my

newly found paternity, I was continually at odds with him—
for Favorite Son, even though he weighed slightly less than
forty pounds, was a forty-pound mass of perpetual motion.

And temper.

Thankfully, he wasn't with us during our brief but daz-
zling honeymoon, but afterward he was with us for everything else, purposely putting himself between me and his
mother. Not knowing what to do with the boy, I sought
counsel from an ill-advised source. My friend and band
chief, White Bear. Now, the reason that asking his advice
was something of a blunder was because White Bear—
legend, leader, and Orator of the Plains—was also a prank-
ster of near mythical proportions. Of course I was well
aware of this. A person would have had to have spent his
entire life in an isolated cave not to have known it. But at
the time I was in such distress that I truly believed that
seeking help from a man who was himself a father at least
twelve times over was the appropriate thing to do.

Oh, he gave me advice, all right. He said that what I
ought to do was spank Favorite Son. Well, that went contrary to our custom. We didn't spank our children. When
they became hard to handle, we packed them off to aunties
or uncles who did the hard disciplining. This custom saved
harried parents from bouts of guilt as well any ill feelings
from their own offspring. Even so, White Bear assured me
that for adoptive fathers, customs were different.

No, they're not.

I found that out just after giving Favorite Son's round
bottom one measly swat. That daring act was quickly followed by Crying Wind chasing me through the camp,

hitting me on my head with a broom. I am told that White Bear laughed so long and so hard that he was weak for nearly two days.

I next turned to my best friend, Skywalker.

His name in Kiowa was Maman-ti. Meaning, He Walks In The Clouds . . . Skywalker. He was an Owl Doctor, a member of the society of prophets and seers, and he was the best of his kind. He was also a father. But even with all of these gifts, the best he could do was toss his hands in the air when it came to advising me about Favorite Son. But the thing I should have paid attention to was his saying, "As long as you are a slave to your lust for his mother, that boy will have power over you."

Two years of marriage should have dampened my lust for my own wife, but it didn't. Crying Wind was one of those freakish women who only became lovelier with the passing of time. And every time she took her dress off, I promptly fell to my knees in adoration. The upshot of all this lustful worship was that my son became worse, his unbridled anarchy controlling our lives. Finally in the early summer of 1868, the constant tensions in our home broke.

My life was beginning to fall apart just after our nation gathered at Medicine Lodge Creek, the same place we'd camped the previous summer. This time we were there for our Sun Dance. The summer before had been for the Medicine Lodge Treaty—a treaty that wasn't working. The United States government blamed us, saying that Bad Boy Kiowas were tearing the treaty up. We Bad Boy Kiowas blamed J. H. Leavenworth.

Following the treaty signing, we had been told to go to

Fort Cobb because the country around the fort would be our reserved land. But when all of our bands reached the fort, the band chiefs were told that Leavenworth had decided to move the agency to the Eureka Valley. We'd also been promised in the treaty that we would be within riding range of our allies, the Comanche and Cheyenne. What happened was, the Cheyenne and Comanche were sent up north, and Leavenworth chose a valley for us that was over three hundred miles to the south.

Col. Jesse Henry Leavenworth was a lot of things, but organized wasn't one of them. On account of the distance between our agency and the fort—and Jesse Henry's inept organizational skills—we Kiowa spent the winter season of 1867–68 huddled around waiting for the goods and foods promised to us for giving up our rightful homelands. After a few months everyone had run out of coffee and sugar—items we Kiowa had become addicted to. Not having these promised staples made everyone mad. Leavenworth begged for us to be a bit more patient. We tried.

Into this valley of frustration came a wily old Caddo known as Caddo George Washington, a notorious trafficker of whiskey. He also sold guns. As we had a surplus of tanned hides from the previous summer hunts, young men were able to buy both whiskey and guns. Pretty soon, both by day and at night, young men were staggering around drunk and shooting at the sky. Leavenworth's answer to this noisome problem was to lecture the chiefly councils, expounding his "Great Vision." He'd barely finished drying the tears streaking his face and putting away the white wiping cloth inside his long coat pocket when he went on to say—and without qualm or emotional quiver—that any

7

Kiowas who did not share in his dream would be punished.

White Bear, along with his equally notable nephew, The Cheyenne Robber, took exception. Then they took all of the horses in the agency corral. Leavenworth, of course, demanded the return of the horses. White Bear refused, saying that he would no longer try to hold (restrain) his "Bad Boy Kiowas." Enraged, Colonel Leavenworth sent for the army from Fort Cobb. It took over two weeks for the soldiers to arrive, and by the time they finally did, Leavenworth had changed his mind, ordering the soldiers to "leave his red children" alone. Well, that made the captain of those blue jackets pretty mad because just to get to the agency had meant a long wintery slog from Fort Cobb. Having arrived in "fighting kit," the soldiers were quite ready and willing to give chase to the horse thieves. As for our side, a mass of hot-tempered Kiowa warriors were wanting to be chased, rattling their war shields and sounding their hollers, trying their best to goad the soldiers to come out and fight. But because one man had been unable to stick with any one decision, all that happened was the absurdity of soldiers and Indians just sort of milling around.

Not long after that, White Bear decided to take himself off to Fort Dodge and make a formal complaint against Colonel Leavenworth. I decided I would go with him. Mainly because I needed to get away from my wife. We were bickering almost constantly, and the tension within our home was steadily rising. I thought that if I just went away for a little while, my wife would simmer down. Now, basically I'm an incurable homebody. Especially during the cold season. But that particular cold season I was desperate, so I layered myself with my warmest clothing, which included a fine fur hat my wife had made for me, and chose my sturdiest horse: a short-limbed, round-bodied little brute that looked more like a goat than a horse but never seemed bothered by cold and was so surefooted that it could almost walk straight up a tree. There were eight of us making the journey: White Bear, The Cheyenne Robber, Skywalker, Hears The Wolf, Raven's Wing, Big Tree, and Returned To Us—or Returned, as we simply called him—and me.

We were not well received at Fort Dodge, and were it not for the kindness of the fort's sutler, we would have been left to sleep out in the cold and beg scraps from the kitchens. The sutler sheltered us in a room in his big store and gave us food as well as pot after pot of hot coffee. The sutler was named Tappan, and by his generosity he proved to White Bear that he truly loved Indian people. Secure in this man's protection, we waited three days for the fort's commander to consent to speak with us. Once we were finally granted an audience, we suffered that man's air of total indifference as White Bear formally requested Leavenworth's dismissal and that Mr. John Tappan be made our new agent. Through his interpreter the commander officially said that while he regretted our troubles, Father Washington only wanted Leavenworth. But that wasn't what the commander had said at all.

We knew on account of Returned.

That young man was our secret weapon. Being only half Kiowa, he'd spent a great deal of his young life among the whites, and he knew their talk just as well as they did. It was cold in that hallway just outside the commander's office, and Returned's words floated out like frosty clouds as we were treated to what the commander had actually said:

"I'm not in the habit, nor do I intend taking it up, of accepting orders from a trounced old Indian. Tell him anything you want, just as long as whatever it is effectively sends him back to the dung pile from whence he came."

White Bear stood silently, his face completely leached of blood. Then he turned, and with head high, shoulders squared and in measured strides, he walked the length of that long murky corridor.

We were only a few miles out of Fort Dodge when the slate-gray skies suddenly opened, and we found ourselves caught in the frigid heart of an ice storm. Within minutes the sleet had turned into long, thin icicles that hung from our protective clothing, and we held knifes in frozen hands as we cut saplings and hurriedly fashioned a shelter. It wasn't big, and once we were inside it was certainly crowded, but it kept the worst of the weather off us and allowed a warming fire. Considering the scant availability of burnable fuel, we were lucky to even have a fire, and to keep it going we spent the remainder of that awful afternoon trying to protect the meager flames from the howling winds. We had some of the poor provisions we'd brought with us, but thanks to Mr. John Tappan, we also had a little bit of coffee, sugar, and bacon. In these coarse conditions we boiled up coffee in the pot White Bear always carried with him, and we fried up the bacon by skewering pieces onto sticks and holding the sticks over the flames. Because of the dripping bacon, it got very smoky in that pitiful shelter, but we didn't care. We were all together, we were safe, and we were reasonably warm. On the trail, that was as good as it ever got. Warriors were used to such deprivations.

Personally, I couldn't stand it.

The storm raged all night long. Somehow we managed fitful sleep, waking late the next morning to find the earth icebound. We shook out our robes, relieved our bladders, and made a breakfast of dried meat. We had no more coffee, and from the look of things, having it would not have done us any good for there wasn't a hope of finding so much as a dried twig for another fire. Wordlessly, we plodded through the slippery ice and mounds of snow to retrieve our horses.

My little gelding's thick coat was encrusted in ice, but its eyes were alert. None of the horses cared very much for our beating the ice off their backs, then burdening them with saddles. I passed around a clay jar containing tallow. After we protected our faces with a good smear, we quietly set to work applying it to our horses' legs. After that, each of us lost to our own private concerns, we were somberly homeward bound, riding in single file. I was the last in that line. About midmorning, with the sun a blur behind oppressive clouds, all of us were bunched down in our robes, chins near chests, hats pulled low on foreheads. I was so cold that there was a danger I would fall asleep. Fighting a doze about to overtake me, my head jerked up. And that's when I saw it. Or rather, them.

The trees.

The small forest we inched through was so loaded with sparkling ice that the older leafless trees had lost innumerable limbs. But the little scrub pines, unable to stand against the sheer weight of the ice, were bowed like penitent servants before the passing of the sluggish parade of horsed men. I reigned up, and my breath fogging the crisp air blurred the image of the others continuing forward. The silence of that frozen place was absolute. Until that moment I'd never been one for premonitions. Personal premonitions, I mean. I have to say that it was a highly unpleasant experience, for I knew in that moment that something evil lurked.

Because denial is a strong protective instinct, I flung myself headlong into banishing the notion, talking myself right out of my first genuine forewarning. And that made me thoroughly unprepared for the events that were to come.

Colonel Leavenworth remained our agent, and the young men of our Nation were still spending the winter drinking all the whiskey Caddo George could supply and pestering the peaceful Chickasaws, Caddoes, and Wichitas who all lived on farms over there in Cottonwood Grove. The Cheyenne Robber was the worst of these offenders, but the agents for the peaceful Indians could never prove to Leavenworth's satisfaction that The Cheyenne Robber was the culprit. Besides, by now the man was mortally terrified of his "red children." I wasn't an innocent during all of this whiskey drinking. Crying Wind and I were fighting even more, mainly because of He Goes Into Battle First, our son's paternal uncle. That man was determined to have our boy, getting his hands on our son whenever the opportunity presented itself, filling his now six-year-old mind with wonderful stories about his dead father. I wanted all of this stopped, mainly because it had me competing against a dead hero. Crying Wind shouted that she was doing her best, and I would let loose that she wasn't even trying. Life was getting nastier by the day, and we finally stopped speaking altogether. That's when I decided that if all the other men could amuse themselves with the crazy water, I'd have a go at it, too. I gathered up a few things to barter, went to Caddo George's camp, and traded for a single bottle of whiskey.

Foolishly I took it home to enjoy. No sooner had I entered our lodge than Crying Wind diverted my attention and got her hands on the bottle. The next thing I knew, she was standing outside with the bottle cork in her mouth, pouring the whiskey out onto the ground. All Indian people are stubborn, but I seem to be stubborn all the way to my toes. So while Crying Wind was busy pouring out the first bottle, I was busy gathering up a few more things to barter, and off I went again, back to Caddo George. Well, he wasn't all that interested in the new items I had to offer, but he did like my determination to become a drunk. Clutching a new bottle in both hands, I went home again. Crying Wind knew that it was impossible to fool me twice, so this time she didn't bother trying. Just as I was ducking inside our door, she hit me on my head with a little iron pan. My head was swimming with stars while she poured out the second bottle, but my hearing was clear enough to hear her say, "I can keep this up as long as you can."

According to the terms of the Medicine Lodge Treaty, Leavenworth's time to make good on the promised annuities was fast running out. Yet even this failed to spur the man into haste. Which is why White Bear abducted Jesse Henry, hauled him out onto the prairie. Finding a good-sized tree, he strung him up and told the dithering agent that if he refused to make one final promise—to leave the agency just as quickly as he could—then he could count on dying. Funnily enough, the man did not dawdle. The last sight we had of him were quick glimpses of the iron shoes on the bottom of his horse's feet.

And so it was that Mr. S. T. Walkley, the agency assistant, and in a somewhat confused condition, found himself to be our new agent. Not wanting the job, he quickly suggested we go to Ft. Larned for our annuities. That plan suiting us just fine, family bands began packing up, heading first for Medicine Lodge Creek.

The Sun Dance was our highest religious celebration. It was always held in the month of June and lasted about two weeks. It was also my busiest time, for I was steadily gaining a reputation for being a very good doctor, and with the Nation gathered in one place, hordes of patients sought me out. During my early adolescence, my father realized just how inept I was with weaponry—the term *fearless* would never be applied to me—so he made certain that his only son was a very good runner. And I was. My ability to run long distances and at great speed was the primary reason I remained trim all of my life. However, when the time came for my induction into the warrior class, my runner's ability failed to impress anyone. That was why I became a doctor.

But my calling could at times be a bit irritating, especially when there were as many as thirty people waiting directly outside my little doctoring lodge, and I needed to be with my family, the three of us preparing for a special event. Namely, our son's induction into the Rabbit Society. I worked as quickly as I could, and after the last patient was seen, I raced home, only to be met by a weepy Crying Wind.

"Our son"—she hesitated, took a deep breath, expelled it slowly—"has gone . . . to his uncle."

I tried hard not to panic. The boy had many "uncles."

But there was one uncle that my wife and I had especially chosen to sponsor Favorite Son's induction into the Rabbit Society. I prayed he was the uncle she meant. I stopped praying when she averted her eyes.

"He has gone to . . . He Goes."

TWO

Skywalker and I only last year had pledged to act as our sons' sponsors. To seal the pact, a feast had been given and gifts exchanged. Both families had been happy. All of that was gone now, destroyed by He Goes. I was so livid that I stormed past my wife, going straight for the storage box that contained the three blankets, the two tanned deer hides, and a pair of long silver earrings. I shoved all it into a bag and left Crying Wind weeping into her hands.

Skywalker's camp was set up about five miles from ours. I chose to ride there on my worst horse, an old swayback that really should have been put down. I hadn't done it because children loved to play with this mild-mannered creature, and it didn't seem to mind. Today, riding the dilapidated nag fit the occasion. My arrival at Skywalker's camp engendered none of the usual greetings. As gossip is the fastest wind that sweeps the prairie, I knew that everyone glancing at me, then looking quickly away knew the thing my son had done. Because of Favorite Son, one of the most powerful men of our Nation had been grievously insulted. Everything good about my life had been given to me on account of Skywalker. And what he had given, he had the power to take away. My heartbeat was as rampant as the jogging gait of that old horse taking me toward the group of men standing just outside Skywalker's lodge. At first I didn't see my friend, who was somewhere in the middle of this group. What I did see were the many pairs of openly hostile eyes watching my ungainly approach. The most hateful gaze came to me from Skywalker's adopted younger brother, The Cheyenne Robber. This young man, the most splendid of our nation was not only unusually tall, he was unnaturally handsome. He was, more importantly, the blood nephew of White Bear. His gaze locked on me, he stepped away from the group. That baleful gaze did not waver during his advance. If anything, it became more intense as his upper lip curled back in a half snarl, and the muscles along his jawline bunched. The man looked exactly like what he was: fury on two long legs. He reached me just as I was reigning up the old horse. His hand quickly grabbed hold of the bridle.

"You are in so much trouble," he said, his voice husky. He began listing those troubles, summing them up as the natural product of my being such a terrible father. Then he launched himself on the subject of my son. According to him, Favorite Son was ruined beyond hope. Amazingly enough, his saying this sparked something deep inside of me—a something I found profoundly irritating. The burning need to defend my errant child, which my own astonished ears heard me do as I clambered down from the middle of my poor old animal's ailing spine.

"You know as well as I that this is not the boy's doing. The blame belongs to He Goes."

The Cheyenne Robber may have been the most magnificent human ever to walk the face of the earth, but he suffered the witless' curse—snappy retorts were simply beyond him. So he just went on burning with anger while I unloosened the cord holding the bag to the saddle and walked away from him. As I rapidly closed the distance between me and the waiting assembly, a rail-thin man stepped out of its center. He was dressed in a pair of leggings and matching shoes. His narrow chest was bare, and his untied hair was being lightly tossed behind his shoulders by a playful breeze.

He was my dearest friend. He was Skywalker.

All at once I was so filled with sorrow for my loss of him that my grief became lodged in my throat. I was choking on it as the two of us stared at one another across the small divide. Then, without yielding his gaze, Skywalker opened his arms. I have no idea how I got to him—if I walked, ran or flew. All I know is that in the next instant I was hugging him hard and weeping against his neck as he embraced me, made tiny shushing sounds, and said, "It's all right. I know. I know." When gradually I was just a bit more collected, he, with one long arm still around me, turned to face the others.

"Tay-bodal, I am pleased you have arrived in such a timely fashion. I've sent the mother of my son, Tehan, to bring him out."

Astonished, my mouth fell open.

Skywalker chose not to notice. Instead, he continued to speak in a voice loud enough for everyone to hear. "He is a somewhat lively boy, but I trust you to instruct him in the way of our fathers and prepare his first step on the Man Road. Your acceptance of this responsibility proves you are my good friend. My good brother."

Still too flabbergasted to speak, I was a stone mute when Skywalker hugged me again.

The bag I had carried into his camp had been light. It was heavy carrying it out because Skywalker had stuffed it with even more gifts, the most costly of which was a brand new gun. And somehow the old swayback had vanished; in it's place was a three-year-old brown mare. As I rode for home, Tehan, on his own little spotted pony, rode beside me.

As his name implies, the boy was not a blood Kiowa, for Tehan means *Texan*, Texas being the place Skywalker had found him as a baby. In other words, Skywalker's son was white, with fire-red hair, grass-green eyes, and dark-brown spots dotting his cheeks and pug nose. Being six, his two top teeth were missing, and he liked to run his little pink tongue through the gap like a snake tasting the air for the scent of prey. I found this rapid tongue sticking to be a tad annoying, but he was a child, and children relish any opportunity to annoy an adult.

Living with us in our lodge, Tehan was attentive to the stories I taught him and excessively polite to Crying Wind. Then again, my wife was so happy that the child was in our home, and despite our son's misbehavior we weren't in total disgrace, that had Tehan been the worst child ever born, she would not have complained. Neither of us mentioned the fact that Favorite Son was living with He Goes and would remain there until after the Sun Dance. In fact, we shared no conversations at all. When we went to bed at night, were it not for the vague outline of her body beneath the blankets, I would have sworn I was sleeping alone.

Came the day the candidates for the Rabbit Society were to be brought forward by their sponsors, Tehan was dressed in his finest clothing and wearing the brand-new bead-decorated shoes that Crying Wind had made for him. Placing his little sun-browned hand in mine, we took our place among the other sponsors and candidates forming a human circle.

In the center of this circle stood Owl Man, the leader of the Owl Doctors. Behind the circle the relatives and friends of the young candidates proudly watched. Directly to the left stood the drum; around it, six singers. Tehan's little hand gripped mine more firmly as the slow pulse of the drumming and the singers' voices lifted, calling down the attention of the Grandmothers to witness the babies about to step into boyhood. I lightly swung Tehan's little hand as we of the circle did a little sideways dance, carrying on the pattern of the circle until we were all back where we began. With four loud beats of the drum, the singers finished. Behind us the people lifted their voices in *kaws* and *yips*.

Then everything became quiet. From across the circle, He Goes deliberately avoided looking in my direction, and I just as deliberately did the same. But my son's gaze was so steady that despite my best attempts, I couldn't stop my eyes crawling to the corners. He wasn't looking at me; he was staring at Tehan with a hurt expression. I know this will sound foolish, but I felt vindicated. I also felt an enormous pride that everyone could clearly see that I was the sponsor of Skywalker's only son. Bolstered by this pride, I refused to allow my eyes to slide in Favorite Son's direction again as we all listened to the things Owl Man had to say.

The leader of the Owl Doctors was an ancient, and at some point during his exceptionally long life he had gleaned the knowledge of how to hold fast the attention of little boys—a thing that, even during the most sacred of circumstances, is about as long-suffering as a gnat's. Thanks in total to Owl Man's supreme wisdom, the ceremony of induction was over before any of the little candidates could scarcely begin a good fidget, and the singers began the Rabbit Song. We sponsors dutifully stepped back, getting out of the way as the newly initiated Rabbits proceeded to demonstrate their very own society dance, which consisted of a lot of head bobbing, hopping, and shrill-toned yipping. Those little boys, every one of them serious to the core while doing their less-than-rhythmic hopping, were just so adorable. As I looked back over my shoulder and scanned the sea of adult faces behind me, I saw those faces beaming with joy, for a new generation was coming up. Soon these little boys would be men. Today's induction was their first step in preparing them to take our places. This was the way of the Creator. This was His perfect circle. And because of Skywalker's generosity, I had a place in it.

I was grinning like a fool as I looked back at the others. Then I saw Crying Wind. Simultaneously the smiles on our faces collapsed. We stared at each other for a space of seconds; then she turned her face away. My throat closed, becoming so tight that a drawn breath could barely squeak down into my lungs. I went back to watching Tehan and the Rabbit Society dance, a thing for me now that just went on and on without mercy. When the song finally ended, I realized that Tehan had managed to hop his little self directly in front of me. So it was Skywalker's son that I welcomed into my arms, Skywalker's son that I hoisted up. While holding him, turning to show him off to the cheering crowd, I saw my wife's lovely face contort with sorrow, saw the trembling hand she placed just over her mouth. Then as the crowd surged, I lost her.

Following the ceremony, the families of the inductees held separate feasts. As Tehan's sponsor, I was taken off to attend the feast being given by Skywalker. Before any eating began, he had me sit in the place of honor, and then he made a lengthy speech about what a grand fellow I was.

I didn't feel very grand.

Divorce in our culture was an entirely unspoken event. It was deemed much too personal, too private, to discuss. Especially during a celebration. I wasn't actually divorced, and everyone around me knew that, but they and I knew that I was dangerously close to being so. Determined to maintain a brave face, I laughed, ate, made jokes, and ate more. In fact, I ate too much, intentionally making a perfect pig of myself because would a man about to loose his wife, his family, have such a hearty appetite? No, he would not. So I choked down food, only to feel it sit inside my hollow body like a festering lump. I managed to hold it down until I had ridden at least a half mile from Skywalker's camp; then that lump started kicking up rough, and I had barely dismounted when I was spewing the contents of my sickened belly all over innocent grass.

When I arrived home, I was pretty mad at Crying Wind, thinking that she and that son of hers had managed to ruin what should have been a very special time in all of our lives. I also thought it was time she understood that I was tired of always feeling unwelcome in my own home. Tired of her placing Favorite Son's feelings above mine. Pouting up a fury, I decided she should be the one to decide about our marriage, and whatever she decided would be just fine with me. So on that huffy note, I went directly to my little doctoring lodge.

Even though the festivities of the Sun Dance were taking place all around me, and I certainly wasn't sleepy by any means, I kept to my lodge. I wasn't up to being with people, and I now had a real dread of being offered more food.

Following a completely sleepless night, my right eye was peeking out the side seams of the lodge, spying on my home. Amazingly, all of the judgments I'd laid out in my mind during the night were melting with the sunrise. Perhaps I'd been overly hasty. It didn't seem fair now that I'd put all of the decisions about our future onto her. But I had, and now there was nothing for it but to wait.

The wait was excruciating. To make the time pass, I worked out in my mind just how loving, how gentle, I'd be with her when she came looking for me. I'd say something like, "I only stayed away because I didn't want to wake you on account of I knew how hard you had to work to make everything just right for our son." Then she would say, "Oh, you are too kind to me, Tay-bodal. I truly don't deserve you." And I would say, "My darling, you deserve all the good things I am able to give. So now let us forever put away the past."

23

Ooh, that sounded good.

Even more anxious now, I pressed my one eye right up against the wall seam, not minding at all that the rough stitching abraded my face. Or my eyeball. Everything hinged on what my wife did. If she came out with a bowl of food, brought it to my lonely little lodge, we were still married. Probably still fighting but married. I was reasonably sure that I could live with the fighting. I was just a little shaky on how I would do with being divorced. My heart stopped when I saw her come out.

There was nothing in her hands.

I couldn't breathe, and my heart steadfastly refused to beat the whole time she simply stood there staring at my little lodge, seemingly struggling to make up her mind. Then, wiping at her face with the flat of her hand, she walked off. Away from me.

We were divorced.

In the days that followed, Crying Wind seemed to be carrying off our separation rather admirably, whereas I was living with a continuously clenched stomach and skulking around hoping for, yet dreading, any little glimpse of her. The nights were the worst. I stayed awake as long as I could throughout the on-going celebration mainly because my doctoring lodge was cramped and untidy. I was quickly learning that I hated sleeping alone. Then, too, I didn't have Crying Wind's knack at making a lodge snug and cozy. So while I tossed and turned, I suffered drafts and the scampering noises of tiny feet as little creatures freely roamed the interior of my hovel. The one bright spot in our divorce was it had taken place during the Sun Dance—a time when everyone is required to be warmhearted and generous. So women did, albeit with bit of scorn glinting from their eyes, make certain that I was at least fed.

The day after the ceremony there was the subsequent breaking up of the bands. Which meant that now I had to make a decision. I could either beg White Bear to allow me to remain with the Rattle Band, or I could go back living as I had before: on the fringes of other camps. As I packed up my things and wrestled to take down my small lodge, White Bear took my personal matters into his own hands.

He was a wall of a man, tall, wide, and entirely solid. When he walked, his great strides eating up any distance between himself and his goal, he habitually led with a stubborn chin. This was exactly how he came bearing down on me. Then there he was, standing so close that I was melting from the sheer heat of his enormous body while he yelled at me at the top of his voice.

"I've heard all about the ridiculous thing going on between you and my sister-cousin. And I'm here to tell you right now that I'm not going to put up with it. If either one of you has it in your mind that all I have to do with my life is worry about scraping up husbands for her, then the two of you had better think again." He flung his huge arms around dangerously. "If you want to live apart while you're having your little huff, that's fine. I've always said it isn't healthy for a man to spend all of his days and nights with the same woman." A pointy finger hurtfully jabbed my chest as he lowered his voice, his tone oozing menace. "But what you will not do is go off and leave my band. Do you understand me, Tay-bodal?"

"Y-yes," I faltered.

Breathing hard through flaring nostrils and staring at me with barely controlled hostility, he grunted, "Good. We are going up to that Pawnee fort"—by which he meant Ft. Larned—"and during our travel, you will not linger because if I have to go looking for you, you won't like what happens when I catch you. Have I made myself completely clear?"

Images of dismemberment flashed behind my eyes. "I think so."

Satisfied that his point had been taken, White Bear strode off. As I watched him go, my relief that he still considered me to be a member of his extended family, bordered on ecstatic.

The vast majority of the Nation scattered. It was only three bands of us who made the journey to Ft. Larned. I have always been amused by the popular notion that all Blue Jackets rode around on fast horses. A lot of them did, but only those belonging to the calvary. Other soldiers, like the ones at Ft. Larned, marched everywhere, tagging after one or two officers who were riding horses. The soldiers we saw as we made our way into their area had heavy-looking packs on their backs and carried rifles close against their chests. Riding my favorite horse, I kept to the rear of the bands guiding the horse pulling my small travois and bringing along my small herd. As I watched the distant Blue Jacket soldiers dogtrot behind their leader, I remembered what little I knew of the ordinary soldier's life: the too many rules, the bad food, the crowded sleeping quarters, the sameness of clothing. I was wondering how anyone could possibly stand all of that when I was snatched back into the moment by three warriors riding fast and directly toward me.

The three were Dangerous Eagle, Lame Crow, and Big Tree. When they drew up beside me, each looked sweaty and vexed. Big Tree did all of the talking, gesticulating wildly as he spoke.

"White Bear is so mad at you. He says you are trying his patience. He sent us to help you keep up."

I was opening my mouth to say that I was keeping up as best I could when Dangerous Eagle seized the reins of my horse, and the other two took charge of my meager herd. Having rounded me up, the three prodded me forward.

When the camps were made, our three bands all but encircled the eastern side of Ft. Larned. That was all right because that was the side we wanted. The eastern side was directly behind the longhouse belonging to the fort's sutler. On the western side of the fort, and meandering on around to the north, was Pawnee Creek. When the fort had originally been planned, it was felt that the creek was an effective barrier against Indians. And it was. But only against the Pawnee Indians. That creek didn't mean anything to Indians coming from other directions. So I suppose that even though we were only on one side, I guess you could say we had the army surrounded. Although I wasn't really thinking about any of that as I set up my humble little lodge. I'd just finished doing that when I was told by Big Tree in no uncertain terms that I was to live in the bachelor lodge he shared with his brother Dangerous Eagle and The Cheyenne Robber's best friend, Lame Crow.

The trouble with that was their shared lodge was even smaller than mine. The only good thing about the situation was the stream of sisters and aunties always bustling in and out, making certain that their precious boy-men were clean and well fed. I, by way of reflected attention, was cleaned up and fed well, too. But sleeping in confined quarters with three men was not pleasant. I don't know. Maybe I was old even then, or maybe I just missed Crying Wind. What I do know is that I was miserable.

The very next morning began with my awakening to the unmistakable click of a hammer being drawn back on a revolver.

I was curled up on my left side when my eyes snapped open and my fuzzy brain registered the sight of Big Tree, who lay facing me, holding a readied pistol.

"Don't move," he whispered. "It's an easy shot."

My terrified gaze followed his, and to my horror I saw the biggest diamondback in the history of creation coiled up and sleeping near the heated stones of the smoldering fire pit. Because of the lodge's confines, the fire pit was just a scant distance shy of my midsection. Or, more accurately, my groin. There were a lot of targets I would have chosen for a crack shot like Big Tree to take aim against, but a snake that close to my pelvic area did not make the list. So it was for the sake of the children I someday hoped to sire that I commenced to yell. And thrash. And kick away covers. And leap around in that lodge like a demented fool. My persistent screams of *Snake!!* immediately got my other two lodge mates cavorting around with me. Big Tree jumped, too, but the bad part of that was he was still armed and still determined to shoot the snake. Blankets were now tossed all over the place, and the snake was just as awake as we were. We knew this because we could hear it rattling a warning. That thing was ready to strike, but Big Tree no longer had a clear target. Undeterred, he began shooting at anything and everything that was a trifle lumpy. Before he killed us all Dangerous Eagle charged against his brother.

"Stop shooting that thing in here!" Dangerous Eagle yelled.

"I have to! It's going for Lame Crow!"

Lame Crow commenced to tear around the lodge interior in a totally panicked attitude, knocking loose lodge poles and then crashing into me, landing me flat on my back.

"Now it's by Tay-bodal's head!"

Issuing a lung-bursting cry, I sprang to my feet, only to be almost knocked down again by Dangerous Eagle and Big Tree, who were still battling for control of the pistol. Scrambling out of their way, I joined Lame Crow at the narrow door where he and I became hopelessly wedged in the doorway's limited opening. Then the gun went off again, and everything went dark gray on account of the entire lodge collapsed, taking the four of us, twisted up inside covering hides, with it.

I have no idea what happened to the snake.

The worst thing was the laughter. Extracting ourselves from the demolished lodge, the sight greeting us was the gathered crowd. Now, no one can tease quite as effectively as Indians. Most of the time teasing is subtle, but on an occasion such as this, the three of us were treated to full-voiced hilarity. And pointing. A lot of pointing. So was I pleased to see my wife among the mocking crowd and standing close beside the warrior known as Wolf Blanket?

I wouldn't especially say so, no.

For a homely, mediocre person, I have an unusual

amount of pride. Seeing my wife with that man wounded every ounce of it. She, of course, had every right to be with someone else. This is exactly what the reasonable voice living inside my brain commenced to tell me. But I wasn't able to listen to my reasonable voice. Or anything else. Which is why White Bear standing right in front of me and shouting my name caught me entirely unawares. With a jerk of his head and quick twist of his lips, he indicated that I was to follow after the others who were already shuffling away. I stole a glance over my slumped shoulder. Crying Wind was walking off in that sultry hip-swaying way of hers, shoulder to shoulder with Wolf Blanket.

By the time we reached White Bear's lodge, the other three were already making jokes about the event, reliving it in all its formerly traumatic detail and hooting with laughter. Because I was such an emotional wreck, I didn't find any of it one bit funny, so it was with a sullen thank you that I accepted a platter of food being held out to me by a grinning woman. I sat down in the rear of the lodge and picked, without interest, at my breakfast. As there were a lot of men breaking their morning fast with White Bear, it was easy to hide in the back while I pouted, gloriously wallowing in self-pity. It needn't be said that I wasn't listening to any of the low-voiced talk. What I did eventually hear—and this couldn't be helped because White Bear had begun to yell—was that he was reorganizing his elite council. The instant he said this, enraged men were jumping to their feet, one of them bumping against me, causing me to spill the platter of food in my lap. I was still unconcerned about the political brawl because in the lives of notoriously

30

ambitious men, there were always loud disputes. I had learned never to mix in. But I really should have been paying attention this one time. After all, the premonition I'd had in that frozen forest had tried to warn me.

THREE

I stopped worrying about my stained breechcloth when I realized something was seriously wrong. A large number of men were storming out while those remaining packed together and closed in around White Bear. A stony-faced Skywalker, his eyes glancing from one man to another, stood protectively against White Bear's side.

"I have made my decision!" White Bear's deep bass bellowed. "Anyone disagreeing is free to follow a different chief!"

The man I had seen walking with my wife, Wolf Blanket, was among the group surrounding White Bear. I suppose I hadn't noticed him before because I'd been too busy thinking of slow and torturous ways to kill him. Now that I was sitting alone, without the hindrance of larger backs and heads blocking my vision, I was able to have a good, clear look at him. I'm afraid that in those moments I was too involved with examining my rival, so I didn't hear word one my good friend Hears The Wolf, and the acknowledged leader of this minor rebellion, had to say. In my study of Wolf Blanket, I noted that he and I were of the same height, but he was brawnier. He was a stylish dresser, wearing a dark-blue breechcloth over softly tanned leggings with a flowing fringe that puddled around well-shod feet. Two wide silver bands embraced thick biceps. Smaller versions of the armbands clasped each wrist. Around a trim waist, casually riding his hips, hung a Navaho belt. The silver disc belt was a style recently introduced by The Cheyenne Robber and like White Bear's favorite nephew, Wolf Blanket, too, wore his hair braided on each side of his head, the remainder left to hang down his back. This was not the Kiowa way of wearing hair. Traditionally, it was cut short on one side and worn long on the other. But The Cheyenne Robber enjoyed kicking against tradition. His slavish devotees kicked right along with him. I next grimly noted that the whole of Wolf Blanket's bull neck was covered by an elaborate bead-and-polished-bone choker and that his impressive chest was bare. I was afraid to look at his face, but I eventually forced myself.

He was good-looking—not handsome, just good-looking—but even that was more than I would ever be. His final coup was that he was of the Ondegup'a class. Our very militaristic culture was based on warrior status. From this came our four distinct classes. The highest were the Onde, meaning wealthy. The second highest were the Ondegup'a, meaning less wealthy. The third—mine—were the Kaan, meaning poor people. The absolute last class, the poorest of the poor, were the Dapone. My wife was a born-to Onde, meaning that she was a princess . . . but only if by embracing this concept you are able to strike from your mind the fact that none of the Indian cultures had kings, making any likelihood of princesses somewhere beyond impossible. The laid-bare facts are these: My wife was a highborn lady, a rightful member of the elite group that comprised less than 10 percent of our entire Nation. I was her commoner husband.

Now a man infinitely more worthy of her stood before me.

I hated him. My hammered pride unable to endure a moment longer in his presence, I scurried out.

The sleeping lodge I'd shared with Big Tree, Dangerous Eagle, and Lame Crow was no longer a tumbled-down mess. During our absence, unknown women had set it to rights. A few yards away stood my lodge. I went to it, with no other purpose in mind beyond a bath and doing what I could to make myself presentable. Scooping up my very best clothing and bathing supplies, I mounted my horse and rode for Pawnee Creek. Once there, I spent a good deal of time attending to my bath, washing my hair, scrubbing every inch of my skin. I rinsed myself by floating on my back in the creek. As my ears were under water, I only vaguely heard the commotion in the camp. Those sounds were easily dismissed as nothing more than the building excitement of people anxious to flock to the sutler's store.

After the long float, I finally waded out of the creek, shivering in the gloom created by cottonwoods grown so closely together that their limbs entwined high overhead formed a leafy canopy so dense that only spots of sunlight penetrated. Still shivering, I hurried up the incline, coming to stand in the blast of warm summer sunshine. Except for the drone of insects, the occasional *whoosh* of breeze through the cottonwoods behind me, everything was peaceful. My horse was grazing contentedly as I lay down on a blanket. Once I was stretched out, the tall surrounding grasses effectively swallowed me up. I was snugly hidden, and, with the sun warming my body and the sound of my horse steadily crunching as it grazed, I drifted off.

Waking up was not quite as peaceful. Shadows blocked out the sun, and when I opened my eyes, I found myself looking up at a circle of stern faces. My startled gaze flitted from face to face, finally settling on White Bear.

"Well," he said gruffly to a smirking Skywalker, "you were right. We found him close to water." His voice quickly rose to a yell. "You know, Tay-bodal, you have a bad habit of crawling off and going to sleep whenever I'm having a crisis."

During the ride back to the camp I was clothed in all my best things: a short vest of bleached doe hide and matching leggings, a black breechcloth with a blue design woven into it, my nicest shoes. But even in these things, because I'd had to dress with haste, I still felt tossed together. I hadn't been allowed to brush out my hair, so it was flying behind me wild and free—and hopefully shaking loose the bits of grass that my nap had tangled into it.

We rode in a hurry. Why we were in a hurry no one bothered to say, and judging from the ridged set of the jaw-lines, it wouldn't do to ask. It seemed to me that whatever had prompted the search for me, the reason had to be extremely important. Explanations, none of them good, flickered through my brain, and I was caught in a clutch of dread as we closed the distance between ourselves and the unnaturally quiet camp.

Dismounting, the first thing I noticed was that except for the inestimable population of camp dogs, our home camp looked abandoned. From one of the lodges I heard a baby let out a cry; then that cry was quickly hushed. The Cheyenne Robber and his always-eager-to-please best friend, Lame Crow, took the reins of all of our horses, the two of them leading the horses to pasture. The rest of us followed behind White Bear as he led us toward his primary lodge, a huge red conical shape that from any angle dominated the eye, pulling it away from the duller, smoke-blackened-topped lodges comprising the extensive settlement of the Rattle Band. Immediately set up around the looming red colossus were the private homes belonging to his eight wives, those giving way in a circular pattern to the lodges occupied by his bachelor sons. Behind those were the homes of his married sons and daughters, bringing the number of lodges belonging to White Bear's family to about thirty. After that came the near relatives, then the less-near relatives and their relatives, and then friends and their families, and so on and so on. On a day when I hadn't had anything better to do, I'd counted over two hundred lodges belonging to the Rattle Band before I became bored and simply stopped counting. It was sufficient to know that White Bear had successfully created a nation within a nation. Just one of numerous reasons why his enemies, both white and red, were mortally afraid of him.

Following behind as he strode toward that massive red creation, I was watching only the ground, rapidly placing one foot ahead of the other. As a consequence, seconds after he reached the door, stopped, and turned, there was I, slamming into his barrel chest.

"Tay-bodal!" he shouted. "I have no idea what has gotten into you today, but I want you to stop it. Right now!" He pushed his angry face into mine. "One of my most valuable men is in trouble."

"Why?" I dared to ask.

He clicked his tongue. "Well, if you hadn't gone for your little swim and then stopped to have yourself a nice long nap, you'd know. But as you don't know, here is the short version." He straightened, then pointed his arm like a lance toward the lodge door. "The one inside, the one needing your help, stands accused of killing Turned The Horses's youngest son."

It took me several seconds to work out whom he meant, for I barely knew Turned The Horses. Then the answer came to me, and I was stunned.

Three Elks was was one of my "almost" friends. The reason behind the "almost" was, of course, rank. I was a near nothing while he was an Ondegup'a, the son of a chief. I liked to think that he and I were on excellent terms, but we were never more than that.

And now he was dead.

A hand clamped down on my shoulder, and I turned at the waist. Skywalker's expression was taut, his tone so hushed that it neared a whisper. "The one accused is innocent. But I can't prove it. Not without your help. If you refuse to give that help, there will be a lot of trouble because

37

White Bear will not give this young man over to Turned The Horses without a fight." The hand tightened, his whispery voice becoming urgent. "Will you help us?"

"Of course!" I cried.

Skywalker's hand relaxed, becoming almost weightless as it rested on the muscle of my shoulder. "You've answered much too quickly. As this is a dire matter, I would prefer a more thoughtful response. So I put it to you again. Do you swear you will do everything possible to help us in this most urgent matter?"

As instructed, I gave the question a more dignified think and then responded gravely, "Yes. I give you my solemn promise."

Satisfied by this, White Bear turned and ducked through the door hole. Skywalker's hand remained on my back as I followed. That hand was clamping my shoulder again as I stared at the man sitting all folded in on himself. The man covered in another's blood, splashes of it marring his chest and the arms adorned with silver bands. The blood in my veins turned to ice when he lifted his face and I stared into the eyes of Wolf Blanket.

Knocking Skywalker's hand away, I rounded furiously on him. "You tricked me!"

"Yes, I did." Skywalker responded mildly. "You left me no other choice."

Now, anyone not knowing Skywalker would be asking themselves, How did Tay-bodal know that he'd been tricked? Or more to the point, How did Skywalker know he would need to trick Tay-bodal? The answer to both questions is painfully simple. Very little ever escaped my friend the Seer. Being best friends with a clairvoyant is the most annoying thing imaginable. With him for my friend, nothing about my private life was ever truly private. Of course, he knew without having to unnecessarily strain his uncommon gift that Crying Wind and I were separated. The next thing most probably brought to his attention, by way of his own wives, was that Crying Wind was walking about with Wolf Blanket. Without having to read my mind—a thing he did without a great deal of effort—Skywalker knew how deeply her keeping company with another man would hurt me, how jealous I would be. So he, in order to secure my aid, had no other choice.

And now like a snagged fish I was caught on his hook.

Sensing the firestorm welling up inside me, he placed his hand on the small of my back as he formally introduced me to my worst enemy. "Wolf Blanket, I would like you to officially meet a most honored member of my family. He is called Tay-bodal."

Gazing at me, that man's face twisted as if he'd just tasted something extremely sour. It was utterly repellent for a lofty Ondegup'a to address a lowly Kaan. But the worse thing for this particular Ondegup'a was that the Kaan he now found himself badly needing had turned out to be none other than me. Somewhere in the back of my mind, I swear, I heard the Ten Grandmothers laughing, for that old trickster, Old Man Coyote, had done it again. He'd successfully befouled the lives of unwary mortals.

"I found him," Wolf Blanket said softly, simply, his Adam's apple moving so slowly that for a second it appeared to have become stuck just above his expensive choker. Then he opened his mouth and took in a deep breath, swallowing the air, the act sending the pointy blob in his throat down where it was once again hidden behind beads and polished bird bones. He'd made this statement not to me but to Skywalker and White Bear. We had all seated ourselves in a facing half circle, me in the middle, in his direct line of sight. Intentionally he kept his face averted, addressing only White Bear. Tired of his game, I forced him to acknowledge my existence.

"Exactly where did you find him?"

For a moment Wolf Blanket didn't answer. He merely repositioned himself, drawing parted knees close to his chest, hugging them with his arms as he inspected the folds of the blanket I was sitting on. Still looking only at White Bear he finally said, "I was walking away from the home of my sweetheart—"

"She is not your sweetheart!" I cried. My hands were fisted. I was ready to fight him when White Bear's hand brushed my arm. My head turned swiftly, and I stared at him as hatred flowed inside my blood, hissing in my ears with each pulse beat. I must have made a menacing sight, for White Bear's expression was immediately startled. I turned away from him, glaring at the one before me, the man I would gladly walk away from, happily abandoned to Turned The Horses's wrath. But because of that infernal promise Skywalker had swindled out of me, I was trapped. Still, no one had made me promise not to hate him—and certainly nothing had been said about me having to coddle him. Standing on my knees and in a threatening manner I pointed my hand straight at his heart.

"You will *not* refer to my wife as your sweetheart!"

He was looking at me now. Oh, yes, he was. Then his

eyes skittered back to White Bear. I have on several occasions felt grateful to this larger-than-legend man. But this occasion is the one I choose as my most indebted moment. For when Wolf Blanket turned to him, expecting White Bear to admonish me, White Bear's lips bowed in a smile. The next thing I knew, White Bear was playfully hugging the living breath out of me and braying laughter.

"Tay-bodal is quite a little stallion. Especially when he's protecting his only broodmare."

Locked inside his powerful arms, my heartbeat began to ease back from its near bursting boom as I watched, with immeasurable satisfaction, Wolf Blanket's arrogance begin to whither. Unfortunately Skywalker and White Bear succumbed to unbridled snickering, so I'm afraid that this is the place where all my remembrances of gushing gratitude comes to a rude end.

The first thing that needed doing was to move Wolf Blanket to a more secure place. A place even Turned The Horses would not dare invade: the little lodge belonging to one of the Grandmother icons. A sanctuary for felons until their fates have been decided. The same place my wife had once been forced to hide from the howling mob accusing her of being a witch. The same old couple responsible for the Grandmother, the very two people who had taken such tender care of my wife, would now lavish this same concern on a man I heartily despised. A man, for all I knew, was indeed the true killer of my "almost" friend—for I only had Skywalker's word, and sometimes even Seers can be wrong.

Wolf Blanket and I walked in the center of armed and anxious warriors acting as escorts. I couldn't see anyone, but I felt the hundreds of hidden eyes on us. I think this

41

was when the gravity of the situation settled down around my shoulders like a ponderous cloak. One of our own, an illustrious member of the Rattle Band, was accused of the death of another chief's son. Even though the dead man's blood was all over him, streaks of it dried into his skin, his fine clothing stained with large splotches, White Bear was determined not to give him over. His continued refusal would mean an internal war—band chief against band chief.

In the main, I understood why White Bear was being stubborn. In our culture, warrior societies were brotherhoods, and their chiefs were more like second fathers. I realize this may be a hard concept to follow, for the world has gotten too used to measuring all leaders by what they know about army generals. The difference is that generals demand to be feared and obeyed whereas chiefs expected a son's loyalty. And he expected it because that's what he gave. So yes, White Bear would stand up for Wolf Blanket. He would even go to war against another chief for him. He would do it because when the time came to direct his men against an enemy—any enemy—he expected his men to follow him without question.

And they did.

Which is also why I knew that Turned The Horses would go to war. He would have no choice because what kind of a chief refuses rise up to avenge his own son? That's the very question every man in the Nation would ask if Turned The Horses simply rolled over like a submissive dog at White Bear's feet. All of this musing lead me to wonder why two of Turned The Horses's sons had chosen to leave his band and come over to White Bear. In the case of the still living son, Raven's Wing, the answer was apparent. He had married one of White Bear's women. Just which woman and how closely related to White Bear she was, I didn't know. I prayed she wasn't a daughter or a niece. That would make everything twice as horrible. I glanced at Dangerous Eagle, who was marching along on my right and muttered the question.

"Oh," he grunted. "Raven's Wing is married to Always Happy."

I inwardly groaned. I knew something about that woman. Even though she was very young—about fifteen, I reckoned—she was one of White Bear's nieces. All right, that explained Raven's Wing, but I still had no idea why Three Elks had chosen to defect, chosen a different chief. His being an "almost" friend, it hadn't been my place to ask him. All I did know was that his defection from his father had nothing to do with marriage because Three Elks was a bachelor. I was thinking along that line when it occurred to me that there had been something I'd heard once, something my gossipy wife had once tried to tell me. But I couldn't recall what that something was because, frankly, my wife loved a good scandal so much that almost everything she shared naturally hinged on that. Otherwise she couldn't be bothered. So if I wanted a repeat of the juicy details, I was just going to have to ask her. Realizing that my needing to know now gave me a legitimate reason to seek her out, my stomach began to flutter with excitement. But I had to let go of the exciting prospect of talking to my own wife because the escort had come to a stop, and Big Tree was formally addressing the keepers of the Grandmother.

The old couple were known as Deer Trail and Medicine

Woman. They were very good people, worthy of the honor of tending the Grandmother. But they made me laugh. Not out loud, just deep down inside. Medicine Woman was a very roundish person, and as she was half Comanche, she was, well, squat. Being a small woman meant that for her, being fat was like having a handicap. When she walked, she looked as if she was merely swaying from one foot to the other, the landscape inching past her rocking bulk the only indicator that she was actually moving forward. Before any offer of assistance could be made, she invariably said, "No, don't help me. I'm doing fine."

But I think I fell almost in love with her about a year ago while watching her participate in a warrior society scalp dance. It was a very hot day, and the women—the mothers, wives, sisters, and daughters of the men belonging to the society—were all dancing. Medicine Woman was doing her toddling steps, and beside her was her even more portly and ancient sister. It was already evident by the water-soaked cloth that she wore on her head to keep her cool that Medicine Woman was feeling every bit of the day's muggy heat. Then suddenly she grabbed hold of her sister's arm, whirled her bodily, and loud enough over the drumming and singing for everyone to hear, she cried, "You and I are going to dance in the shade! Let the young women sweat in the sun!"

Now, the scalp dance is a serious thing, so you can imagine how difficult it was for us, the spectators, to hold in our chuckles as the two older women wisely, but in a thoroughly disruptive style, arranged themselves in the one shady spot the dancing field had to offer. But that was Medicine Woman. That was how she was. And we all loved her.

Deer Trail was physically his wife's complete opposite.

Where she was short and bulgy, he was tall and lanky. Where her face was round and smooth, his was elongated and deeply creased. When she listened to people, her mouth remained snapped closed as she squinted up at the speaker. The instant anyone spoke to Deer Trail, his eyebrows rose to meet his scalp and he gasped, his lower jaw dropping as if whatever was being said was the most amazing thing he'd ever heard, even if that thing was simply, "I hope you're feeling well today."

Yet despite these noticeable differences, the two had been devotedly married for so long that they thought exactly alike and were able, and with ease, to finish the other's statement—a thing they did without either one of them noticing. As a consequence, talking to them together could be very disconcerting, a bit like having a conversation with an echo. Young people found this annoying. I know Big Tree certainly did.

"We have come," he began.

"We have a guest for the—" Medicine Woman interrupted.

"Grandmother," Deer Trail finished.

Big Tree launched himself again, talking just as rapidly as he possibly could, without even a pause for breath so that neither older person could wedge in a word. "White Bear says it is his wish that you receive as a guest to the Grandmother the one known as Wolf Blanket on account of his life being under threat, and if you will consent to this, White Bear will furnish all that you may require, including fresh meat, and all this on your promise that you will not allow the one known as Wolf Blanket to leave the Grandmother's keeping until White Bear summons him."

Each wearing their separate trademark expressions, Deer Trail and Medicine Woman stared at Big Tree for an uncomfortably long moment. Then Medicine Woman's shrieking lambaste broke the stillness. "Young people always shout. I just hate that."

"Rude," Deer Tail promptly agreed. "I don't know where they get it. It isn't as if they weren't raised properly."

Every rotund inch of her fuming mightily, Medicine Woman interrupted, "No respect. That's what's wrong with the young people today. It's enough to make a mother cry and pour ashes on her head."

"And a shamed father to hide himself under a blanket," Deer Trail finished huffily.

Without any further delay, Big Tree quickly hustled Wolf Blanket and me inside the Grandmother's lodge.

FOUR

A low fired burned in the central fire pit. To the right of it, a single bed had been made. To the left, a small altar stood before the icon of the Grandmother, the Grandmother herself hidden beneath a protective covering. Following Medicine Woman's exit, other than the Grandmother's sleeping presence, Wolf Blanket and I were completely alone. I remained standing as Wolf Blanket gave the sanctuary a cautious perusal, mixed emotions playing across his too-good-looking face. Then, with shoulders slumped, he looked at me and spoke in a tone that was low, brittle.

"This is not how I expected everything to end. I am the son of a worthy man, a noble woman. Never did they . . . or I . . . expect"—he waved a vague hand—"this."

I was unmoved. How could I be otherwise when part of his great destiny included marriage to a woman that I still

47

considered to be *my* wife. Now, I want to be perfectly fair in all of this, so while I may have hated the man, he did have a valid viewpoint in our dispute. Ordinarily, any divorce was deemed final on the day a married couple separated. But in this instance—and this was the hope I clung to—Crying Wind and I were not divorced until White Bear gave his approval. Which meant that White Bear expected me to do something that neither he, nor any other Kiowa male, for that matter, would have ever thought of doing. That thing being taking time to cool off and then talk to my wife and do my part to work out our marital problems. He wanted this strictly because I was of value to him. As we were not related, the best way for him to keep me was to seal me to him in a marriage with one of his relatives. Which was actually a little tricky, but never mind. His recognizing my divorce from Crying Wind would leave me free to go anywhere I chose, and any future favors I did for him, he'd have to pay dearly for—something he didn't have to worry about while I was his relative because his being my protecting band chief was considered to be payment enough. Not wanting to buy anything he was used to having for free, White Bear expected me to do my best to win Crying Wind back. As I hadn't even had a chance to try that yet, Wolf Blanket was being totally presumptive in pressing ahead with his plans for my wife.

And if I didn't stop thinking about all this, I was going to hit him.

Fuming, I crossed the small floor space and sat down on the one available place: the bed. Taking this as some sort of cue, Wolf Blanket quickly did the same, the two of us coming to sit chummily cheek by jowl on the same cushion. For several moments we sat with our legs drawn to our chests, arms atop our knees, foreheads pressed against our arms, listening to the faint pop of the fire, breathing in the cloying but sacred cedar smoke. On such a warm day, a fire burning in a closed lodge caused us to sweat buckets, but there was nothing we could do. The Grandmother required the steady inhalation of cedar smoke, and we weren't allowed to roll up the walls since exposing the holiness of the Grandmother to the elements, even mild sunshine, was strictly forbidden.

"I'm beginning to feel a bit better now," Wolf Blanket said weakly. As he hadn't bothered to raise his head, he was speaking to his lap. Then with a dispirited sigh he muttered, "You have my permission to ask questions."

Raising my head, resting my chin on my arms, I looked steadily at the shrouded figure of the Grandmother. "You said you found him."

"Yes."

"After you left . . . Crying Wind."

There was a long moment of silence, followed by a muffled, "Yes."

"Why is his blood on you?"

"I—" His voice caught, causing him to pause. Then, his voice still so low it was an effort to listen, he continued. "I picked him up. I was taking him for help. The first person I saw was Raven's Wing." He raised his head and took a deep, calming breath. I continued to stare at the Grandmother. Following a lengthy moment, Wolf Blanket went on.

"I had him in my arms when I tried to explain to Raven's Wing that I'd found him, but Raven's Wing was furious. I put his injured brother down because he was so heavy, and when I righted myself, Raven's Wing hit me. So hard that he knocked me down. And because he had the advantage, all I could do to protect myself was curl up into a ball. The next thing I knew, there was gunfire and people surrounding us. It took quite a few men to pull Raven's Wing off of me. Then Skywalker was beside me, whispering in my ear for me to stay very, very still. That sounded like good advice."

"Was—" I very nearly said Three Elk's name out loud. An act that would have stirred up his ghost. I cleared my throat, tried again. "Was the one you found still breathing when you carried him?"

"Yes," Wolf Blanket rasped. He raised his head just enough to peer at me over the curl of his arm. "I know because he was gargling."

That statement perked me right up. My spine immediately straightened, and I looked Wolf Blanket fully in the face. "Gargling?"

"Yes," he said meekly. "It sounded like this. . . ." He sat up a bit straighter and proceeded to make a deep gurgling sound in the back of his throat. I knew that sound. It was the death rattle.

"What were his eyes like?" I asked.

He had to think for a second. "Well, when I found him, he looked straight at me. Then his eyes started—I don't know—rolling around. After that I didn't really notice because I was picking him up. A lot of blood was coming out of his throat. Someone had cut it. And, from my experience in such matters, the cut had come from behind."

As loath as I was to display my ignorance, there was nothing for it but to ask. "What is the difference from a behind-an-enemy cut and a standing-before-an-enemy cut?"

Wolf Blanket had to think again, gather his thoughts in order to explain this basic knowledge to a thorough-going novice. Finally, with a frown and frustrated expulsion of breath, he said, "The best way to explain it is to show you." Well, any thought of exposing my throat to the knife of my wife's suitor certainly made me a bit leery. Sensing my hesitation, he snorted, "I will only use my finger."

"All right, then," I replied. "Show me the back way first." I maneuvered around on my buttocks, turning my back on him. The next thing I knew, his hand had hold of my hair, and his finger swiped my throat, all within the space of a single heartbeat. "That was too fast!" I yelped.

His hand still had hold of my hair as he shouted next to my ear, "That's how you kill an enemy! Fast."

"Yes, but I didn't feel anything."

"With a sharp knife, you wouldn't."

"But I need to feel it. Do it again, this time slowly."

"I don't know if I can."

"*Try!*"

I sat very still. I didn't even breathe as his finger skimmed over my neck, causing my skin to tingle along the curve he traced from my left ear to my right. I really could have done with him doing it a third time, but his grip on my hair and the spine-cracking angle of my pulled-back head were proving painful. "You can let go of me now."

As his fingers eased open, I heard him murmur, "You have good hair."

Since this had come from an expert scalp taker, I certainly didn't care for the intent of his comment. I quickly

51

scooted around and faced him. "Now show me the front way—as slowly as you possibly can." While he complied, I watched as I felt his every move. When he sat back, I said, "Show me your knife."

Wolf Blanket wore the scabbard suspended from his breech string. The elaborate sheath hung low and was tied tightly against his right leg. The long tie string was decorated with beads, hanging below his breechcloth. The length and heavy beads of a warrior's tie string was consciously phallic, meant to set the hearts of maidens trembling. I couldn't help but notice that Wolf Blanket's ended just at the top of his knee and that the series of heavy beads were about as big around as my index finger is when touching the tip of my thumb.

What a braggart!

He handed over his most prized weapon, and I examined it carefully. The blade alone made the knife hefty. It was a polished steel that bowed to a point and felt sharp enough to split a frog's hair. The handle was wood and wrapped in strips of deerhide. No blood stained the hide wrapping. I handed him back his knife.

"I have to leave now."

Sheathing the weapon, he looked steadily at me, worry filming his eyes. Of course I could have eased his mind by explaining the reason I needed to leave, but this was a man I hated, so I didn't.

White Bear refused to allow me to ride alone. It was one of the few times I'd ever known him to show genuine concern for my safety. Oh, I knew that because I belonged to him, he always worried about me, but he'd never been one to be so overt. Now he was, his disapproving mouth pressed into a thin line, his beady eyes boring into mine. It was the look he used whenever he wanted to rattle fear into a man's bones. It worked. Every one of mine was rattling away when he said, "No, you are not going alone. And that is all I have to say."

With that, he began choosing a guard to accompany me. Then he dispatched his eight wives to go and gather together valuable gifts for me and my escort to present to Turned The Horses. When everything was ready, he turned without saying good-bye, closing the door in all of our faces.

Turned The Horses had earned his name in his youth, during the time when the Cheyenne had been one of our bloodiest enemies. Our only allies way back then had been the Comanche and the far-flung Crow. Our primary enemy was the Lakota, but any Nation even slightly aligned with them was considered to be our enemy, as well. That meant a lot of enemies on account of the Lakota were conquerers. Like a whirlwind they came sweeping down from the north, and their moving in displaced a lot of Nations. They took over the Black Hills, the very place the Kiowa people were born, though we weren't there when they came in. We were already south. But because we still thought of the Black Hills as ours and the Lakota as trespassers, we warred against them and they us.

The Comanche are our good friends. So are the Crow, but when it comes to a fight, they can't be counted on for very much. That was not their fault. Those people were virtually surrounded by the Lakota, constantly harried. How they managed to stand them off and hold on to their homeland, I don't know. The Crow are an extraordinary people.

Anyway, the leading members of the Lakota confederation were the Cheyenne, Arapaho, and Osage. Our endless wars with all of these people were terrible. Little Bluff, our principal chief before Lone Wolf, realized that if any of our Nations hoped to survive, we had to have a confederation, one that was formed against a common foe. That enemy was, of course, the encroaching whites. But years before this great alliance, a large number of Cheyenne warriors attacked one of our villages.

The young man who would be called Turned The Horses was then known as Runs Over The Hill. He'd been of Herder Society age and of a humble family. During the attack, Cheyenne warriors scattered the village horse herd. This was diabolical in that the defending Kiowa would have to fight the invaders at a severe disadvantage: on foot. But the boy-man Runs Over The Hill, unarmed and alone, found the courage to place himself in front of the bolting herd, frantically waving his sleeping blanket and shouting. He must have been a very good herder, for those horses listened to him. They turned. The young man's risky effort sent the panicked horses back toward the burning village, where the defending warriors did not question the miracle. All they thought about was that they were able catch a horse, mount up, and chase the marauding Cheyenne off. When the truth was eventually known, Runs Over The Hill was declared the true hero of that fight, and his name was changed to Turned The Horses. By this one deed he advanced from Kaan to Ondegup'a, and for the remainder of his rather lengthy life he prospered, gaining as many as five wives and producing eleven children. Of these, there were only three

daughters. Which meant that aside from his notable courage, Turned The Horses was also an exceptional breeder.
Eight sons survived infancy and grew into full manhood.
Six had chosen to remain loyal to their father, but the youngest two, Raven's Wing and Three Elks, had gone over to
the Rattle Band.

The modest-sized village was in understandable turmoil, and
it was apparent to those of us riding there that their very
vocal grief was not at all understood by the commander of
Ft. Larned. Responding to the wails and steady drumming,
a large number of armed and wary soldiers were sent to
prowl the boundaries of the fort. Skywalker, Big Tree, Returned, Hears The Wolf, and I pulled up short of the camp.
Turned The Horses had been in such a rush to have the
things the army was supposed to be giving out the next day
that he had positioned his band ahead of the other camps,
less than a quarter mile distant from Ft. Larned's eastern-
most long building. When Skywalker signaled for us to stop
and rest our horses, we were so close that the expanse of
gently billowing spring green grassland between us and the
fort was little more than a short canter away.

Because of the army, the miles of prairie land surrounding the fort was out of balance. This was because of the
whites' abhorrence of the Red Buffalo: fire. In an effort to
protect their fort from the threat, the earth all around the
fort had been turned, the disturbed sod formed into about
a knee-high barrier. Along with this firebreak, soldiers
rushed to beat down any evidence of naturally occurring
fire. What they accomplished with these measures was the
slow destruction of the prairie.

This large open country was known to us as the Land Where The Sky Was Formed. The whites called it the Great Desert, but it wasn't a desert at all. It just didn't have a whole lot of trees. What it did have was four different types of grass, a multitude of flowering plants and valuable herbs, and more wildlife per square foot than any forest country could sustain. All of this was because of fire. The Red Buffalo caused the prairie to live and thrive in perfect harmony. My grandfathers and theirs before them all knew this. The newcomers, however, wouldn't listen. To them fire was another enemy, one that had to be conquered. Because of their relentless efforts, the tallest of the four grasses, the giant bluestem, a grass that by midsummer grows higher than a man is tall, was taking over.

That was bad because buffalo couldn't eat the tall grass, and when there was too much of it, they couldn't graze. And so the herds moved on. Next, there came the problem for the profusion of flowering plants. With the tall grass choking them out, their numbers had dwindled to only a few spots of color here and there. The vanishing flowers affected the lesser animals, insects, and birds, all of them dependant on the seeds of the other grasses, the blooms of the flowers, and, finally, each other as sources of food. Listening carefully, I recognized the warble of a bird white men have named shrike. We called it Little Singing Hawk because it sings as beautifully as any seed-eating songbird, but the little hawk follows the way of its bigger brothers, feeding only on field mice and lizards. What I should have heard but didn't was the deep-throated *whooping* sound of prairie chickens. Not hearing those sounds, sounds normally so loud that you couldn't hear yourself think, meant that this was yet another animal that had moved on.

I bowed my head as a summer breeze whispered by me, a breeze absent of the perfume that a healthy prairie ought to have. In that nearly sterile wind I sensed change. When I raised my head, I was partially blinded by the tears welling in my eyes. I blinked rapidly in order to clear them, training my sight, my entire concentration, on the cause of my grief.

Ft. Larned.

Ft. Larned was an open fort, meaning no walls, just buildings made from quarried sandstone and constructed in a way that made the layout look like a large square formed around a central grassy area. Two long buildings made up the east and west sides. The north had a series of small buildings and dark wooden sheds. The northeastern corner, just before the long building making up the east side, consisted of a squat, funny-looking building that had eight sides rather than four.

Earlier, when I'd ridden off for my bath, I studied this oddly shaped building and its close proximity to the northern bend of Pawnee Creek. It was so near the tall and densely stationed cottonwoods that their spring abundance of deep silvery green leaves shaded most of the eight-sided roof. Another thing I'd noticed was that on each of the blocked-sandstone walls there were narrow horizontal and rectangular openings that stared blankly back at me. Those cuts in the walls had to be gun holes. Then I'd begun to wonder just how intentionally this particular building had been erected so closely to the creek. If it had been an accident, then it had been a supremely lucky one. But knowing what little I did about the army, I didn't believe that anything even remotely connected to their rigid mentality allowed for any type of accident. Therefore, there had to be a secret, hidden path leading from that building to the life-giving water, a pathway that would supply the needs of the building's inhabitants during times of siege. I began thinking that maybe I should mention all of this to White Bear as I studied the south side of the fort, a side consisting of only four evenly spaced from each other clapboard houses, all of them painted snowy white. Those houses would be where all of the officers lived. Knowing this, I also knew that I was staring into the face of Ft. Larned's greatest weakness. That a surprise attack launched first against—

"You have a wonderfully tactical mind," Skywalker said. I was confused for only a passing second when in a humorous tone he continued, "It's a pity this gift was bestowed on a craven."

His broad smile and the snickering of the others turned my expression sour. Skywalker had been at it again, eavesdropping on my private thoughts.

"Are you going to tell him?" I asked crisply, meaning White Bear.

"Of course," he chuckled. "And I'm also taking the honor as being the one to have worked it all out."

I shook my head as he laughed louder.

As we were White Bear's representatives, we'd come bearing gifts. We were taken with haste and grim pomp to Turned The Horses's lodge. Walking through the village, the noise of its shared grief beat against my ears. My nerves were jangled as we passed somberly, our arms filled with White Bear's offerings, through a gauntlet of shrilly keening women who paused just long enough in their wailing to spit on us. Our faces were drenched with spittle when we finally reached, then ducked to enter, Turned The Horses's private sanctum. I was clearing the entry hole when Skywalker whispered to me, "Expect bluster. But don't be alarmed by it."

Turned The Horses's six sons were present, all of them silently standing along the circular walls of the lodge and staring malevolently. I forced my eyes to remain focused on the backs of my pitifully few comrades as Hears The Wolf began to speak with the authority granted him as White Bear's intercessor.

"We of the Rattle Band are heartily sorry for this thing that has happened. The young man that has been lost was well thought of by all of us. White Bear says to tell you that he loved that young man. From this day on through to the remainder of his life, White Bear says he will grieve for your son."

The ancient Turned The Horses lifted his eyes. The interior light was murky, but even in the dimness I could see that his hair was almost white, his skin was profusely wrinkled, his brow was a solid bone set without a break, and his hooked nose jutted from that bone. Eyes as cold and emotionally void as two black pebbles stared at Hears The Wolf.

"White Bear has always been a good talker," the old man finally rasped. "It was his . . . talk that took from me two of my sons. Now on account of him, one of them is dead." Moments of awkward silence ensued as Turned The Horses's shaky left hand wiped the corner of his mouth. "You go on back to White Bear. You tell him Turned The

Horses does not forgive him. You tell him the only way he can make it up with me is to hand over the one known as Wolf Blanket."

Flustered, Hears The Wolf offered, "White Bear has called for a council trial and—"

His voice was drowned out when Turned The Horses's six sons began shouting. They didn't stop until their father raised his hand. When again there was silence, and Hears The Wolf was able to continue, I became more intent on Turned The Horses's now violently trembling hand than I was with listening to Hears The Wolf's speech. Now, Hears The Wolf was always a man that I've considered to be my very, very good friend, despite the fact that he had an extremely annoying trait. He was a devoted planner. His wife Beloved claimed that from the moment he opened his eyes in the morning, he was busy detailing the way the day could be used to its absolute best. I believed her. And being a man of organized temperament, during our ride to Turned The Horses's camp he'd practiced out loud exactly what he was going to say. Knowing my friend preferred death over deviating from a plotted course, I already knew every word about to come out of his mouth. So instead of listening, I fixed my attention on Turned The Horses.

There was something the matter with him. Something other than old age. The symptom was in the uncontrollable shake of his hands, the drool that would not stop leaking from the corners of his thin lips. I despised the fact that the light in that lodge was so bad and I was standing so far back that I couldn't get a clearer look. I turned my attention to his stony-faced sons, beginning with the eldest, a man in his late middle age. His formal name was A Watchful Hawk

Sitting On A High Mound. He was better known as Watching Hawk, and other than the common knowledge of his being a decent, slow-to-anger person, not a lot was known about him. This wasn't unusual, for our Nation was a big place and mild-mannered men were all but invisible.

The first thing I noted was that he was terribly lean. Skinny. Skywalker was skinny, too, but there was taut muscle over bone. Watching Hawk's muscle mass seemed to hang beneath flaccid skin. He looked haggard, as if he hadn't had a good night's rest in months. He held a lance, the blade pointing up, the broad shaft crossing his chest, the butt end imbedded in the bare earth floor. Both hands gripped the weapon, and he leaned forward and against it. The thing that entered my mind was that if the lance was kicked away, Watching Hawk would promptly fall forward and land on his exhausted-looking face. His hands were big, bony, and white knuckled from his grip on the lance.

And they trembled.

Not as badly as his father's, but the tremor was definitely there. I quickly glanced at the remaining five. They ranged in ages from Watching Hawk's fifty-odd years to late thirties. Everyone of them was rail thin and displayed the same exhaustion overshadowing Watching Hawk. One, Red Sash, a man close to my age and someone I remembered from our shared herder days, manifested the uncontrolled tremor in the right hand hanging limply by his side. The shake was so slight that if I hadn't been looking for it, I would have missed it entirely. But Red Sash was aware of his affliction, for the instant he felt my stare, that hand crept for safety behind his back as he pulled himself upright and fixed me with a hostile look. My eyes darted forward, and

I tried to appear absorbed in the continuing exchange between Hears The Wolf and Turned The Horses, but that effort was short-lived.

"Get out!" the quaky-voiced Turned The Horses managed to shout. "Tell White Bear I refuse his gifts. Tell him what I demand is the killer of my son."

We went out carrying the gifts we'd brought in. The visit hadn't gone at all the way I badly needed it to go. There was no use saying this to Hears The Wolf, for the man's face was a hard mask of anger as we again found ourselves walking that irksome gauntlet of shrieking and spitting women. Turning my face away just as a glob sailed past my nose, I whispered urgently to Skywalker.

"I have to see the body. That was the whole purpose of our coming here."

A wad of spittle found his upper cheek. He ignored it as he spoke to me, his words weaving in and out of the din surrounding us. "We came . . . White Bear wanted . . . I should have done the . . . Let me . . . think . . ."

Well, I certainly didn't have time for him to mull. Given the mood of the camp, it wasn't likely I'd have another opportunity. Holding tight the basket in my arms, I darted off, crashing through the line of women, knocking one of them down. The mob turned its anger away from my companions and set it on me. And this is where my father's training of me paid off. I knew exactly what direction to go. Not because I'd ever been a visitor to Turned The Horses's camp but because of our burial customs.

I ran east, and I ran very, very fast. Even though I was burdened with a heavy basket, I managed to stay ahead of the men, women, and camp dogs following in determined pursuit. The mob skidded to a combined halt as I entered the immediate area of the death lodge. Although by now the mob wanted every inch of my sweaty hide, it maintained a respectful distance as the woman who was seated before the doorway stood.

FIVE

She was a big rawboned woman, absolutely nothing delicate about her. Her work-rough hands were as large as mine. Because of her grief, the dress she wore was in a dingy state. Her braided hair looked white, but that, I realized, was from the ashes grimed into it. Placing herself in the immediate vicinity of Three Elks's remains meant that she was either a professional mourner or his nearest female relative. She appeared too calm to be a professional, a widow dependent on the gifts a grieving family would pay. Professionals work hard at keeping themselves het up, giving full measure in order to earn a good-sized fee. I quickly decided that this woman must be an auntie, for her unlined face caused her to appear much too young to be the mother of a fully grown man.

"Are you here because of my son?" she asked, her mild tone reflecting curiosity.

All right, she *was* Three Elks's mother. Proving yet again that I am a terrible judge of age. Clutching the basket, I stepped nearer. "My name is Tay-bodal."

She parted her mouth slightly, sounded a knowing, "Ahhh." Then she looked beyond me, considering, I suppose, whether to let the angry crowd have me or continue to extend her protection. My being chased by her relatives was not a good sign of friendliness, but other than the basket I held, I was not armed. Finally, shifting her gaze back to me, she decided I was not a danger to her. With a wave of her arm she sent away her sullen relatives, who didn't seem to care for this decision very much. Just for good measure, someone spit on me again, the stream hitting the center of my back. Seeing this, a slight smile tugged her mouth as Three Elks's mother turned, took up her vigil once again, eased her round body down on the sitting blanket placed before the lodge door.

"My son spoke of you." She said, patting the space on the blanket to her right. I accepted the invitation while she continued, "He thought a lot of you. He said you are a good doctor." Before I could reply, she hastened to ask, "And what is that you've brought me?"

I handed over the basket. The instant she had it, she pulled away the covering cloth, hurriedly examining—no, hunting through—the contents. Then she sat back, severe disappointment playing across her plump features. That confused me. Dried buffalo tongues are a delicacy. As there were ten tongues in that basket, this was indeed a generous gift. She sighed deeply as she looked up at the sky. I looked up right along with her, and for several minutes we did nothing more than watch streams of white clouds being pushed by the high prairie winds.

"He trusted you," she said at last.

"It touches my heart to hear his mother say this."

She looked away, the wealth of her bosom rising, slowly descending. "Yes, well, I suppose his being able to trust someone from the Rattle Band made him feel better. His older brother pushed him around, and he confided to me all the troubles he had with The Cheyenne Robber and the one known as Lame Crow. It did me good to hear that he had a famous doctor to call his good friend." Her meaty hand patted the right knee of my crossed legs.

For a moment I was speechless. In no way did I consider myself famous, nor had I ever thought of Three Elks as my good friend. But what I puzzled aloud was, "Lame Crow? I wasn't aware of any trouble between your son and Lame Crow."

"Oh," she scoffed a bitter little laugh, "there was trouble all right. I lay all that on The Cheyenne Robber. He's a bad, bad person. And every one of his friends must do exactly as he says since he is such a hero and White Bear's favorite. Lame Crow is the first to do whatever he says, and The Cheyenne Robber told him to hate my son, so he did. Those two taunted him without mercy, determined to drive him off. But my son was stubborn. He said he wasn't going to leave the Rattle Band just because those two wanted it. He said he was going to get power and then make them sorry."

"How was he going to do that?"

She shrugged. "I don't know. He wouldn't tell me." After another moment of quiet, she said, "I suppose you didn't know about Big Tree, either."

I turned an aghast face toward her. She sneered.

"Oh, yes, Big Tree was another one he had to watch out for. My poor son was surrounded by enemies, but I was maddest about Big Tree."

"Why?"

"Because my son saved him once, and Big Tree repaid him with his contempt."

I found that too hard to believe, and so I blurted, "If he felt that way, why would your son stay on with the Rattle Band?"

Staring off into a middle distance, she said crisply, "You weren't listening. I told you, he was stubborn. But most of his stubbornness had to do with Raven's Wing. They weren't full brothers, but when my son was small, Raven's Wing, being almost ten years older, used to look out for him, take care of him. Then Raven's Wing went over to the Rattle Band. When my son became old enough, Raven's Wing came back, but only to claim my son for his warrior society. We all grieved when he took my son away. My son was glad to go with the one brother he felt truly loved him, but the years they'd been apart had changed Raven's Wing, made him hard. Too hard, I say. There was no love left in him. Certainly no forgiveness, not for anyone. But mostly, not for his younger bother. He was determined that my son would be the best at everything. That the two of them would be White Bear's finest. My son tried very hard, but there was just no pleasing Raven's Wing. My son began to hate him, but not enough to quit. He kept saying to me, 'One day I'll show him up.' " She became quiet, reflective.

After what proved to be a goodly wait, she said introspectively, "He was so positive, so . . . determined."

As her introspection was leading me exactly nowhere, I changed the subject. "What did your husband Turned The Horses think of two of his sons leaving him for White Bear?"

She waved a hand and made a hissing noise that was quickly followed by a grunted, "Him." There was a lot of stored up anger in that one word. "Truth be told, both I and my sister wife, Raven's Wing's mother, were secretly glad that our sons got away." Canting her head, she looked me straight in the eyes. "This used to be a big band. Years ago when I came into it as a bride, and known more by my true name, Red Flowers, than the one I've become used to, Turned The Horses's Last Wife, there were over two hundred lodges. Now there are less than fifty. That's because he's a bad chief. My sister-wife and I knew that our sons had no future with him."

I thought it best not to press her further; after all, she was telling me more about her husband than a good wife ought to. "I am a new member of the Rattle Band," I said. "I came in about two years ago."

"Yes," she replied, "I heard all about it." She smiled faintly. "Your coming in made a bit of a stir. My son visited me right after White Bear gave Crying Wind to you for a wife. He said there were a few men who weren't pleased with the match. He was talking about men who'd had their own hearts set on her. He laughed about their complaints that White Bear had thrown a fine woman to waste."

She turned her face away, and I was glad on account of mine was flushed with anger. I wanted her to name names, but she really didn't have to. Wolf Blanket's name was already being screamed inside my head.

Looking over to the horizon at nothing in particular, she sighed deeply. "It was only after you treated the wound he'd received from that strutting jaybird, The Cheyenne Robber, and then you were gracious enough to wait for any type of payment, that he came to see you differently, talked about you being his friend."

I remembered the incident she referred to, for it had only happened the previous summer while our Nation had been making its way toward Medicine Lodge. The Cheyenne Robber had, accidently he claimed, shot Three Elks in the posterior. Three Elks hadn't much taken to the idea of me digging the bullet out. In fact, he ran away. We had to chase him. Raven's Wing had been among the chasers. And as I thought about it, I remembered it had been Raven's Wing who'd brought him down, tackling him around the waist. I hadn't known then that they were brothers. As a matter of fact, I still hadn't known until midwinter, when Raven's Wing came to my home, interrupting a heated argument between me and Crying Wind. Because we were not in the friendliest mood to entertain an unexpected guest, Raven's Wing kept the visit short, staying just long enough to ask one question.

"Has my brother ever bothered to pay you for your services?" He'd first had to make it clear to me just who his brother was. Surprised to learn that he meant Three Elks, I'd stammered a no, then looked to my wife for confirmation (because too often my patients paid her rather than me). She was shaking her head when Raven's Wing said disgustedly, "He will." Then he left, and we got back to our arguing. Two days later I was paid in full, a tense Three Elks appearing at my door offering a fresh deer liver and eight shiny new bullets for my rifle. He'd seemed vastly relieved when I accepted all of it, shook his hand, and declared us even. He'd been very friendly after that. Now I believed I understood why. It had been his older and very stern brother, Raven's Wing, who'd forced him to face me like an honorable man. He'd probably been expecting me to be stern with him too, but it had worked out that I was flexible enough to happily accept his small payment. It was after that that he began smiling and waving or walking with me when we were headed in the same direction.

"Are you thirsty?" Three Elk's mother asked rather suddenly. "I'm thirsty," she said. "And I have no more water. You stay and guard him while I replenish my water."

The next thing I knew, she was toddling off, the large empty water gourd dangling from her hand. My stomach began to flutter. This unexpected chance was exactly what I'd hoped for. When Red Flowers was a good distance away, I scooted inside.

Being an interloper in someone else's private place has always made me nervous. But, oddly, it has always made another part of me excited. Maybe both are caused by the fear of being caught. But intruding in a death lodge made me *too* nervous and excited. My hands were shaking, my entire body was dribbling cold sweat, and my head was spinning. Taking a deep breath, locking it in my throat, I rushed to the body and removed the covering blanket.

My heart instantly seized.

No one had closed his eyes! Three Elks's blank orbs were

70

staring straight back at me. Well, I couldn't stand that. Nor could I imagine how I'd have the courage to ignore those cloudy eyes while doing an examination of the fatal wound. I felt caught on the proverbial horns of the dilemma for I had promised myself that I wouldn't disturb anything, leave no evidence of my presence in this somber lodge. Closing his eyes would be indisputable proof that the dead man had had a visitor. I thought and thought, trying to convince myself that it was all right that he was looking at me because dead eyes can't see. This isn't an easy thing to convince oneself of when a pair of eyes are staring fixedly at you. Then there was yet another stumper. Three Elks was dressed in all of his finest clothing. Clothing that included a many-strand choker that began at the base of his jawline and ended at his collarbone. To see the wound meant I would have to remove the choker, which meant that I was now up to two ways of disturbing this dead man. Taking a deep breath, expelling it, I forced myself into the first violation: closing the eyes. After that you'd think everything else would have been simple, but it was not. Removing the choker meant that my face came too close to his. I kept my eyes squeezed firmly shut as my fingers fumbled with the choker's tying knot secured at the base of his neck. After what felt like an eternity, I finally managed, despite the tangle of Three Elks's long brushed-out hair, to loosen that blasted knot. With a long, relieved sigh, I sat back on my legs and while looking only at the ruined throat, I lightly ran a finger across my own, remembering the two patterns Wolf Blanket had demonstrated.

"Come out of there!" a furious voice ordered.

I jumped as if I'd been scalded. Then I hurried to repair

the damage, the whole time loudly blathering one apology after another. I had no idea how many people were waiting for me outside as I worked, frantically putting Three Elks back into a reasonable state, the choker tied down, hair smoothed out . . . I'm afraid I couldn't get the eyes to open again. At least not completely. The lids lay across his eyeballs in a sleepy sort of way, and that would simply have to do because . . . well, I don't know if you've ever touched a dead person, but take my word for it, lifeless skin is viscous, and once it fully enters the decomposition process, it does pretty much whatever it wants to do. What those lids wanted to do was remain half open, and what I did not want to do was touch them anymore, so I left him like that and dashed out, fully prepared to make yet another run for my very life. But any headlong flight I'd hoped to make was thwarted by Red Flowers's amazingly strong hold on my arm.

"*What were you doing to my son!*" she shrieked.

"I-I was praying—"

"Liar! I saw you!" she cried, hysteria raising her voice. If she took her hysterics to Turned The Horses, I was as good as dead. The only thing I could do now was trade unmercifully on a grieving mother's love.

"I meant no disrespect. My sole aim is to find the one responsible for his death."

Her fingernails dug painfully into my forearm as her furious face came within inches of my own. "We already *know* who killed him," she said, her words coming at me like a menacing hiss. "All we need is for White Bear to hand him over for justice."

"Wolf Blanket says he didn't do it. He says he merely

found him, that he was taking your son for help."

"Another liar!" she hollered. "The Rattle Band is a home of liars."

"Listen to me!" I shouted over her. "I am many things, but I am not a liar. For you to believe that, you must first believe you raised a son so simple that he would be fool enough to profess our friendship to you, a wise and noble woman."

Her mouth snapped closed. Amazing how a bit of flattery never fails to render an angry woman speechless. But she did not let go of my arm. Which meant she was busy figuring out what to do about my transgression, no doubt including whether to take my crime to her husband. So I jumped in, hopefully talking faster than her mind could think.

"Wolf Blanket is not my favorite person. As a matter of fact, I'm quite sure I hate him. But my feelings have nothing to do with the truth. The right person must pay for the violence done against your son. Otherwise his death will not be avenged, and his spirit will wander and cry. For this reason I cannot accept without question the word of one man, even though this word comes from the mouth of your son's own brother. The risk to your son's eternal well-being is simply too great."

Her hand fluttered away. Fresh tears formed and fell, adding more streaks to her face. "He was my only child," she said, her voice dwindling in a sob.

A mother's deepest fear is that she will outlive her children. This fear comes in a rush at the moment of birth. Death is a seeker of tiny lives, which is why mothers are so protective of their infants, their children. An easy breath is not drawn even when their children become adults, for sons become warriors, daughters become wives. One faces death on the war road; the other, in childbirth. Through all of this, a mother can only stand and pray.

I wrapped my arms around Red Flowers's bulky body and pulled her in close, allowing her tears to soak my vest. I felt terrible. To save my miserable self, I'd manipulated, abused a mother's sorrow. The image of my wife's face was in the tears that swam across my eyes. During our constant bickering I'd belittled her love for her son. Now, mixing up Red Flowers with her, I begged my wife's forgiveness.

If it hadn't been for the horses, I wouldn't have seen my traveling companions, for they were hidden by in the tall grass as they lolled around waiting for me. Keeping my line of sight on the saddled and grazing horses, I stomped through the lush green growth. When I was halfway there, a head bobbed up. Big Tree's. He had a long stem of grass sticking out of the side of his mouth. He looked down and poked someone. Another head came up, Hears The Wolf's. He had a long stem of grass in his mouth, too. He tore it out just before yelling at me.

"You've been gone long enough!"

"I apologize," I called back, my tone thoroughly unapologetic.

Hears The Wolf appeared ready to let fly another complaint, but Skywalker, sitting up now and watching my approach with a one-eyed squint, nudged Hears The Wolf into silence. They were all standing by the time I reached them.

"I know it was bad. I'm sorry," Skywalker said somberly.

His word offering did not make me feel better. Still confusing Red Flowers with Crying Wind, I was miserable with guilt and seething. All right, the seething had more to do with that little nugget that Three Elks had confided to his mother: that there were men in the Rattle Band who felt giving Crying Wind to me was tantamount to a good woman being thrown to waste. If I lived to be nine hundred years old, that remark would continue to affect me. Just as I would always be mad at the person who I believed actually said it. Wolf Blanket. And believing that had me aching to be the one to haul him to Turned The Horses and cry, "Here he is! Cut him up!" With all that churning around inside my head, I badly needed to fight with somebody. Skywalker looked like a good enough somebody to me.

"What you *know*," I said icily, "is nothing more than the shadows you see in your mind. But now *feel* this." I grabbed his hand, forced him to touch the left side of my vest. "Feel the tears of a grieving mother."

Skywalker did not fight me, did not try to pull away his hand. A puzzled expression swept across his face. In a disarmingly calm tone he said, "I feel the wetness, but I feel no tears."

Now, that made me just as mad as I knew how to get.

"And I feel something else," he continued. "I feel your need to hit someone. If that's true, I am here. Swing away."

I did.

My fist connected with his jaw, and the blow sent him flying backward. As he lay sprawled on his back, he raised a staying hand to the others who were about to rush against me. Skywalker pulled himself up into a sitting position and waggled his injured jaw from side to side. "Good hit," he grunted. Then he laughed, "I hope you enjoyed yourself because, truthfully, had I'd known you were so strong, I would have said for you to hit Hears The Wolf."

We went to the place where Wolf Blanket claimed he'd found Three Elks. While the others—all of them practiced trackers—prowled the area looking for sign, I remained on my horse, my narrowed focus judging the distance between this spot and what I could see of my wife's lodge. Typically Crying Wind preferred to set up house within a close proximity to water and a good firewood supply. In this place those two things were not possible because the fort was too near the creek, and there wasn't any wood to speak of except for the few water-hungry cottonwoods lining the creek banks. To gain water the women had to travel, twice a day and with a guard of warriors, to the creek. While filling the waterskins, the women would naturally hunt around for fallen limbs but they would only find enough to add to the fires feeding on a steady diet of dried buffalo chips, the one fuel source that could be found virtually everywhere. And, no, burning buffalo chips did not smell bad. Actually, a fire made from this wholly reliable fuel smelled a lot like a prairie fire. It was also smoky. Which was a good thing on summer nights, as the dense smoke kept mosquitoes at bay.

Not only did Crying Wind prefer to live within an easy walk to water, she was also an enormously private person, and during our marriage she'd invariably set our home as far as she could from our closest neighbor. Far enough, anyway, that my patients complained. I, in turn, complained to Crying Wind, but she just shrugged that off. Ironically, because of our separation she was now denied privacy. Unmarried women were required to live within the easy range of hawk-eyed, sharp-eared aunties so that their virtue could never be called into question. All of this meant that Crying Wind's lodge was anything but a simple stroll from her door to this place.

Which also meant Wolf Blanket had lied.

SIX

Deep in thought, I stared off at a large half-dead scrub bush poking spiky limbs above the high grasses and the few dried up leaves clinging to those branches twisting furiously against unrelenting breezes. The prairie is also the land where the winds were born. Winds that come as a hundred gentle sighs or as a mighty howling thing. But today the winds were sighing, against my face, playing with my hair, as I stared at that lonesome scrub, my mind drifting. While I was doing that, Skywalker was hunting for signs. He came into my view as he neared the immediate area of the scrub and gave me a start when he yelled, "Ho!" A second later the other men were running toward him, and I was clambering down from my horse.

"He was attacked here," Skywalker said. With a hand

he indicated the edge of the bush. He began to move again, and we silently parted, allowing him to pass. He looked up at Hears The Wolf. "Do you see it, too?"

Hears The Wolf nodded. Then, one after the other, the remaining men nodded. Everyone except for me since quite frankly I couldn't see a thing. Which is not my fault because prairie grass is the most resilient thing imaginable. Within hours of being flattened, either by the cloven hooves of thousands of buffalo or a week-long encampment of humans with horse herds and the constant trampling that all of this implies, the hardy grasses will spring right back up.

"Two paths," Hears The Wolf muttered absently.

Skywalker hunkered down and began rooting around. On account of the high grass, he virtually disappeared. Then he jumped to his feet and startled the pure liver out of all of us. Not because of the speed of his movements but his eyes. They'd gone all mist covered, and then they rolled back into his head. His lower jaw hung, and a frisson of fear raced through me, causing me to shudder when he began to gurgle. Knowing him as well as we all did, none of us reached out to touch him. A Seer's trance state is a perilous thing, a danger not only for himself but for anyone near him because when in a trance, a Seer is a doorway between two worlds. One touch—one small concerned touch—might be more than enough to send a mortal through or unleash the wrath of a vengeful spirit. Terrified of either possibility, we all stood absolutely still, barely breathing while suffering the sound of that awful gurgle.

After an eternity the sound stopped. Skywalker's face began to twist and kept on twisting until his very familiar features were so contorted that he was unrecognizable. His mouth was set in a vicious sneer when in a raspy, barely audible voice he hissed, *"Die."*

His knees buckling, Skywalker slowly fell to the side in a deep faint.

Owl Man, the venerable leader of the Society of Owl Doctors, chanted softly, his croaking voice oddly soothing, as he briskly waved a feather fan across Skywalker's unconscious face. The walls of his lodge were rolled up, the smoke hole braced wide open. Breezes rushed through but did little to obliterate the old-man smells saturated into the hide walls. They weren't bad smells, merely the aromas of joint ointments and burned herbs, the smoke helping to ease old lungs while he slept. Then there were the smells of the things he owned, everything old and, like the owner, slightly decayed. Only half listening to Owl Man's little healing song, I thought of the combined effort that had been required to haul Skywalker's amazingly heavy and floppy form, load him across the saddle of his horse, then carefully lead the horse toward the camp while Big Tree raced on ahead. I thought then of Three Elks's more solid weight, the effort required for one man to pick him up, then carry his bleeding body as far as Wolf Blanket supposedly had. If this one part of his tale was actually true, then Wolf Blanket was the possessor of gargantuan strength. But that wasn't the thing worrying my mind. The thing I couldn't shake was the memory of Skywalker's face, the full-of-hatred tone of his voice.

Even the recollection gave me a case of the skittering chills up and down my spine and it was while I was in the middle of a really good shudder that I asked, "Will he remember?"

The fanning and chanting instantly stopped as Owl Man raised his eyes, fastening them on me. "No," he answered. "His gift is too powerful for one mortal man. Sometimes, like now, he has to go off, hide from that power. If he didn't, he would go insane. Which is why, I believe, he never remembers the truly bad things that flood into his mind. Hiding is the only way he has to protect himself. But he can't control the hiding any more than he can control the images that come at him. Both things cause him terrible frustration."

I knew that what Owl Man was saying was the truth, mainly because I'd heard it all before and from Skywalker himself. He often felt defeated that after a lifetime of study and effort, he could not control or harness his great flashes of insight. He said it was like trying to catch the wind. I'd been with him during many trances, but this was the first time I'd ever witnessed one to cause him to fall into a death-like faint.

"W-where he is now," I stammered, "is it a safe place?"

With one hand Owl Man wrung water from a small cloth, then applied the cloth to Skywalker's brow. "It is as safe as someone like him can know. Right now he's walking the Black Road—the road that stretches in between the next life and this one." He drew in a deep breath, and once again he was chanting and fanning the length of Skywalker's body with the feather fan.

In his prime Owl Man had been very tall and lanky. He was stooped now, shoulders rounded, muscle tone beneath his sagging skin all but nonexistent. White stringy hair framed a face beset with wrinkles so broad and deep, they were like pleats. His deep voice was rough because of the cigars he habitually smoked—cigars he rolled himself from the green tobacco leaves he bought in abundance from Caddo farmers. The cigars were then stored until they were a little bit brown and reasonably good for smoking. But when his supply of properly seasoned cigars ran out, it was not unusual to see a greenish cigar sticking from his mouth. Yet another curious thing about him was his form of dress. Or rather, lack of, for my only memories of him are of him wearing a tattered breechcloth and scruffy shoes. In the winter when everyone else was dressed in layers of clothing, warm hats, and fur-lined shoes, Owl Man acknowledged the season by throwing a robe over naked shoulders. His perpetual disheveled state was the complete opposite of how he'd been as a young man. I was told that back then he'd been exceptionally vain, dressing himself in the finest clothing and tending his hair with the same conceit as a beautiful maiden. I was also told that in those times he'd been a sincere flirt and seducer. I found that hard to believe of a man who wore just enough for modesty, had never had a wife, and to my personal knowledge never so much as glanced in the direction of a female.

The other thing about Owl Man was that he was yet another of my "almost friends." In the first days of my tending patients Owl Man declared my form of doctoring dangerous. As far as I know, he never wavered from this opinion, but because of Skywalker's support of me, he eventually stopped his public denunciation and put up with me as best he could. Through all the years Owl Man and I were civil, even, at times, helpful to one another, we were always too uncomfortable with each other to be real friends.

I didn't want to leave, but Owl Man suddenly remembered that because of my being an outsider to his Owl Doctors Society, my jug ears should not be hearing the society's private prayer songs. As if all of this was my fault, he harshly ordered me out. I lapsed into deep thought as I trudged along, trying to bring forward a memory clinging to the back of my mind. Then I thought of Crying Wind. That memory had everything to do with her because in my mind's eye I could see her face, see her lips move, almost catch the words she whispered. Then the memory was gone again. Which meant that I would simply have to do what I'd formerly made up my mind to do: Talk to her.

After a lot of wandering around, I finally found Crying Wind with a large group of women, all of them sitting on their heels as they laboriously ground slabs of thin, dried meat to a powder. They were preparing pemmican, the staple of our winter diet. Although Crying Wind's back was to me, I immediately noticed that she was wearing her short summer dress. She had several dresses, but her summer dress was my favorite. Mainly because it was so short and she'd been blessed with the finest legs I have ever seen on a woman. Kneeling the way she was while she busied with her task, the skirt cut across midthigh, revealing a sight I'd missed so much that my entire body ached. During the first two days of our "divorce," one man, embarrassment evident in his tone, had hesitantly said, "I'm sorry you lost such a fine wife." Then he'd moved on, and, watching as he hurried off, it occurred to me that she hadn't died nor had I misplaced her. She was very much alive, and I knew exactly where she was. So if anyone was lost, in the truest sense of this word, that person was me. Because without her I felt dead inside, and I was alone, bewildered, adrift. Then came the hurtful knowledge that I could so easily and quickly be replaced. By Wolf Blanket. That thought suddenly had me building up a good case of mad.

When one woman caught sight of my determined advance, she nudged another, who quickly looked up and even more quickly nudged the next woman. The nudging made the rounds, and by the time I was there, standing barely a foot away from them, other than the grating noise of grinding stone against grinding stone, there was a cold silence.

"I beg your pardon," I said.

Not one female head turned. Stones worked harder against stones.

By now I was so angry that I felt I'd swallowed a wildcat whole, and it was trying to claw its way out of my skin. I cleared my throat, tried again. "White Bear has charged me with a duty important to our band, and it is on account of this that I must speak privately with Crying Wind."

The grinding stopped. The other women looked directly at me, but Crying Wind merely straightened her spine, brushed hair from her face, refused to turn her head. Then she announced, "Whatever you need to say, you can say it before my sisters."

My blood was boiling, steam practically coming out of my ears as I snapped, "That's just fine with me, for the only thing I need to talk to you about is your murdering lover."

Crying Wind gasped sharply. A twitter went around the group as the women unsuccessfully fought the urge to giggle and grin. Throwing down her grinding stone, Crying Wind stood to her feet and, on those splendid legs of hers, moved in a determined way toward me. The next thing I knew we were toe to toe, and she was waving her arms and screaming straight into my face.

"I don't care how many favors you're doing for my cousin, my life and how I chose to live it is no longer your concern!"

"Yes, it is!" I yelled right back. "Because according to your cousin, you and I are still married!"

"That's a lie," she spat.

"It is not. Why do you think I'm still with the Rattle Band?" Before she could sputter an answer, I charged on. "Because he won't let me leave. He says he doesn't have time to scrape you up another husband, so whether you like it or not, I'm still yours."

She slapped me so hard, my head almost flew off my neck.

The formerly suppressed giggles erupted into gales of hearty laughter. I stood there for a second, the side of my face stinging as if it had been burned, staring stupidly at the mocking women before my fuzzy brain cleared and I realized that my wife was gone. Quickly looking back over my shoulder I saw her running. If she reached her lodge . . .

"Oh, no, you don't!" I hollered.

The members of the Rattle Band witnessing this race were immediately vocal, the women sounding shrill cries urging Crying Wind to run faster, the men whooping for me to catch her. Crying Wind put on more speed and so did I, my gaze concentrated on those beautiful, sprinting legs. I was still a good distance behind as she rounded the side of a lodge, and her own was now just a small distance away. She was almost safe.

This is where my boyhood training really paid off. I dug deep for that reserve of speed every good runner knows. I poured that speed on, and before Crying Wind knew what was happening to her, I had her by the hair. A second later she was swinging a fist at my midsection. Instinct saved me. Still holding her by the hair, I sucked my belly in just in time, and she missed her target. To prevent another attempt, I choked up on her hair, brought her in close enough to get an armlock on her waist. She tried to kick me, but her being slightly off balance was exactly the leverage I needed. With very little effort I was able to sling her under my arm. Everyone became instantly silent as Crying Wind hung at my side like a slain doe. Rapidly recovering from the shock, the women began screaming, calling me some really bad names. Then they began flocking to her rescue. I was saved by the men, who, laughing uproariously, held the women off. This gave me just enough time to run away.

And that was how I ended up kidnapping my own wife.

No sooner had we cleared the encampment than the squirming Crying Wind settled down. Which was good because she was heavy, and her squirming was killing me. I carried her as far as I could, praying with each step that my arm wouldn't break, but after only another few yards my strained muscles began to shake in an unseemly way, so I had to set her down on her feet. But before she could do anything tricky, I grabbed hold of her arm and pulled her along after me. She didn't struggle anymore because she obviously knew by then that I was fuming mad. Two years of marriage had taught her that when I got that way, she shouldn't keep pushing me. So while I dragged her along, she thought the situation over. Which was good. She had a lot to think about because my carrying her off in such a brazen way had, in effect, overturned our divorce. I was thinking, too—about just the right words to say to fully win her back. Frantically, I remembered our courting days, shrinking my concentration down to the one thing I used to do that Crying Wind had liked the best.

Groveling.

A young man in love is known to bend a knee before his beloved, begging pitifully for a kiss, a word of encouragement . . . sex. I'd spent an enormous amount of our courting time on both my knees and in a totally agitated state while Crying Wind played at trying to decide what I might be worthy of. Finally on our honeymoon I'd assumed my begging days were over.

I'd assumed wrong.

The troublesome thing about marriage is that not long after the honeymoon, a man finds himself lumbered with the one thing he hadn't even considered during the days of heated courtship. Pride. This sudden emergence of a stubborn spirit quickly has the woman looking askance, wondering what, if anything, she'd ever loved about him.

The encampment looked small behind us when I stopped, fell to my knees, my arms raised in humbled supplication. And considering that I was so woefully out of practice, I thought I sounded pretty good.

"You are everything—the beat of my heart, the air in my lungs. Without you to sustain me, I am good for nothing."

She raised a hand and looked at it, flicking the nail of her third finger against her thumb. The *click, click, click* reverberated against my ears. Then she put the hand away, folding her arms beneath her breasts as she looked down at me with unveiled disgust.

"That's it?" she asked crisply. "After everything you put me through, that's all you have to say? That I'm a bodily function?"

Stunned stupid, my eyebrows shot to my crown. Gathering my wits, I hastily stood, going at her with the last defense of any truly desperate man.

Flagrant truth.

"All right, have it your way. I'm an idiot. And my past behavior has been unforgivable. But before you congratulate yourself on being the exemplary wife, I must remind you that you are a bad-tempered, jealous-natured woman who—"

"Jealous?!" she hooted. "Why would I ever be jealous of *you?*"

"I have no idea!" I shouted. "But you are! And you know that's the truth because anytime a young woman came to me as a patient, you were mad at me for days."

She tossed her arms wide. "Well, that's because you always want young women to take off their clothing!"

"No, I don't. And if you are honest with yourself you will recall that the few times I've needed to see a woman *partially* unclothed, members of her family were also present."

Her teeth scraped the corner of her mouth as she glared at me. In the fading sunlight, I caught a glint of a tear sneaking along the curve of her cheek. Bristling with barely contained anger, she quickly brushed the tear away. "What I do know," she said hotly, "is that too many women are more than willing to take their clothing off in front of you. And if you must know, that makes me mad!"

My eyebrows were on top of my head again.

"I don't understand," she jeered, "why you even trouble yourself to be married when you can have all the women you want without any of the bother. But what I have been lately made to understand is that you now have a new wife in mind."

Now I was completely befuddled. "What are you talking about?" I cried.

She advanced on me, coming so close that if I had dared, I could have reached out and touched her. I didn't. And I think that made her madder. *"Don't play the innocent with me!"* she screamed. "I've been kept informed about Twelve Trees's daughter. How he is saying he will be glad to receive your courtship of his girl."

My lower jaw fell as I quickly remembered the daughter of the man known as Twelve Trees. Then I started yelling. "She's a child!"

"Yes, she is," Crying Wind hotly agreed. "A very pretty child. And according to rumor, she's going around saying that you are the handsomest ugly man she has ever seen."

There was a compliment in there somewhere, but I didn't have time to wedge it out. "No one has talked to me!" I hollered, "Not Twelve Trees or White Bear. Because if either one of them had, I would have said that I already have a wife. The only wife I want!"

Crying Wind's hands flew to her face. Tears began to flow unchecked. Tears were always her best weapon—I guess because they always worked. They were certainly working now. My temper dropping with each falling tear, I gathered her in my arms and held her close. And as I held her, I said a prayer of thanks that she still loved me enough to cry.

"We have a lot to talk about," I said, my voice shaky. Adding hesitantly, "That is, if you still want to be my wife."

A breath later, I felt her slow nod.

The sun was now slanted in the direction of late afternoon, and together we watched the first faint traces of dusk gradually darkening the thin blue. The white clouds had a lot of gold in them. It wouldn't be too much longer before orange and purple were added to the gold. Then the sun would set, and, just like that, all colors would be wiped out. The sky would be an impenetrable black dotted with uncountable stars and one big fat hazy moon crawling groggily up out of its secret sleeping place. I couldn't help but marvel that these miracles happened every day. But for me, the biggest miracle was that I was lying side by side with Crying Wind while she talked and I pretended to be listening. To be honest I wanted to make love, and, frankly, I've never understood why women need to talk so much, solve all the problems in the world, before they deign to consent to sex.

I was also hungry.

With my body pulling me in two different directions at once, and because I felt it was maybe a tad too soon in our reconciliation to ask her what she was planning to cook for supper, I grumpily settled for lying beside her, holding her hand, our fingers intertwined. So, no, I wasn't listening to her. Not until she casually asked, "How are you doing about Wolf Blanket?"

My head rolled toward hers. "What?"

"You know," she said, "this business about him killing Turned The Horses's son. Do you really think it's true?"

All of that brought me back to the excuse I'd used to hunt her down. But I couldn't tell her that. She'd quickly decide that that was the only reason I came after her and then we'd be in a mess again. I turned onto my side, rested my head against the crook of my arm, and said softly, "You know what I missed most about you?"

She laughed, made a face at the sky. "Of course. You missed making love. But mostly I think you missed my cooking."

The woman was uncanny.

My face crunched into a frown. "Yes, all right, but that wasn't what I was thinking."

Another laugh gurgled in her throat.

"I was thinking about the way you always helped me solve puzzles."

She blinked rapidly. "I did?"

"Of course you did. You always listened, always offered good advice, and you kept me informed about camp gossip."

"You hate gossip," she jeered.

"True, but . . ." I sighed for effect, "whenever it comes from you, I know it's dependable."

Her face turned toward mine, her eyes wide. "You *want* me to tell you gossip?"

Once again I began to worry. I stopped worrying when her eyes took that predatory gleam I knew so well. "Because I will," she said in a rush, her hand tightening in mine. "Helping her husband is what a good wife ought to do. But first, would you like the real truth about Wolf Blanket?"

"Yes," I answered simply. I was more than ready to listen to some of that. We sat up, the knees of our crossed legs touching. Finally, because she was saying things I badly wanted to hear, my mind did not drift. The first thing she said—and in no uncertain terms—was that she could not stand Wolf Blanket.

"Then why were you seeing him?" I demanded.

Her anger was just as swift. "Because you were only gone for one day when I began hearing stories concerning you and the daughter of Twelve Trees." She threw her hands toward the darkening sky. "What was I suppose to do? Let you think no one wanted me?"

She was jealous and I loved it. "I swear on my life," I said feigning great patience, "I didn't even look at another woman."

She gave this a considerable think. Then, slightly mollified she continued, "He is extremely good-looking, but he doesn't have any humor. And he's too . . . ambitious."

I knew exactly what she meant. Wolf Blanket was an Ondegup'a desperate to have an Onde wife. He must have felt himself very lucky when Crying Wind had suddenly become available. Even the suggestion that he had been more interested in her rank than he'd been in her as a person made me hate him more. Then a tremor ran through me as the thought occurred that if it hadn't been for the thing that had happened to Three Elks, Wolf Blanket could have too easily ended up being Crying Wind's new husband. And I would have been consigned to a maelstrom of torment. Hears The Wolf had lived in that deplorable condition for years after the woman he loved was given into marriage to someone else. I'd pitied him then. Now I couldn't stop wondering how he'd been able to stand it. Crying Wind's voice brought me back to the moment, and in that moment I vowed that from then on I would always listen to her sweet voice. Always, always, always.

"But he isn't nearly as ambitious as the one who died today."

My lower jaw dropped. "*He* was courting you, too?"

"Yes!" she cried. "I thought you knew!"

I was still in a state of complete disbelief when I fired back, "How would I know a thing like that?"

"Well, don't yell at me! He was your friend. Besides, he said he had your permission." Her eyes narrowed as she thrust her face into mine. "Tell me that was a lie."

"It was a lie," I said vehemently. "He never asked. If he'd had, I would have hit him."

Looking smug, she sat back. "That's what I thought." She looked off into a middle distance. "Anyway," she said with a vague wave of her hand, "I wouldn't have considered him for a husband even if you had approved of the match."

"Why?" I asked, simmering with rage on account of my "almost friend's" duplicity but at the same time morbidly curious about her reason for rejecting him.

Her expression broached startled. "Because of his family, of course!"

Now I was completely confused. "What about his family?"

She looked down as she paused and thought for about a minute. Suddenly her head shot up. "Now, this is only gossip you understand."

I braced myself.

SEVEN

"It's well known that Turned The Horses's health is not good," Crying Wind said in a matter-of-fact way. "It's also commonly known that he refuses the services of reputable Owl Doctors or Buffalo Doctors. He says they're all thieves. But I have heard some talk about Burned Hand going in and out of his camp."

I couldn't believe what I was hearing. My loud tone conveyed this. "But he can't be more than nineteen!"

"Seventeen," she corrected.

Seventeen, I quickly thought. What was I doing at seventeen? Ah, yes. I was studying why birds did not eat a particular butterfly, the most magnificent of all butterflies—the very large orange-and-black one swarming the prairies in an uncountable number. It's the only butterfly that I've ever observed to actually migrate south. Their migration is a hard thing to miss, actually, because until they pass, the sky is totally blackened with them. The puzzle of why birds would refuse such bounty had taken a lot of working out, but I finally realized that the big orange-and-black butterfly feeds on the nectar of the bright yellow-to-orange-to-red flowers of the milkweed plant and lays its eggs on milkweed greenery. Further investigation had led me to the fact that the birds also avoided the fierce looking fat caterpillars, which was why they were allowed to grow up into such marvelous butterflies. That was when I became incurably fascinated by plants. I had already known that the root of the milkweed was widely used for many types of cures, mostly nasty cuts, but the birds—by their avoidance of both the plump, juicy caterpillars and then the adult butterflies— were telling me that this plant was also a poison. Now, being absorbed with an investigation of the hidden properties of a plant may have been an odd way for a seventeen-year-old male to be spending his days, but it was certainly harmless, for during this age I was in no way representing myself as a doctor. The very idea that a seventeen-year-old Burned Hand . . .

"Why hasn't Turned The Horses called for me?" I demanded furiously. "If he is too poor to pay, I would have treated him for nothing."

Crying Wind thumped me right between the eyes. "You weren't listening," she said tartly. "I said he is greedy, I did not say anything about him being poor. And, yes, I know you are a generous person, but a greedy person doesn't understand generosity."

95

I settled down, thinking hard about what she said. Finally I asked, "Any word on just how Burned Hand tends his patient?"

She scowled darkly. "No. He's as bad if not worse than you about sharing information."

I tried very hard not to smile.

"But what he refuses to say doesn't really matter because Burned Hand's father told his third wife, who then told the woman Many Gifts, who then told my sister Carries His Lance, who then told me . . . all in the strictest confidence of course—"

"Oh, of course."

She glared at me. Taking a moment to smooth her ruffled dignity, she went on. "Well, what has been said is that Turned The Horses must be bled . . . a lot." She nodded sagely as if this actively garnered bit of information should be perfectly clear to me.

It was. Buffalo Doctors believed that all illnesses had to do with the condition of the blood. When a patient was very ill, that patient was bled, sometimes a bit too generously.

Crying Wind's voice broke into my hurried thoughts. "I know you know my cousin Rainy's girl, the one known as She's Always Happy."

I nodded that I did—never mind that I didn't. I knew of her, of course, but I didn't know her. Nor did I know where this newest tack was taking us.

"Well," she said, "my cousin's girl should change her name to She's Always Upset on account of her marriage to Raven's Wing. I think she hates him. I know she certainly hated his brother. His whole family, now that I think about it."

I was very confused. "If she hates her husband, why doesn't she just divorce him?"

"On account of her being so close to her time to deliver."

"She's having a baby?"

Crying Wind blessed me with a look that was able to convey complete disapproval as well as certain level of self-satisfaction. Just how she managed to make faces like that was something of a wonder. "Yes, she is. Now *there's* a story," she declared. "One that every woman understands. Raven's Wing might let her go without a fuss, but he will not let go of the child. And that's something I find very strange on account of there's a lot of whispering going on about that child."

"Why?" I was beginning to sound like an echo.

Crying Wind leaned in, speaking quickly and barely above a whisper. "This is something only we women know. Which means you'd better not tell another man or I will hurt you."

"I promise," I swore.

A smile radiated her face as she leaned in closer. We were almost nose to nose as she said in a rush, "She's Always Happy is not carrying Raven's Wing's child. But guess who seemed to know and even told me so to my face!"

"Three Elks?"

She slapped my arm. "Why do I ever try to tell you anything?"

Rubbing my upper arm, I cried, "It was a guess! A lucky guess! And please stop beating me up. You know I—" Our eyes quickly met and held, amused smiles tugging the corners of our mouths. It had taken less than an hour for us to slip back into the good part of our marriage as if we'd found, then put on, a comfortable old shoe. I offered out my other arm. "Go ahead and hit this one now. You know you want to."

Laughing, she obliged.

It was getting dark. Holding hands, we made our way back to the camp, strolling into the shadowy light of the camp's central bonfire. Spotting us, Dangerous Eagle came on the run, skidding to a stop that almost cost him his balance.

"Everyone has been looking for you!" he exclaimed. "White Bear's going crazy!"

"Why? What's happened?"

"It's The Cheyenne Robber. He's been attacked!"

The first thing I did was race for my medical supplies. Dangerous Eagle raced right along with me. Once I had the heavy bag in hand, we took off again, Dangerous Eagle leading the way. We did not, as I'd expected, charge for The Cheyenne Robber's enormous blue lodge. Instead we were going toward Owl Man's. A large group of warrior elite surrounded that mean little lodge, many of them standing in separate clumps, hotly arguing among themselves, but a goodly number, heavily armed, stood guarding the door. These guards sent me flinty glances as I passed through the doorway about a half step behind Dangerous Eagle. It was clear to me that had I not been with him, they would not have allowed me to pass. I took that as a good sign, a sign that The Cheyenne Robber was still alive. But for how long I wouldn't know, not until I saw him.

Skywalker was wide awake and cradling his younger

brother's head in his lap. He was also doing something I'd taught him to do: applying direct pressure to the deep wound on The Cheyenne Robber's chest. The central fire was high, flames rising dangerously. Owl Man, even more dangerously, was sitting close to it, shaking a rattle as he chanted into the dense cedar woodsmoke coiling up toward the smoke hole. In the meantime, White Bear was doing what he did best: He was raging, venting his shock and fury against the half-dozen men doing their best to stand as far away from him as they possibly could. Every last one of those men were bloody. Coated, I guessed—for not one of them looked wounded—with The Cheyenne Robber's blood. As I came near the bed, Skywalker raised pleading, sorrow-filled eyes.

Being stabbed in the chest was nothing that should have ever happened to The Cheyenne Robber. For one thing, the man was just too beautiful to be scarred. For another, he was a heroic person; he deserved far better than a coward's knife. For that, I thought as I began to work frantically, was what the attacker of Three Elks and now The Cheyenne Robber, was—nothing more than a thorough-going coward.

Knife wounds can do far more injury than a passing bullet because a knife gets everything in its path—muscles, large veins, vital organs—severing them too often, beyond my abilities to repair. That was the kind of wound Three Elks had suffered. With his windpipe cut in half, gushing blood had raced in and then entered his lungs. The gurgling sound Wolf Blanket had described was the sound of a man drowning. All things considered, a stab wound to the chest high and to the left was extremely lucky. I forced away the blood-soaked cloth Skywalker was applying to the wound.

The instant he let up on the pressure, more blood, gushed up. The wound was deep, and I would have to work fast before the last drop of The Cheyenne Robber's blood supply was drained. I quickly gave Skywalker a new cloth, and he went back to putting on the necessary pressure.

"Get out!" I shouted as I glanced back over my shoulder. White Bear's reaction was immediate, his broad face registering full surprise. Before he could collect himself, I hurried on, "Question them outside. I need room to work."

"Oh," he blurted, as if the idea that his temper tantrum was crowding up valuable space was a new and strange thought. The men were glad to go, all of them filing out as rapidly as possible, White Bear dogging the heels of the last man.

The instant they were gone, I began issuing orders to the hovering Dangerous Eagle. "Go to the old woman known as Duck, the mother-in-law of Hears The Wolf. Tell her I need a large bowl of hot water and the use of her valuable hands." Dangerous Eagle nodded once; then he was gone. To Skywalker, I said, "When I begin to advance, ease back on the cloth but not on the pressure."

Skywalker did not waste his time or mine by asking any questions. He kept The Cheyenne Robber's head steady between his legs, the clean cloth pressed firmly against the skin directly beneath the wound. I turned and yelled at Owl Man, interrupting him midchant, as I tossed him a sealed clay jar. The old man caught it nimbly and, holding it in his hands, blinked several times as I issued orders.

"Empty the contents into something you can set directly into the fire. I need it to be melted but not so hot that it will burn his skin."

Owl man offered no comment, but while I concentrated on making the tiniest stitches I've ever sewn into human flesh, I felt him staring at me, and I felt his anger. My ordering him around, even during a dire situation, was not something he handled very well. Finally he turned and set himself to the task I'd dictated. As for The Cheyenne Robber, he didn't so much as twitch each time I jabbed his skin with the long and slender metal needle, then pulled through the fine thread of sinew. His eyes were open and he was looking at me, but it was like he was unconscious. His breathing was shallow, taking in just enough air to keep him alive, and every time his heart beat, large drops of blood beaded up directly under my carefully made stitching. I was so agitated by the sight of it that my hands were shaking. For his sake I forced myself to think of something else. So I thought about the needle I was using, how I'd purloined it and two more just like it out of Crying Wind's sewing basket.

If she knew I had those three needles, she would have throttled me. They were very hard to obtain and expensive. I have a friend, Ha-we-sun—Hawwy—a white man in the Blue Jacket army who is also a practical doctor. I suppose in a way he's a relative because he married the woman known as Cherish—who just happens to be another of White Bear's nieces and The Cheyenne Robber's younger sister. Officially that makes Hawwy a member of the Rattle Band. But he didn't live with us. He lived over near the Wichita Mountains with the army. Ever since last summer, Cherish, as his wife, lived there with him. Anyway, Hawwy is a generous person, always giving me gifts of things he uses in his doctoring. One of the things was a set of little needles, but I threw them away. They were curved funny, hard to hold on to. But what I had liked was that they were fine and sharp. So were the straight ones that Crying Wind had. My filching her needles was dangerous because she set great store in that little package containing the ten metal needles.

It was sometime during this past winter that Crying Wind discovered three of her needles missing. By then we were squabbling almost night and day, and I was not about to admit that I had taken them. Or that I'd also helped myself to some of her delicate sinew. Fortunately she hadn't imagined for one moment that I would have had anything to do with the missing needles and threads. What she did was accuse her sisters—which I confess did give me one or two pangs of guilty conscience. But not guilty enough to step forward and take the blame. Even now as I used her possessions to save a valuable man's life, and even though she and I had made up and with the earnest promise that everything we'd said and done during the winter was completely forgiven, I still didn't relish the notion of her learning the truth.

Duck bustled in carrying a big bowl of steaming water, just as Owl Man was pouring the liquified tallow into a little bowl. Duck was one of the most quarrelsome women I've ever known, but she was also the best nurse I've ever worked with. Having lived to a great age, she'd seen every type of wound there was to see, delivered more babies than she cared to count, and best of all was a storehouse of information on the types of healing herbs her grandmothers and mothers had used during her childhood. I was always learning something new and valuable from Duck. I was also constantly mad at her on account of her barbed tongue. But when she knelt down beside me and without a word proceeded to lend me the use of her highly capable hands, I blessed her name to the heavens.

Backlit as we were to the fire, our shadows—Duck's and mine—moved on the surface of the lodge wall like two dark specters bowing in acknowledgment of each other. Duck's shadow bowed deeper as she relieved Skywalker's pressure point hold, replacing the cloth he held with a clean, dry one. I was still stitching, doing to my mind an admirable job. Duck didn't think so.

"You're being too slow."

"I'm being thorough."

"No, you're being wasteful of your time and his blood. Make bigger stitches."

"Big stitches make big scars."

"So what?"

"I intend to save his beauty as well as his life."

Duck muttered something unintelligible. Following that, she addressed Skywalker. "You're at the wrong end. Come down here by his legs and put his feet in your lap."

Skywalker looked to me. "She's right," I said. "He could do with a bit more blood flowing to his brain."

"Won't the blood spill through the cut?"

"Not anymore," I said, stubbornly carrying on making tiny stitches. "I'm almost finished."

Duck left me to retrieve the prepared tallow from Owl Man. The second she had it, Owl Man commenced chanting again, softly this time, the music of his prayer soothing, pleasing to the ear. The instant Duck handed the tallow to me, I tied off the final stitch and bathed the sewn-up wound with the healing substance. Then out of my medical bag, I took, a mixing bowl, several little bags of powdered herbs, and a battered canteen. The contents of the canteen sloshed as I stood to go to sit on the other side of the fire Owl Man was singing into. Duck used the big bowl of hot water she'd brought in as bath water, cleaning dried blood off The Cheyenne Robber's chest, out of his ear, and as much as she could from his hair. What I did was pour the liquid from the canteen into the mixing bowl, adding to it the water I'd taken, finally dusting in pinches of several herbs already ground into a powder. I stirred all of these ingredients until the mixture began to thicken to about the consistency of a runny soup. I then had to work quickly. Place the bandages in the bowl and then work them around so that every part of the soft cloth could absorb the liquid mixture before it did what it was suppose to do, which was form itself into a paste. When I softly said that I was ready, Duck moved away slightly, and, holding the drippy bandage by the top corners, I shuffled on my knees to my patient, carefully laying the sodden strip over the wound. Some details about the way I worked are mine alone to know. I have no war honors or trophies, nothing special about my life to confer on an heir. But I do have my healing paste. And because it's my only legacy, the thing I am proud to bequeath to a worthy recipient, I alone know its secret.

It's marvelous stuff. It effectively seals a wound shut, eliminating the dread of dirt getting inside an ordinary bandage and causing the wound to go sour and turn green. But the absolute best thing is the near miraculous healings that have occurred. Healings that without this treatment would have resulted in horrific scaring. Not only that, this paste was simply amazing whenever I used it on burns. As I lay the bandage across The Cheyenne Robber's chest and then gently pressed it into place, I began to think of the young man Crying Wind had mentioned.

The novice Buffalo Doctor known as Burned Hand.

His father, A Bull Standing Alone And Far Off, also known as Standing Alone, was himself a Buffalo Doctor and a fairly notable one. Which is why he came to me in secret bringing with him his son who was during this time only about ten years old. The boy had severely injured himself in an accident, the kind little boys are doomed to have whenever they are being rowdy and their mothers aren't looking. Standing Alone's son and his playmate were being rowdy on a rainy day, which meant their rowdiness was confined to the lodge. In an effort to calm them down, Standing Alone's harried wife decided to fry the boys some bacon. It was frying on a flat pan when she turned her back for barely a minute. That's when the boys, as a joke, grabbed for the half-cooked bacon and in the tussle tipped the pan, spilling hot meat and grease. Standing Alone's son was the only one of the two boys who was injured, severely burning his hand and wrist.

The Buffalo Doctors did what they could, but after several days the boy's hand began to curl inward. Quickly, the Owl Doctors rushed in, doing what *they* could. Another day passed, and the hand was more like a claw. Even more alarming, the boy was becoming fevered. Standing Alone knew the fever could kill his boy. He also knew that even if the fever spared him, there was a real possibility that his son would be a cripple for the rest of his life. Needless to say, Standing Alone was a desperate man.

During those days I was a recent widower, and having no family, no alliance with any band, I lived on the edge of any camp I chose. I did so as a virtual hermit, for my form of healing was not recognized as being worth very much and so only the truly desperate ever sought me out. But that was all right with me. I had been a bitter person back then; my little wife and my parents were dead, and the illness that had taken them away from me, smallpox, had left my face ravaged. My self-imposed isolation had suited me just fine, left me free to experiment with plants and herbs, and in that process, I came up with the healing paste. Not having many human patients, I used the paste on horses that suffered sores generated either by saddle rub or gaping bites that stallions invariably inflict on each other during fights over in-season mares. The results were amazing, but as I said, at that time I had no idea what it would do to a human.

I had the chance to find out when Standing Alone brought me his sickened and terribly injured little boy.

The first thing I had to do was tell that distraught man the truth: I didn't know if I had the proper knowledge to help his boy, nor could I be held responsible if while I used an unproven treatment on a human his son worsened and died. I remember vividly how that man sobbed as he knelt over his gravely ill boy and in a choking voice freed me of any blame. The instant he finished making this vow, I pushed him aside and set to work.

That boy was in a terrible state. He had cuts on his arms and legs where the Buffalo Doctors had tried to bleed out the fever as well as the poisonous thing afflicting the burned hand. He was also covered with a white powder the Owl

Doctors had coated him with to draw out any evil spirits trying to take over the child's body. The first thing I did was wash off the powder, then clean and close with tallow the series of cuts. The boy was awake but groggy, almost like he was drunk on whiskey. His being awake was a good thing because he was able to swallow the herb tea I forced into him. A tea I knew would fight down the fever. I knew because it had fought down the fever I'd had during the worst days of my suffering the pox. But at the time I hadn't known it would do that. I'd just buried my wife, my mother, and my father and I'd made up that brew for one purpose: to kill myself. Well, it had worked in reverse. It saved my life. After the fever broke, I remembered exactly how I'd made it, and the one ingredient that I had been completely certain would kill me.

Alkali water.

Alkali was a common household substance that women kept in order to set dyes into fabric and porcupine quills. Well, my dead little wife loved to sew, create beautiful designs. Being an artist, she always kept a good supply of alkali water. I found it, boiled some of it up, throwing in a few herbs to make it taste a bit better because when I'd tried swallowing it on its own, it was such a foul experience that I couldn't stop myself spitting that rank water out. If I didn't want to go on foiling one suicide attempt after another, I had to improve the taste. So I made a somewhat pleasant tea, drank every drop of it, and then lay myself down to die. Imagine my surprise when I woke up again. I was still sick, my body covered with sores and every bone I owned felt as if it had been broken in half. Even more desperate to die, I made the tea again, this time making it twice as strong and adding a dollop of honey for good measure.

That second dose cured me completely.

When the boy was crying, on account of he didn't want to be force fed any more tea, I allowed him to rest while I made up the bandage. Standing Alone very nearly went gray headed right there on the spot when I forced that little hand open, and the child rent the air with piercing screams. I ordered the stunned man to help me as I coiled the sodden bandage in and around those little fingers and then around the wrist. Standing Alone and his son stayed with me for almost a week. Within two days the fever was gone and the boy was eating well, his father quick to supply as much fresh meat as either the boy or I cared to have. The boy continued to put up a terrible fuss whenever I changed the bandage—most especially when I scraped away dead skin before reapplying—but by the fourth day those little fingers were wiggling, and the boy was finally well enough to go home. I never saw him up close again, and as the years passed, I forgot about him. As for Standing Alone, he took all the credit for the cure. That did not surprise me. His admitting that he, a celebrated Buffalo Doctor, had turned his son's life over to an eccentric would have ruined him, and, quite honestly, I really didn't care about my reputation or his. The only thing I cared about was that I'd had the opportunity to try out my paste bandage on a human being, and the outcome had surpassed even my wildest imaginings.

We could hear White Bear. He was right outside and in a rage. He bellowed a question, and then there was a muttered response from someone. Whatever was said set him off again. Skywalker raised his eyes to me and gave a quick lift of his chin in the direction of the doorway. He and I left Owl Man to chant and Duck to continue bathing a now-sleeping The Cheyenne Robber.

The sight greeting my eyes as I cleared the doorway just behind Skywalker were over a dozen guards, armed with shields and lances, staving off a goodly number of the camp's population, with scores more rapidly arriving. The Cheyenne Robber was a hero. News of the attack against him ranged between disbelief and outrage. The people had come to keep vigil over him, pray for his return to health and strength. But White Bear, because he was in such an outrage, did not want to be fettered by the presence of a lot of praying people. No longer shouting at his own men, he turned on the people his guards struggled to hold back.

EIGHT

Waving his arms broadly, White Bear shouted at the gathered crowd, "Everyone go home!"

The crowd did not budge; instead, anxious questions began to fly. Grappling to maintain the brave pretense of still being in control, White Bear did answer one or two questions but only those concerning the safety of the people. Clearly a knife-wielding crazy person was running loose, and not knowing just who that person might be, people were giving relatives and friends sidelong glances, the unspoken question hanging, "Are you the one?" The smell of fear was pervasive. If the mighty The Cheyenne Robber could be attacked, then everyone was at risk. These people stood stolid, waiting for a guarantee that they would not be murdered in their sleep, and they were not moving until their chief gave them one.

In an attempt to relieve their worry, White Bear said, "The one who struck down my nephew is not one of us. I say he came from Turned The Horses's band, and he came here on Turned The Horses's order."

For too long a moment no one said a word. Then angry muttering rolled through the crowd. Skywalker and I were standing well back, so near to the lodge walls that we were in immediate danger of stumbling over the ropes that lashed the walls to slanted wooden stakes. Skywalker ran a hand over his face—a hand bearing the dried blood of his younger brother. He looked emotionally drained, but as White Bear warmed to the theme of the unknown assailant belonging to Turned The Horses's camp, Skywalker hastened forward and hurriedly spoke into White Bear's ear. His expression was tight, but at least White Bear was listening to whatever his closest adviser was saying, and that filled me with a modicum of relief. Given the prevailing mood of the people, one more word from White Bear about his fellow chief and Turned The Horses's camp faced the real threat of being wiped out. As the Rattle Band was hundreds more than Turned The Horses's camp, it would have been a fast and easy victory. But the win would also mean White Bear's even quicker downfall.

Lone Wolf, our principal chief, had not been pleased with White Bear for well over a year. Twice during this last year, Lone Wolf had come drastically close to declaring White Bear an outcast. If White Bear persisted in going to war against a weaker chief, this would be all the excuse Lone Wolf would need to cut him down once and for all. The gravity of this settled over my brain like a dense fog as I gazed dully at the blackness of the night that was displaced

here and there by the yellowish glow of bonfires. The fire-
light was doing strange things to the faces of people I knew,
people who were my family. It heightened and deepened
their contorted-with-anger faces, changing them from the
friendly people I knew into frightening apparitions. So
caught up in the illusion, I almost screamed when Big Tree
pulled on my arm.

"Skywalker said to tell you that he must stay with
White Bear. But he says that's all right because he trusts
you with the other."

Looking around, I was surprised to see that the crowd
was moving off, people going their separate directions, and
that White Bear and Skywalker were gone. I turned to Big
Tree. "What 'other'?"

He wagged his head, then shrugged, showing me the
palms of his hands. "All I know is that I am to keep close
to you." He quickly added, "For your protection."

There were only a few lingerers now, the crowd having
dwindled down to the kind of people who would not budge
because they harbored the hope that something else halfway
exciting might happen. This kind of spectator rarely talked
to guards standing sentinel, much less tag after the guards
now busy making another bonfire, this one on the back side
of Owl Man's lodge. The guards were preparing for a long
night of watching over The Cheyenne Robber. Off to the
left and out of the gloom came Hears The Wolf trailed by
two women. One woman was his wife Beloved; the other,
his daughter White Otter, the wife of The Cheyenne Robber. When Hears The Wolf came closer, he paused, but the
two women passed me by without a word.

Worry etched Hears The Wolf's face, tinged his voice, as he asked, "Will he live?"

"I believe yes, but the wound is serious, and he's a lost a great deal of blood. The most serious threat, of course, is the wound becoming fevered. If anything will kill him, it will be that."

Hears The Wolf sagged as he looked off into the night. Finally he said, more to himself than to me, "Maybe his dying is the thing my daughter needs."

Unfortunately, I knew what he meant. Even more unfortunately, I agreed. Both Hears The Wolf and I cared a great deal for The Cheyenne Robber, but we were men, immune to the heartache he was prone to cause women— his own wife in particular. It was a hard thing for Hears The Wolf to stand back, to do nothing while his daughter cried and The Cheyenne Robber proved over and over again that he was not a good husband. Then it it came to me. The thing that had been hovering in the recesses of my memory, resisting all effort to bring it forward, the initial reason I'd sought out my wife, only to be distracted. I grabbed hold of Hears The Wolf's cold hand and shook it while giving my hurried words of departure.

"I've told Duck to stay with him. She knows just what to do. But I will return. I promise."

Big Tree stayed with me as I ran for home. And as we were running in the opposite direction, I missed seeing Skywalker rushing back to Owl Man's lodge.

My sudden entrance startled Crying Wind. As it did the four women cluttering up our home. I should of course have known that this would happen, but I'd been too absorbed in my own misery to consider hers. In our culture women never live solely on their own. In all probability I had been just barely gone when the widow I recognized and then the three other women I vaguely knew leaped at the chance of better accommodations. Widows lived at the mercy of generosity. The other three were married but were lesser wives. The widow needed shelter, but the others had no doubt pushed in on Crying Wind just to get out from under the control of dominating first wives. With all four women came their children. What with the recent excitement, it was apparent that Crying Wind had yet to tell them that she and I had agreed to reconcile. Either that or she'd been waiting for me to do it. Now she was fervently avoiding my eye, lightly dry washing her hands as the four women glared at me.

For an exceedingly long and awkward moment, I noted with no small degree of shock that gone from our home was the strict order my wife normally maintained with a near religious fervor. Our lodge was a mess, filled with the things the women had brought with them and had haphazardly tossed about. Naked toddlers sat on rugs playing with chewable toys while older children crawled in and out of the laps of the four steely-eyed women. It took a bit of doing, but I finally spotted my son sitting off in the shadows. When my eye caught his, his expression turned hopeful, a trembling attempt at a smile tugging one corner of his mouth. Craning my head forward and crooking my finger, I beckoned. It was the first time I'd ever known that boy to run to me with his arms extended and with the glad cry of "Father!"

I grabbed him up, swinging him to straddle my hip. His

little arms went around my neck, and when he stole a backward glance, I felt a shudder run through him. With one hand I massaged his back as I addressed my wife in as calm a tone as I could manage.

"I am taking our son. We will be gone only for a little while. When we come home, I expect to find things set to rights and a meal ready. That is all I have to say."

Crying Wind all but bowed before me. Favorite Son, smiling, patted me on the back during our duck through the entry hole.

Standing outside, Big Tree opened his arms, inviting Favorite Son to come to him. I was happily surprised a second time when he shunned the invitation, twisted away, wrapped his little arms more tightly around my neck. Hearing the arguing female voices inside, Big Tree glanced anxiously at me. I didn't want to totally abandon my wife in case the eviction of her sisters got ugly, so I led Big Tree around to the back, and there we hunkered down, my son straddling my bent-at-the-knee leg. For a while we did nothing more than listen to the raised female voices, the bawling of babies.

A visible tremor shook Big Tree as he murmured, "Women are scary." He looked at me hopefully. "You know, we could always go someplace a bit . . . safer."

"Not just yet," I whispered. "I want to make certain my wife will be all right." Patting my son on his tummy, I asked, "Was it terrible?"

Favorite Son nodded with his entire body. "Mommy cried. She wanted you to come home." He became hesitant, unusually shy. "You left on account of I was bad."

His saying that wrenched my heart. I hugged him

against me. "You are not a bad boy. You are my son. I love you. I'm sorry I'm not the kind of father you can be proud of."

Big Tree snorted disdainfully. Jabbing a finger against Favorite Son's arm he said, "Your father is better than a warrior." Favorite Son fixed his concentration on him as Big Tree went on to explain, "It's true. Warriors only know how to rub out lives, but your father knows how to give life back to those about to die. I've seen him do that many times. Many warriors owe him for that. Just like your uncle, The Cheyenne Robber, now owes him."

Favorite Son's eyes widened, and he let go a tiny gasp. Big Tree smiled and duck walked closer to us, his face very near my son's. "As big and as powerful as The Cheyenne Robber is," he said, making my doctoring sound like an exciting tale of a brave hero's deed, "he was in terrible danger. Only your father knew just what to do to save him. Without your father, your uncle would need putting in the ground. I believe this is something a boy ought to brag about."

Before Favorite Son could respond, a shriek came from inside my lodge, and something hit the wall.

"Please," Big Tree whisper-hissed urgently, "can't we hide someplace else?"

"I really do want to," I whispered back, "but I have to know my wife will be all right."

"I wouldn't worry," Big Tree huffed. "I've seen her take on women before."

So had I. "True," I hastened to say, "but there's something I need to ask her."

"What?" Big Tree sneered. "What question can be more important than three male lives?"

"It concerns some talk about the one who died and The Cheyenne Robber."

Big Tree lifted the corner of his upper lip in a sneer. "Would it happen to do with the talk about that dead man trying to favor himself up to White Otter?"

"Yes!" I shouted. Our gazes slid toward the lodge wall as everything suddenly became too quiet inside my home.

"Now we do have to get out of here," Big Tree said, rising to a crouch.

Favorite Son was clinging to my neck as I half stood and moved to follow the escaping Big Tree.

"I know all about that," he said, flinging an arm to the side. We were walking upright now, like real men. Of course, we'd only begun to do this after we'd managed to put a good distance between us and my home. "The talk wasn't just among the women. We men talked, too. We even made bets on how much longer The Cheyenne Robber's marriage would last."

"Isn't that a bit cruel?" I snorted. I shifted my son's weight as I reduced our hurrying walk to a casual stroll. Big Tree was able to continue without his words coming out in puffs.

"It would be if it wasn't The Cheyenne Robber we were betting on," he said with a half laugh. "He's always been a bit . . . loose about his marriage. At least, his part in the marriage. His idea is that he should be able to do whatever he wants while he holds White Otter on a short rein. While she was pregnant, he didn't worry about her too much. After she delivered and got her figure back, he began demanding to know just how she spent every hour of her day. They were fighting all the time when that other one started coming around."

"I didn't know they were fighting," I said, genuinely amazed.

"Why would you?" he laughed. "The Cheyenne Robber and White Otter don't fight the way you and Crying Wind do. They aren't loud. They don't carry on in front of their neighbors. And White Otter wouldn't dare chase The Cheyenne Robber around with a broom."

Instantly, we three were remembering White Bear's little joke. How his advice had won me a sore head and then a lot of teasing from everyone who'd witnessed the spectacle. Even Favorite Son thought this particular memory was funny. Not being quite so amused, I brought Big Tree back to the point of the conversation.

"White Otter's problem," Big Tree reflected, "has always been that she loves him too much. On account of that, she gives in too quickly whenever he says he's sorry. Her own mother tried to tell her that if she'd be a little harder to persuade, he'd respect her more, but she wouldn't listen. Not until there came the talk about him fathering a child by another woman. She confronted him, but he only put her off, saying she shouldn't worry about the talk. I believe she tried to put the gossip out of her mind, but the thing that made her unsure was that he hadn't bothered trying to deny the rumors. That's when that other one, the one who died this morning, started doing her . . . favors. Letting her know that if she divorced The Cheyenne Robber, he would be glad."

"So," I mused aloud, "The Cheyenne Robber shooting him wasn't an accident."

"No," Big Tree said with a heavy sigh. "And we all knew it. Just as we knew that the area where he shot him"—meaning Three Elks's rump—"was meant to humiliate."

"Do you know who the other woman is?"

Big Tree shook his head. "The Cheyenne Robber only wants exceptional women. He likes it even better if they are unavailable and are the daughters or wives of powerful men. The risk of seducing women like that makes him excited. Then, too, those kinds of women are just as anxious to keep everything a secret, so whenever he talks about a new sweetheart, no name is ever mentioned."

I picked up our pace.

"Where are we going?" he asked as the speed increased.

"To talk to Raven's Wing."

"He's under guard, you know."

No, I didn't. But I should have at least considered it, for following the attack on his nephew, placing a guard on the in-residence son of Turned The Horses would have been the first thing White Bear would have done. Then again, his gifts being rebuffed by Turned The Horses might have been all he'd needed to order a guard before the attack. That was the question I put to Big Tree.

"You're right to think that way," he replied. "No sooner had Hears The Wolf repeated the things Turned The Horses had said than White Bear ordered the guard. But the guards couldn't find him for a long time on account of his being in his father's camp for his brother's funeral. No one expected him to come back. But he did. The guards have been with him ever since."

"Turned The Horses has already buried his son?"

"Yes. He did that not long after we left his camp."

"Wasn't that a bit hasty?"

Big Tree pulled a frown. "Not for Turned The Horses. Waiting until tomorrow would have interfered with his receiving the army's gifts."

"The man is that greedy?"

"Yes," Big Tree responded flatly. "I have a fine broodmare to wager that when the sutler opens his doors in the morning, Turned The Horses's face will be the first thing that man sees."

I didn't take the bet. I merely shook a perplexed head.

"I wouldn't go in there," one of two of the guards—both of them standing several yards away from Raven's Wing's home but close enough to watch the door—said ruefully.

"White Bear won't allow him visitors?" I asked.

Both men turned their faces away and snickered. Eventually, the first guard answered. "White Bear doesn't care who goes in. He just doesn't want Raven's Wing coming out."

I set my son down on his feet, took his little hand, and held it. "Then I don't understand."

"It's simple," the second guard offered. "Always Happy went in a while ago and was not at all happy to find that her husband had come back. They've been shouting at each other ever since. We"—with his head he indicated his fellow guard—"decided to stand clear. Give them privacy."

I transferred my son's hand into Big Tree's. "Stay here," I ordered softly.

As I walked away, I heard Big Tree say to my son, "Did I tell you that I believe your father is also a very brave man?"

The young woman—girl, really—was heavily pregnant. Which made the sight of Raven's Wing holding her by the wrists and forcing her to her knees, doubly contemptible. Without thinking, I rushed to her aid. Tears streamed down her too-young face as she grimaced against the pain he was inflicting. Raven's Wing was so lost to his fury that he wasn't even aware of me, even though I was frantically trying to break his hold on her. Finally, I balled up my fist and hit him in the face. It was the second time in one day I'd dared to hit one of my betters. This second time was far more satisfying than the first, but it was infinitely more dangerous.

His eyes flared wide as he staggered back, his hands finally letting go of his wife's small, bird-bone-delicate wrists. And then I had her behind me, shielding her, taking side steps, aiming the two of us for the doorway and warily watching Raven's Wing, who was touching his a hand to his nose, then examining the show of blood on his fingers.

In a truly amazed tone, he cried, "You hit me!"

I certainly didn't care to belabor the obvious, so I said shakily, "Stand clear of the doorway, Raven's Wing."

The only movement he made was to touch his mouth, where blood also dribbled. Then he wagged his head as if to clear it. "What right," he demanded in a contemptuous tone, "have you to come into my home and assault me?"

"The right of a doctor protecting his patient."

His eyes slid to his bulky wife sheltering herself behind me. "Her?" He tipped his head back and made an ugly sound that nearly resembled a laugh. When the sound stopped, his eyes made deep contact with mine, and the sharp-edged voice issuing from his lips caused fear bumps to raise up all over my arms.

The girl behind me was shaking violently. My heart hammering, I trembled right along with her. "Have you forgotten the guards outside?" I shouted, praying they could hear me.

He tilted his head as he looked at me shrewdly. "Have you forgotten," he said in a menacing hiss, "that I could kill you before they'd have time to get to me?"

Actually, I had given the thought a panic-riddled flicker, but what I said, as evenly as possible, was, "But you won't. An argument with your wife is not cause enough to take another man's life."

His eyes still locked on mine, he took a deep breath, then slowly expelled it. "Get out," he finally growled. Then shifting his gaze to the girl's terrified eyes, he growled again, "It's not over with us. Do you hear me, woman?"

She let out a tiny cry, and, still shielding her, I hustled Always Happy out. Once we were clear of the door I held her hand as we ran toward Big Tree and the two guards. Like the girl-woman that she was, with each running step, Always Happy cried, "I want my mommy! I want my mommy!"

Big Tree lifted my son, holding him as the girl and I struggled to regain our breath. Looking closely at Always Happy, realizing her distress, the guards lost their former jocularity. I was quite angry with them for their indifference to the marital squabble that had placed the girl and her unborn child at risk. When I spoke, informing them that Always Happy would not be returning and that Raven's Wing was far more dangerous than their indolent guarding afforded, they beset me with earnest apologies and pleas that I not report them to White Bear. Before I could respond, Big Tree stepped between me and the guards.

"They're bachelors, and being younger than me, they haven't learned yet that a marriage can sometimes be more like a war. But I assure you, had this woman screamed for help, they would have gone in there. And not just on account of her being White Bear's brother's daughter. I've trained these men myself. They know their first duty is to protect our women and children."

That simmered me down some—but not enough to stop sending the repentant young men evil looks the whole time Big Tree hurriedly assured them that no report would be made. However, before they were able to take a relieved breath, I demanded their names. Worry shown from their eyes as I was glumly informed that one was called Whistles and the other, Took The Good Road. Leaving them to fret about what I intended to do with their names, Big Tree, still carrying my son, helped me shepherd off Always Happy.

She was still being very adamant about wanting to go home to her mother, but with the welts and bruises steadily rising on her arms, I didn't believe it was advisable for her to be anywhere near her parents just yet. Her father just happened to be White Bear's older brother, and he would naturally demand justice. What we of the Rattle Band did not need was one more dead son for Turned The Horses to have to bury. So I convinced the girl that she would be safer in my home. Possibly this was a mistake, for I hadn't asked my wife's opinion on our having a guest, but things being what they were, I didn't have a choice. I was thinking of a hundred things I could say to ease Crying Wind's objections as we all trooped along. Dimly I heard Big Tree complain about being hungry. Then the girl piped up and said she was hungry, too. Then against my ear I heard my son's soft voice.

"Uh-oh. Mommy's not going to like having all these people to feed."

Knowing the truth of those words, I tried to banish them from my mind, to hear only the sound of thousands of crickets chirping all at once and, down by the creek, the multitude of frogs singing their mating songs. This night before annuity day should have also carried the hum of excitement. Housewives should have been preparing their storage containers to receive the staples they'd come to rely on. The men should have been playing gambling games and talking about how glad they would be to finally receive rations of coffee. The children should have been running everywhere, jubilant that in the morning they would have the hard candy the soldiers so liked to give them. But instead, because one man was dead, another gravely injured, and two camp chiefs ready to go to war against each other, people were keeping quiet and inside their homes. Over in the third camp . . . well, I didn't know about the third camp, but odds were high that the chief of that band, Woman's Heart, a staunch devotee of Lone Wolf, was prepared to pull up stakes and fly the instant more trouble flared. And he would fly straight to Lone Wolf and give him a detailed account of what White Bear was getting up to. Even if his haste to do that required his missing out on receiving any coffee. I was certain that, given the former noise and gunfire, the commander of Ft. Larned was left in something of an anxious state, as well, but I couldn't be bothered with worrying about him.

At my lodge, everything was still a shambles, but a least the women and extra children were gone, and Crying Wind was energetically striving to restore order when we came in. Dismay over yet another female relative's intrusion was written all over her face, but she managed to control her tongue during my hurried explanation of the situation.

"Well," she said, following a considerable think, "I suppose everyone should just find a place to sit"—she waved an arm in a hapless manner—"somewhere."

Big Tree was noticeably uncomfortable with having to remain, but he would have been even more uncomfortable explaining to White Bear why he'd left me on my own, so he found a clear spot near the right of the door. The instant his legs began to fold into a sitting position, Favorite Son wriggled away from him. Crying Wind was mothering over Always Happy—that girl working herself up into another good cry—and I was speaking in low tones to my wife when I felt the tugging at my hand.

I glanced down into my son's upturned little face and did not try to hide my smile as I accepted his hand in mine. Then I turned back to Crying Wind.

"I must examine her, make certain Raven's Wing's actions did not harm the child. I'm afraid I'm going to need you to help me."

125

As every bit of this was one more part of an ever-expanding juicy scandal, Crying Wind quickly consented. Within a few minutes the privacy curtain that normally hung between our bed and our son's was rehung, but for extra measure I sent my son and Big Tree to sit just outside. For all that she was about to be a mother, my patient looked terribly young. I worried—unnecessarily as it turned out—about her being shy with a physical examination. I explained in detail just what I needed to do, and with an indifferent shrug, she lifted her dress. I must admit that I was a bit taken aback by that. That and the fact that beneath her dress there was no female breechcloth. Judging by the way Crying Wind's eyes enlarged, she was a trifle undone herself.

"Uh . . ." I hedged, "exactly how old are you?"

The girl answered proudly. "I have been alive for fourteen Sun Dances."

I stole a quick glance at my wife, who mouthed, "Just turned."

Taking a deep breath, locking it in my throat, I knelt down at the girl's feet. Crying Wind knelt with me, standing on her knees. The girl standing before us wasn't showing any signs of embarrassment, but I noticed a definite flush on my wife's face. Her flush deepened when I placed my hands on Always Happy's bulging abdomen and began to press in various places. Still concerned about my wife, I chanced another glance in her direction only to quickly realize that this type of examination fascinated her completely. Dismissing further worry, I concentrated on finding the baby's placement.

"What are you doing?" Crying Wind whispered.

"Feeling for the head," I answered tersely.

"You can do that?"

"Yes, but only if you keep quiet."

She went back to watching. I really shouldn't have been so sharp with her. It wasn't her fault she was ignorant of such things. During her pregnancy she had been tended only by her former mother-in-law. Throughout Crying Wind's term that woman had neither looked at her nor had she ever touched her. It was only when it came time for the actual delivery that her mother-in-law was even remotely personal with her. From what I understand, Crying Wind's labor had been long and arduous. I strongly suspected that it was because of the experience that she'd never shown any interest in attending another childbirth. I also suspected it was because of her first time that we were still without a child of our own. Experienced women had secret ways of preventing childbirth. The pity was they didn't think it was proper to share this knowledge with younger women. Which was why so many of them got caught out. If I had to bet on it, I'd bet that Always Happy had gotten herself caught. And because of that, she suffered an unhappy marriage.

Even though my wife was a mother herself, she had no experience with the care and tending of expecting women. Hoping to remove some of her lingering fear of the process, I took her hand I placed it just above the rise of Always Happy's pubic area.

"Feel that?"

Crying Wind's hand was trembling, and she looked at me with fear-filled eyes as she nodded.

"That's the back of the head." I slid her hand farther up

the girl's belly. "What you're feeling now is the baby's spine."

Her mouth parted slightly as, on her own, she guided her hand along swell of the girl's belly. Halfway up, Crying Wind's hand stopped, and she gasped, "What are these bumps?"

"Elbows," I smiled. She was about to take her hand away. I hurriedly placed mine over hers, forcing her hand to go higher, to the crest of the breathing mound. "Now you're feeling the feet."

Taking her hand away, forming it into a fist that she pressed against her heart, Crying Wind sat back on her heels and was quiet for a good length of time. Then she slid misting eyes toward mine. "Why is the baby upside down?"

"Because he . . . or she . . . is ready to be born."

"Ahhh," she breathed. That was the one thing she did know, that babies needed to be born headfirst. Still gazing up at the girl's swollen belly, she asked softly, "How do you know so much about all of . . . this." Meaning the mysteries of prebirth.

"I learned. To be a good doctor, that was my duty. To learn. To know."

She stared at me for an indeterminate amount of time, questions she badly wanted to ask filling the air between us. Finally she said almost reverently, "What a wonderful mind you have."

Now, that set me back. Pride for my craft was not a thing I was used to receiving from my wife. Oh, she liked it that I was a doctor, but truth be told she would have liked anything that I did just so long as it didn't involve something silly—such as placing myself in a position to be killed.

Yet her assisting me with the examination had accomplished more than I'd intended, which had been first to protect the modesty of Always Happy, then secondly to relieve my wife's hidden fear of childbirth. It had never occurred to me that I would gain her awe. But I had. And I felt thirty feet tall.

Next we made Always Happy more comfortable on our bed, and I proceeded to examine the girls arms and hands, making sure that Raven's Wing's crushing hold hadn't caused any more harm than the bruising imprints of his hands. Sitting so close beside me that our shoulders touched, Crying Wind studied the girl's arms right along with me. When I held the girl's hand flat in mine and said that I needed a pin, Crying Wind scooted off to find one. Then she was back, and my wife held her breath as I used the pin to lightly prick each fingertip. I didn't need to ask if Always Happy could feel each small jab because the girl flinched, and the affected finger curled inward.

"There are no broken bones," I thought out loud.

"But wouldn't she know if her own bones were broken?"

"Not necessarily. Fingers are not simply five small bones joined to one big block of bone. The four fingers are made up of three little bones, each of them set into three different joints; the thumb only has two bones, two joints. Fingers and thumbs are connected to longer, thinner bones. And because these bones are finer than finger and thumb bones, they are protected by thick muscles that make up the palm. If one of the bones in the palm is damaged, the palm will swell, and a finger will not move, but the person will not understand why. The wrist is even more delicate because this is the area locking all of the hand bones into place and fixing the hand to the two bones that extend to the elbow."

"How many bones are in the upper arm?"

"One. And it locks into the shoulder joint." She didn't have to tell me that she found my knowledge of all of this wondrous. I saw it in her eyes.

But mostly I saw her pride and love.

NINE

Big Tree and I walked along the darkened pathways of the camp. It was early in the night, too early for people to be holed up in their homes, but they were, and their doors were tied closed against any visitors. The people were afraid because the cover of darkness is perfect for an assailant's strike. It eased no one's mind that this particular assailant had been bold enough to strike twice during full daylight. I knew that while women and children slept, armed husbands, sons, and brothers would sit before their lodge fires, keeping awake all through the night. Until whoever was guilty was found out, every person in the Rattle Band would remain nervous, remain on their guard.

Arriving at the Grandmother's little lodge, I left my personal bodyguard to stand watch outside and entered alone. Deer Trail and Wolf Blanket were enjoying an evening meal. The wafting aroma of stew hit me like a physical force, the pungent odor stealing my breath, keenly reminding me that I'd only eaten breakfast—and that, long hours ago. My empty stomach began to twist and squirm. Before it set to growling, I spoke hurriedly to Deer Trail.

"You've heard about the attack on The Cheyenne Robber?"

"Yes, I heard, and I'm still trying to force myself to believe such a thing could happen to that fine young man."

I leveled an accusing hand at Wolf Blanket while demanding, "To the best of your knowledge, has he been here throughout the entire day?"

Wolf Blanket was instantly offended. "Now, look here—"

I yelled over him to Deer Trail. "Answer!"

The old man became lost in a muddle, looking up at me, blinking again and again. His long thought process made Wolf Blanket edgy. Finally Deer Trail said, "I would have to say that, yes, he has been here throughout the entire day."

Wolf Blanket closed his eyes, let go a held breath. Then he shot me the most hateful look a human face can manage.

Still addressing the old man I asked, "Could he have gotten out without your knowing?"

This time the old man took even longer to consider, which caused Wolf Blanket even more distress. In the guise of being helpful, he tried prodding the old fellow's memory. "You know I was here. You and your good wife would have known immediately if I'd slipped out."

"Well," Deer Trail drawled, "I suppose that is true." His face pulling a frown, he looked up at me. "Medicine Woman and I come in and out of here a lot. We have to on account of our duties. Everything for the Grandmother must be just right. And this one"—with a lift of his chin he indicated Wolf Blanket—"never really knows just when we will come in or how long we will be away when we go out." His tone approaching scolding, he admonished my audacity in questioning his diligence. "As you very well know, this one is not our prisoner. He is a guest, merely here for his own personal safety. Which means he's allowed visitors."

Hearing this, Wolf Blanket glared hard at Deer Trail, but the old man wasn't paying him any attention.

"And those he's had—quite a number actually—but had he left this place, for any reason, I wouldn't be allowed to let him back in." Shaking a finger at me, the old man angrily finished, "You, Tay-bodal, should know this better than anyone, that The Grandmother offers her protection to all in need, but she only offers once."

I understood the none-too-subtle inference. Deer Trail was strongly reminding me of my wife's time under the Grandmother's protection and the many times I was in and out of the lodge while trying to help and comfort her. My eyes locked with Wolf Blanket's. I didn't believe he'd remained in place throughout the day. That disbelief shone from my eyes, and finally, under the pressure of mine, his gaze dropped. Satisfied by this small victory, I made my apologies to Deer Trail for any suggestion that he had failed in his duty. I had nothing to say to Wolf Blanket as I left.

I set a brisk pace, almost a dogtrot. Big Tree wasn't troubled by the pace, but even he found it hard to jog and keep a conversation flowing smoothly. I was really glad about that because every word I spoke came inside a pant. "I want you to tell me," I huffed, "everything you know about Wolf Blanket."

"I know a lot," he answered. "But you're going to have to slow down while I do the telling."

I did. In fact, because of a pain coming into my side, he gave me a perfect reason to stop.

"To begin with," Big Tree said, "he doesn't like me. He never has. His attitude has to do with me coming up hard and him being born into the upper class."

"Born to the *second* upper class," I sharply reminded.

Big Tree sighed wearily, rolling his eyes as if my correction made precious little difference. Following this minor pause, he continued on. "He's always teased me, and his remarks have always been personal." He waved a hand as if brushing away a bothersome fly. "Oh, he tried to disguise his teasing, and others simply took it as that, but I knew he meant every word he said. My accusing him would have made me look foolish. The best I could do was pretend I took it for teasing, too. But then he made trouble for me out on the trail. *That* I couldn't ignore, and I'm afraid I reacted badly." His fingers toyed with his lower lip, and I felt the radiating warmth of his embarrassment. "I . . . uh . . . resorted to violence."

Now, this was something I wanted to hear, so I folded my arms across my chest—a clear signal that I had no intention of budging until I'd heard him out.

Striated clouds drifted across the lazily ascending moon, reducing it for a time to a hazy ball. More clouds moved in until only a few stars managed to wink through the thin cover. Neither the overcast moon nor the impish stars were enough to provide anything beyond a glimmer of light, but all around us lodges glowed from internal fires, turning the walls bright gold. Black shadows bobbed in the gold as people inside their homes moved around, and we could smell meals being cooked. The camp dogs smelled the food, too, and were on the hunt, slinking around the camp with heads lowered as they went from doorway to doorway, sniffing hopefully for scraps. It was more on account of the golden lodges than any light from the sky that I was able to see Big Tree, watch his girl-pretty face churn with disgust.

"When we went against the Utes," he said, his tone now conveying anger, "I was a bit more timid with my responsibility as pipe bearer than I should have been. I guess that was because of so many of upper-class warriors accepting the pipe."

His eyes shot toward me as he paused to make certain that I understood. I did. Even though no pipe had ever been presented to me, I wasn't ignorant of the gravity involved when a warrior, no matter his rank, actively submitted himself to a war chief's authority. An act that involved taking the long pipe from a war chief's hands and drawing smoke from it, men literally pledging their loyalty with just that one inhalation of smoke. But it also meant that the raid leader was totally responsible for the lives and welfare of his men. If a man was wounded, the leader had to make certain that that man was saved. If a man died, the loss of his life would be counted as the raid leader's fault. Which asked a lot when considering the way warriors preferred to fight: virtually on their own and for their own gain. Holding together so many hardheaded individuals required an incredibly strong leader, which was why White Bear was so much the way he was. As a seasoned war chief, he'd become too used to shouting, knocking heads together, wading into brawls and sorting them out. White Bear only knew how to shoot or club a problem over the head. On matters of diplomacy, he was like a blind puppy rooting for the tit.

But not Big Tree.

He'd been a young man in the lower ranks during the time when our principal chief had been Little Bluff, a man who'd raised diplomacy to the level of an art. Because Big Tree was almost two decades younger than White Bear, he'd grasped the importance of the very thing White Bear too often chose to ignore. But because he'd also been trained by White Bear, when reasoning talk failed, Big Tree was more than capable of settling issues with whatever force necessary.

"From the very beginning, Wolf Blanket demanded that he be second leader," Big Tree went on. "Deep inside I knew that agreeing to such a thing was dangerous, but I thought that if we worked together, then he would come to respect me more. So I agreed. A few days later I realized my first instinct had been right. That man would not follow my lead without first loudly questioning my judgment. This agitated my men, who numbered about thirty. Feelings began to run hot, and the night before the raid against the Ute horse herds, seventeen of the thirty were ready to follow only him in what I'd planned as a three-pronged attack." Big Tree began to explain, raising his arms to shoulder level, almost as in the sign of surrender. "Two groups would ride like this"—he brought forward the raised right hand. "This group would sweep this way"—the arm arched around—"the second would sweep this way"—he arched the left arm—"and I would lead the charge straight up the center."

His arms fell to his sides. "By flanking the two, the Utes's camp guards would be cut off from the fight, and my men and I coming up the center would draw fire and do the actual fighting while the right and left groups made off with the entire herd."

"That sounds like a very good plan."

"I thought so, too," he grumbled. "But Wolf Blanket said it would only work if he took the center on account of him being older and more experienced. His doing that would have meant that all credit and honors would go to him. It didn't trouble his mind at all that he'd earn them with my plan, my raid party. When I said this to his face, he told me that if I felt that way about it, we should just put it to a vote.

"Well, I needed to think about that, and it's a good thing I did, for while I was sulking, the one who died today"— Three Elks—"came to me and told me that Wolf Blanket already had a larger number of men ready to vote for him. That if I had allowed the vote to go forward, I would certainly loose. Of course this also meant that I would have been ruined forever. Which is what I believe that man wanted."

During Big Tree's pause for air, I recalled something Red Flowers had said: that her son had once saved Big Tree. This had to be the incident she'd referred to.

Cutting into my thoughts, Big Tree continued, "Wolf Blanket left me no choice but to challenge him. As you know"—I didn't and he knew it, but never mind—"a night camp before a raid is kept dark. No fires are allowed. A knife fight in the dark is the most dangerous fight there is. But we went at it anyway, and we kept at it until I finally had him down, my foot on his throat and my knife against his hairline. I was about to cut him when he cried enough. With that cry, I won back all of my men. Four days later we came home with eighty good horses and one Ute scalp. Wolf Blanket acted as if nothing untoward had happened, and to save face I did the same. But I've never asked him to go out with me since that time."

He folded his arms against his chest and looked at me sternly. "I know that White Bear thinks a lot of him, but that's because Wolf Blanket leaps to obey whenever he speaks. For everyone else, Wolf Blanket is more trouble than he's worth. The Cheyenne Robber knows what I say is true. Wolf Blanket likes to act that he's The Cheyenne Robber's good friend, but the truth is, The Cheyenne Robber doesn't trust him any further than he can fling him, and he won't go out with him, either."

I brought the conversation back to Three Elks. "I talked to the dead man's mother, and she indicated that her son and you shared hard feelings. She blames you, saying that you behaved badly after her son saved you. I assume she was speaking of the very situation you just shared."

"That's right," Big Tree snorted. "For a long time I was grateful to him until he squeezed that gratitude dust dry. His brother, Raven's Wing, was all the time mad at him about something, and he in turn would come to me expecting me to stand between them. Once or twice was all right, but constantly became too much. Finally I told him to grow up, be a man, fight with his brother alone."

"And that's it?" I laughed. "That was the extent of your malice toward him?"

Big Tree shook his head and shrugged. "I barely knew him. What else were you expecting?"

Considering what his mother had said, that Big Tree had been another man intent on doing in her son, I'd been expecting something a shade more diabolical. But if Big Tree was to be believed, and I did believe him, this meant that the late and scarcely lamented Three Elks had to have been one of the most thin-skinned men to ever draw breath. Which led me into thinking about what I knew about excessively sensitive people. Being sensitive generally meant a person was deeply insecure and frightened. Now, while this nature was all right for a woman—barely—it was totally unforgivable in a man. Meaning that a sensitive man would go to any lengths to hide this nature. And in my experience with human beings, the ones with something to hide are by habit crafty. Or, more bluntly put, downright sneaky. Three Elks had shown this particular stripe when he took the opportunity to warn Big Tree. At the time his intentions had probably been for good—I had to give him that, at least—but then he twisted it. Raven's Wing, from my personal knowledge, was cruel and stern. So what else would a sensitive young man do except use Big Tree's gratitude to his advantage. But Big Tree wasn't anybody's thug, so when he told Three Elks to stand up for himself, that one had instead gone crying to his mother.

I then set to wondering if Wolf Blanket had figured out that it had been Three Elks who warned Big Tree about the vote. If he had, that would have been more than enough to harbor a grudge. Big Tree, typical of him, had let the incident in the raid camp drop. This was done more out of pride than as a favor to Wolf Blanket, for Big Tree would have seen the entire affair as a failure of his own judgment. He would have learned from it, but mostly he would have been too embarrassed to go carrying tales about the unseemly way he'd had to seize control of his own men. They in turn promptly took their cue from him. Besides, I couldn't imagine for a second that anyone of them wanted to be charged with sedition. So that left only one tongue to fear. Three Elks's. With White Bear determined to reorganize his vanguard, the wrong word in his ear—and from a proven sneak—would have been something Wolf Blanket would have dreaded.

Possibly enough to kill for.

"I have to check my patient," I said, hurrying off in the direction of Owl Man's lodge.

Running close beside me, Big Tree complained, "But I'm hungry. You said we would eat now."

"Later!" I shouted, increasing my speed.

To my vast relief, the posted guards were still wide-eyed, still wary of any approach. As we hurried out of the shadows, they stood to their feet, weapons ready. They saw Big Tree first and relaxed. I intentionally kept behind him as he gained permission for us to enter the lodge. Then, staying behind him, I followed him inside. The first thing I noticed was that there were only two people tending The Cheyenne Robber; Owl Man and Skywalker. Owl Man canted his head, looking back at me over the his shoulder. Then he turned, looking deeply into the low-burning fire as if searching its glow for some type of answer. Skywalker looked up at me, his face drawn. I sat down directly beside him. Big Tree walked around the lodge, sitting down on the far side of the fire—a position that gave him a clear view—expectation apparent as he waited for Owl Man to glance up and notice him. I knew that he was hoping the old Owl Doctor would offer him food. I also knew that his was a vain hope. Even in times of plenty, I have never known Owl Man to offer a guest anything beyond a bowl of coffee. But Owl Man's store of coffee had long ago been depleted. Now that he didn't even have that, his hospitality had been compressed into a grim acceptance of whoever happened to come through his door. And that galled him, causing him to lower an ashamed face and avoid the fact that Big Tree was working hard to catch his eye.

"The women went home," Skywalker said just above a whisper, meaning the old woman Duck, her daughter Beloved, and her granddaughter White Otter. "We all thought it would be best for White Otter to rest."

"But I told Duck to stay here," I said, my tone annoyed.

"Yes, but White Otter was terribly upset. She needed her grandmother and her mother more than this one needed them, for he does have two perfectly capable doctors tending him."

"But," I tried, "I specifically said—"

"What you said doesn't matter," Skywalker snapped impatiently. "Two Owl Doctors are worth more than one old woman, and he is my brother and I . . ." His voice thick with emotion, his words trailed off. He took a moment to collect himself. When he spoke again, his tone was crisp, professional. "He opened his eyes three times. All three times were brief but long enough for me to manage to get him to swallow some broth. I'm keeping cool cloths on his forehead to curb fever. And as you can see, there is no fresh blood on his bandage."

Actually, Duck couldn't have done better than Skywalker was doing, but I was angry that the old woman had just up and left her patient when she'd promised she wouldn't. I'd relied on her, and I couldn't stop feeling that she'd let me down. Still, there was nothing I could do other than commend Skywalker, which I did. In response he lowered his eyes, and I saw a single tear fall. Placing my hand on his shoulder I said, "You are tired. I'm here now. You can—"

"No!" he shouted, giving me something of a start. "I will not leave him."

Skywalker seemed to need a little calming down himself, and the way I did that was to admit defeat. "It's all right. Do whatever you think is best."

"Thank you," he finally murmured. "For all that you've done for my brother. You are truly a gifted doctor. I don't know what I'd do without you."

That warmed one or two of my cockles, and in return I said, "Promise that the instant he wakes that you will send for me."

I felt him tense, and his eyes slid to the corners. "Of course," he responded, his tone brittle. His seething anger at first confused me, but then I reminded myself that a terrible thing had happened to his only brother. It was natural for his emotions to be raw. If snapping at me helped him to feel a bit better, I should not hold it against him. I stood, wordlessly summoning Big Tree.

· · ·

142

Maybe I had gotten a good second wind or something because as we walked to my home, I felt invigorated. Big Tree had not received a share of this newfound energy. The man groused with every step. Mostly about Owl Man, about how he hadn't offered so much as a bowl of cool water. Finally he cried, "There's just something not right about anyone who is mean to his guests!"

I would have responded, maybe sticking up for my old adversary by saying that he hadn't considered us his guests. That at best we were a necessary evil invading his otherwise private residence. I could have even gone on to explain that old people weren't as flexible about such things. I could have said all of that, but I didn't. Mainly because in my mind's eye I was seeing Owl Man's hunched shoulders, the back of his lowered head. The recollection bothered me. Why, I didn't know. It simply did. But I brushed it from my thoughts the instant we neared my home and I smelled something wonderful.

"Flatbread!" I cried, hurrying my pace. Catching the scent of food, Big Tree hurried with me.

Now, I have to be honest. During our separation, I had indeed missed my wife's cooking. Primarily because she was such a creative cook. Sometimes her creativity led to disaster, but more often than not she came up with incredibly delicious innovations. Flatbread was one of those things. It was a little like what the Mexicans did, a little like what the Hopis did. Mostly, it was pure Crying Wind since both the Mexicans and the Hopis used only corn to make their breads, while my wife, because she didn't have a lot of corn flour, blended what she did have with mesquite bean flour.

She also added a pinch of salt, which neither the Mexicans or the Hopis were known to do. Neither did she cook her bread the way they did. My wife favored frying, a thing she'd learned from the Caddoes, a people who believed in frying everything, even—and this makes me shudder—fresh vegetables. Anyway, she would make up a dough, pat it out as thin as a squint, and then lay it in the iron pot filled with all kinds of bubbling oils—she collected grease the way some women collected jewelry—and fried the dough until it floated to the top. The result was a bread as bubbly as the oils it cooked in and all crispy and brown. Because she was always adding different oils to the pot that she kept sealed when not in use, the breads never tasted the same. The corn flour gave it body; the mesquite flour, a nutty bite. But the varying oils gave the bread differing aftertastes. Usually she served this bread with stews and soups, but when she had some extra, she would sprinkle sugar on the hot bread and give it to us as a treat. Smelling the aroma of my favorite food had me sprinting for home. Arriving there, I found my son standing outside, a big piece of bread in his hands and chewing just as fast as his little jaws could go.

"Mommy's cooking again," his words muffled out through the mouthful of bread.

I hesitated, my pause blocking the door. Behind me, a very hungry Big Tree lurked, and his hunger caused him to restlessly shift from one foot to the other. I forced him to wait a few seconds more.

"I don't understand," I said to Favorite Son. "She didn't cook while I was gone?"

His cheeks now were too stuffed, so he simply shook his head.

In the brief time Big Tree and I had been away, my home had undergone a miraculous transformation. Everything was neat, orderly, the rugs swept clean. The girl-woman Always Happy was propped up in my son's bed, dozing. I stopped to look at her, but Big Tree kept moving, aiming himself for the oblong wooden platter heaped with cooling bread. Crying Wind was seated near the bubbling pot suspended over the flames by a chain connected to an iron-legged tripod. Dense smoke from the pot wafted toward the ceiling smoke hole. My wife fished out the bread from the pot and placed it on the platter Big Tree squatted near, stuffing bread into his mouth. When she stood to her feet, a wad of cloth in her hand, I rushed to her.

This was the part about cooking her bread that was dangerous: removing the pot and taking it outside to cool. I knew too well what hot oils could do to human skin, so I never allowed her to do this last task. Taking the thick cloth away from her, I removed the pot from the holding hook. Carefully carrying it, I yelled for our son to stand clear of the entry doorway. Once the pot and I were safely outside, he followed behind me during the search for a place to put it. It had to be a good place because the heat from the pot alone was enough to start a grass fire. Then, too, it had to be high, a place scrounging camp dogs couldn't reach and overturn. That place ended up being a few yards behind our home on a granite outcropping. It was a bit of a tricky climb, but I was finally able to set the pot on the highest part. I placed a few small rocks around the base to prevent its tipping; then I climbed back down.

I took my son's hand, and we walked back home. Favorite Son, his little mouth now empty, was chatty. "Mommy didn't cook on account of protecting her stores," he declared. "She said she needed to save our food for when you came home."

"She said that?"

"Yes," he chirped. "She said you'd come back when you were finished being stubborn. Uncle Skywalker said you were just about ready."

"When did he say that?"

"Yesterday."

I tried hard to remember yesterday. I couldn't. The only day clear to me was this extraordinary day, which after starting off with a rude awakening had proceeded on at a clip. Thinking about the things that still needed doing, I suddenly felt exhausted. And ravenous. All I wanted was a good meal—that is, if Big Tree had left any of it—and to lie down with my wife, hold her close in a way that I hadn't in too long. But snuggling wasn't in my immediate future. Primarily because snuggling wasn't something one generally did under the watchful gazes of a young runaway wife and a bachelor bodyguard. Hearing me heave a resigned sigh, my son quickly looked up, his expression concerned. I sent him what I hoped was a reassuring smile as I gave his little hand a slight squeeze. Evidently both things did the trick, for while hanging on to me, he proceeded to practice the Rabbit Society dance, which basically, amounted to just a lot of spirited jumping. I kept my strides even, doing my best not to interfere with his hopping while in companionable silence we made our way home.

During our separation Crying Wind had lived in an out-of-control fashion with too many sisters and babies crowded in on her. Part of me wondered if the chaos was the reason my son had begun to miss me. Life inside that crowd had to have made his remembrances of docile old me seem blissful. Enough to cause him to love me—for the moment, anyway—more than he ever had before. I had no idea just how long this father and son union would last. What I did know was that I had to make the most of it.

Big Tree was sitting to the right of the door with a cloth covering his lap and a platter of food balanced between his knees. He was still eating. And that upset me because I was certain that he was eating up every bit of the bread. My wife caught my attention, indicating that I should come sit down before a long, stiff hide box. The best way to describe this box is to say *trunk* because that was its size and shape. Crying Wind had several of these big boxes. She made them herself and used used them to store everything from food to clothing to blankets. The box lids were handy in that not only did they protect the contents, they could be used as tables. Which she was doing now.

The box I hurried to had a cloth-covered platter on top of it. I knew that that was my food, and I couldn't wait to get to it. The trouble was, Favorite Son was still hanging on to me, impeding my progress. As I neared Crying Wind, she roughly jerked her son off of my arm.

"Stop pestering your father! He needs to sit down and

eat." My eyes widened when she gave his backside a swat and sent him off to sit on our bed. He couldn't go for his own bed because Always Happy was filling it up. Still befuddled about the swat, I just stood there. Irritably, Crying Wind took charge, pushing me down on a rug, uncovering the platter of food. "Eat," she ordered.

Looking at the platter, my mouth began to water. Not only did I have a healthy portion of flat bread, there were also chunks of fresh meat, charred on the outside, good and bloody on the inside, and a large onion that she'd roasted just the way I liked them. The woman had prepared a veritable feast for her returning husband.

Before lunging for the food, I said a humble prayer of thanks to be her husband.

Finished eating, I washed my hands and arms. Big Tree was beside me, speaking urgently as he glanced askance at our other houseguest, the girl-woman Always Happy. Being a bachelor, he was uncomfortable with a prolonged association with young females. Mainly because bachelors were too readily accused of *styling.*

Hopeful young men "styled" in various ways. The first way was to strut back and forth in front of a young woman's home. Another way required a friend to talk loudly about the bachelor in question's manly prowesses while said bachelor did his best to appear embarrassed. But both of these ways publicly proclaimed the man's affection for a particular girl, and if she rejected him, his pride took a severe hammering. Therefore, the most favorite way to style was to place oneself in a woman's path, be an obstacle she had to go around while acting as if totally unaware of her. If this was done often enough, then perhaps she might eventually offer a coy smile. If she did, then serious courtship could begin.

Now, I said all this to explain Big Tree's anxious state. The more he honestly tried to ignore the young woman sitting across from him, the more she smiled. That girl was young, she was silly. Both of these things had obviously caused her to forget that she was very married and very pregnant. Needless to say, Big Tree—who in truth was considered to be quite a catch—desperately wanted to leave. And that was all right with me on account of my needing to talk to a certain novice Buffalo Doctor.

Drying my hands on the cloth my wife provided, I spoke softly to her, our faces close together. Excitement leaped inside of me when she absently pushed a tendril of my hair back behind my ear, her hand lightly grazing the side of my face. This simple gesture was mind-numbingly sensuous, and it took every ounce of my willpower not to sweep her up in my arms right there in front of everyone.

"I have to find Burned Hand." I handed her back the cloth. "I have to know about the illness affecting that family."

Our eyes slid in the direction of Always Happy, both of us fearful that she'd heard. We needn't have worried. She was still too involved with smiling at Big Tree to pay attention to us. But just in case she became bored with her attempts with him, I kept my voice low.

"I don't know how long all of this will take," I said as I lowered my head toward my chest, stretching out the tight kinks in the back of my neck. Crying Wind placed her hand at the base of my skull, her warmth doing wonderful things for my too-taut muscles.

"Take as long as you need," she said softly. "I'll be waiting."

TEN

Even though people often lived their entire lives within the confines of the same band, it was possible, even preferable, to avoid seeing those deemed disagreeable. This was the way it was between me and many of the men belonging to the Buffalo and Owl Doctor Societies. I had been a member of the Rattle Band for over two years. Burned Hand had been a member all of his life. Yet because his father was a prominent Buffalo Doctor and in that society my form of doctoring was still deemed to be something bordering on fraud, Buffalo Doctors and I studiously avoided each other. We were all so successful with this avoidance that the last I'd seen of Burned Hand was when he was a boy. As Big Tree and I made our way to the lodge Burned Hand shared with two other novice Buffalo Doctors, I wondered if the young man he now was remembered all the details of just how he'd earned his adult name. Or, more to the point, the part I'd shared in the incident.

I tended to believe that because the brain effectively blocks out the full terror and incredible pain associated with any severe injury, and because he'd been groggy with fever when he was brought to me, that he wouldn't. His coming into training as a Buffalo Doctor guaranteed that he knew who I was if only by way of reputation and/or vilification. A good bet was the latter, for the Buffalo Doctors were not fond of me. Neither were the Owl Doctors, but because of Skywalker—and, if needs must, albeit grudgingly, Owl Man—the Owl Doctors had become tolerant. But within the Buffalo Doctors' association, I had nary a soul to speak in my defense, so among them I was a nonperson. And certainly not a doctor. However, one man in their number could speak on my behalf, but that man would go to his death before ever admitting that once, in a moment of sheer desperation, he'd sought me out. Burned Hand's father. He'd gone on to become the second most powerful leader of the Buffalo Doctors. Holding this title, he stood on shaky ground, and I'm sure it must have sometimes kept him awake at night worrying that I could have destroyed him with a word. But I never did because I valued the doctoring ethic. So throughout his long life his dark secret remained safe in my keeping.

When Big Tree and I arrived at the place where the young doctors lived, I stood back and let Big Tree do all the talking. He was someone to be respected, and the men he addressed were all so much younger than me. No matter what era you might find yourself living in, there is one fact that endures from generation to generation.

152

Youth responds only to youth.

Meaning of course that anyone carrying a few wrinkles on his face must either be age addled or thoroughly backward—probably both. Young people don't mean to be arrogant. They simply are. They are also dismissive, shunting aside any thought that one day they, too, will be old.

Big Tree was direct, stating that on account of the trouble with Turned The Horses and the dangers everyone in the Rattle Band faced, it was imperative for us to know all there was to know about the dead man and his family. Burned Hand considered all of this for a goodly amount of time, then turned to his fellow novices for a brief and muted discussion. After a lot of head nodding and utterances of "Ho," Burned Hand made a decision.

"It is only for the good of all that I will speak to you. If things were otherwise, I wouldn't."

Spoken like a true doctor. The boy had promise. I also hoped he had some usable information.

His lodge mates left, giving us privacy. Burned Hand placed two large chips on the low-burning fire and sat back. His good hand continually stroked the scarred one as he slumped against a backrest. Keeping my eyes lowered, peering through my lashes, I took a good long look at the results of my earlier work. The hand that had been burned was a series of large dull-pink splotches smearing otherwise dusky skin. The third and little fingers curled inward at the tips. But the hand was still usable, even if, by the evidence of his unconscious rubbing of it, it was sensitive to the effects of cooler night air. I wondered what pains he must suffer during winters, if the hand had to remain gloved. But these were questions I could not ask. He had not been my patient for a long, long time. Odds were high that he would never be again. What discomforts he felt or did not feel were none of my business. So I let the boy I'd known go, and concentrated instead on the young man who for all intents and purposes was a total stranger.

He was about medium height, his face shining with robust good health and youth. He wore his braided hair covered with beaver fur. His face was pleasant, but he was a touch too serious in his manner. In an attempt to ease some of the tension Burned Hand clearly felt, Big Tree said something halfway funny. Burned Hand did not chuckle, didn't even crack a smile. I don't think this can be blamed on his preparing himself to break a confidence. I just don't believe the young man had much of a humor. Big Tree came to realize this, too, and gave up any further attempt at lightening the mood.

Following a lengthy silence, Burned Hand deigned to speak. "The man you want to know about has honored me by trusting himself into my care." Saying this, he looked self-satisfied to the point of smug. I wondered how long this would seem an honor once he learned that Turned The Horses had used a novice doctor simply because he was too miserly to pay for better care. Ah, well, that wasn't my concern, either.

"He has been ill for quite a long time," Burned Hand continued. "But of late I've had to increase the bleedings."

Now, this is where the Buffalo Doctors and I violently differed. They believed that all illnesses had to do with bad blood, which meant inducing bleeding by way of a series of small cuts over the affected area. I preferred to look for a cause for the pain because, frankly, I never could see that bleeding a person helped in any way at all. But you know who agreed with the Buffalo Doctors almost completely? (And this to me is the irony of ironies.) Army doctors. Or to be more specific, an army doctor well-known to all of us. Ha-we-sun. Hawwy had these special little knives on a big ring, that I have come to realize looked an awful lot like door keys, and he used these knives exactly the same way Buffalo Doctors used their much bigger knives. Of course, he had many other ways of curing illnesses, but he considered bleeding to be highly beneficial. I think the word he used was *invigorating*. I violently disagreed with him, too.

"There is a weakness in his spirit," Burned Hand went on to say. "And it's getting worse."

I craned forward, capturing his eyes with mine. He instantly shrank back as if something foul was coming too near. Then realizing the offense this might cause Big Tree, he recovered slightly, regathered his dignity. I pretended not to notice any of it as I asked, "Have you treated any of his sons?"

No sooner had I finished the question than he was sending me a baleful look, his mouth becoming a hard line. "You only wanted to know about Turned The Horses," he seethed. "Now you're asking about other patients." His eyes narrowed as his stare bore into me. "You know, you are as sneaky as I've heard said."

I could be nasty, too. "You must be referring to your father. A man who would certainly know."

Burned Hand's eyes flared wide. Mentioning his father had apparently niggled a deeply buried memory. Alarm colored his face as part of the memory unfolded, I'm sure. No doubt somewhere in those murky recesses he saw my much younger face, for he was looking at me with panic riddled eyes, and his mouth was moving but produced no sound. Instantly I regretted my act of revenge, and because of that regret, I hurried on with a more professional attitude.

"As you probably know, I was in Turned The Horses's camp earlier today and I witnessed the weakness you speak of. I also saw traces of this malady in his sons. So again, I put the question to you, have you been treating any of them?"

He was still staring at me, still fighting against that blurry memory, when he said in a husky whisper, "No. Turned The Horses would only pay for one patient. Himself."

That fit with the things my wife had to say about Turned The Horses being a stingy old man. I moved the subject on. "How many sons have you determined to be affected?"

My treating him as another professional was gradually having a positive effect, for he sat up straight and gave the question considerable thought. Finally he said, "All but two."

"Which two?"

"Raven's Wing and the one who died today."

"Tell me about the women, Turned The Horses's wives, the mothers of his sons. Have you observed any of the weakness in them?"

Burned Hand, now warming even more to my strategy of treating him as a peer, leaned forward, arms resting against bent knees, hands clasped together. "There *is* something wrong there," he said earnestly, "but I've no idea what. The best I can say is that the women suffer from sluggish blood. Several times I suggested he allow me to thin their blood, but Turned The Horses said his women were all right. That they were just lazy. But I don't think that's the case because I've watched them. It's true that they go about their daily lives just as other women do, but for them everything seems to be a great effort. Almost as if they are dragging themselves through the most ordinary chores. And there's something else. . . ."

"What?" I asked anxiously.

"Thirst," he said, his eyes glinting confusion. "They are always thirsty. So thirsty that they wear canteens hanging from their belts."

"Do the men share this great thirst?"

Burned Hand hesitated, then slowly nodded. "Yes. But their thirst isn't for water." The young man's wary eyes strayed in Big Tree's direction. I then knew that he needed to tell me something that would directly affect the Ondes' code of superiority. Only an Onde could denigrate another Onde and only then by way of challenge. Any of the rest of us found guilty of scandalizing a member of the highest class was immediately subject to harsh punishment. Big Tree knew that this was about to happen. He also knew that whatever was needing to be said was important for me to hear. He vacillated for a moment between duty and the need for me to know the truth; then, muttering something about needing to relieve himself, he stood to his feet and left.

We waited enough time for him to take himself away, but apparently still fearing he would be overheard, Burned Hand said in a hushed tone, "Their thirst is the kind only eased by someone like Caddo George."

All right, I admit I was dense. With a baffled shrug, I

said, "I see nothing wrong with those men buying a few bottles of whis—"

"*A barrel!*" he cut in, his whispered words delivered with explosive force.

I was astounded. Not only by this piece of information but by my personal knowledge of the price Caddo George demanded for only a single bottle. The cost for a barrel seemed incalculable. Maybe Turned The Horses wasn't stingy. Maybe the old man's love for whiskey had reduced him to grinding poverty. That would certainly explain why he could only afford a novice Buffalo Doctor. Burned Hand sensed what I was thinking, and evidently he agreed.

"I know he didn't send for me because of my good reputation. I'm too young to have a reputation. But having studied under my father for my entire life, I do have more knowledge than any doctors my age. It was for this reason that Turned The Horses chose me. Even then he said that I shouldn't be charging him because he was my opportunity to practice on a real human without my father watching over my shoulder. I'm afraid he had a point, but he was so superior in his attitude that I charged him, anyway."

"How much are your fees?"

Burned Hand looked embarrassed as he replied nearly under his breath, "A good meal."

I couldn't help the chuckle in my throat as I asked, "And his wives complied?"

His mouth turned down in distaste. "They tried," he said miserably. "But their food is not easy to eat. Everything they cook is . . . sweet!"

I sat straight up. "Sweet?"

He nodded. "Yes. They put sugar in all their foods."

"Where are they getting sugar?"

"I don't know."

The image of Three Elks's mother eagerly digging through the gift basket, her expression registering disappointment at finding only dried tongues, came into my mind's eye. And in the middle of our conversation she'd said she was very thirsty. The large water gourd should have been more than enough to last a person an entire day, but her's hadn't even taken her into the afternoon. I stored that knowledge in the back of my brain and went on to ask Burned Hand what he knew about Raven's Wing's young wife. If she had come to him voicing fears for her unborn child.

"No," he said simply. "I've never even met her." His eyes crawled away from mine. He concentrated on an invisible something on the floor of his lodge as he muttered, "But I've certainly heard a lot about her." I remained quiet, encouraging him to continue. He did. And as he spoke, I was very glad that Big Tree had made his excuses, for this next turn in the discussion led us to the subject of The Cheyenne Robber, the supreme Onde.

Undone by what I heard, I mumbled my thanks, shook Burned Hand's good hand, and, as I ducked out the doorway, worried that maybe Big Tree hadn't gone far enough. That still acting as my guard, he'd lurked too close and had heard too much. Because it was summer, that would have been a very easy thing to do.

Lodges consisting of twenty-five to thirty support poles used the same covering year after year, but in the wintertime there was an inner wall packed tightly with sage for insulation. Not only did this inner wall keep warmth in, it also kept conversations private. This was a luxury practically nonexistent during the warm season, for during the hottest months a lodge had only an outer wall. And sometimes when the nights were hot and muggy, the covering wall was rolled up and tied in place against the support poles so that the sleeping people might now and again enjoy a refreshing breeze. It was during the summer months that people had to be extremely careful about what they said and did in their own homes because anyone could either look in or stand close enough to listen. Which was why I was concerned about just where Big Tree had gotten to. If he'd remained close by, no matter how softly Burned Hand and I had spoken, he could have heard.

And then the boy would have been in a quandary.

Should he endanger my life by reporting to the Onde council that a member of their class had been demeaned by lessors? Or should he gamble everything he'd risked his own life to gain simply because he was halfway friendly with me? It took only a few seconds for these questions to flit through my brain—the same amount of time needed to pass through the doorway. Farther away was a smear of light coming from an open lodge. In that yellowish glow I spotted Big Tree standing and smoking a cigar. He wasn't alone. Two other young men stood with him, and the three were chuckling about something. I felt relieved, but now I faced another problem.

How to get rid of Big Tree.

I didn't wish to seem ungrateful because he was acting as my bodyguard, and his willingness to place himself between me and danger was exceptionally generous. But be that as it may, I needed to start asking hard questions. Questions guaranteed to grievously offend Big Tree and his fellow Ondes. Therefore, I had to rid myself of my Onde escort. As I strode toward him, a possible way occurred.

Coming to a stop, my voice sounding every bit as tired as I felt, I said, "I must now look in on The Cheyenne Robber."

Big Tree let go a leaden sigh, then nodded as he removed the small utility knife from his waist scabbard, cut off the burning end of the smoldering cigar. The glowing ember hit the ground, and he stomped it out. The remainder of the cigar was promptly stored in his carry pouch. With a word of farewell to his companions, he followed after me as I headed off in the direction of Owl Man's lodge.

That place was even more lit up. Three bonfires burned around the perimeter, and flaming torches stuck into the ground stood between the fires. A cricket couldn't have gotten through that ring of light without the guards seeing. White Bear was not about to take the chance of his nephew The Cheyenne Robber being murdered while recovering in Owl Man's bed. And as for that old Owl Doctor, he was standing just outside his seedy home, off to the extreme left. His bent-by-age bare back was toward me, so he could not see my approach. Nor did he hear me, for he was too involved in an urgent discussion he was having with Sky-walker. As I neared, Skywalker did see me, and he nudged his ancient mentor. That touch was enough, for Owl Man shot right up. He and Skywalker were looking my way, and their expressions were . . . what? It was hard for me to know because within seconds of focusing their eyes on me, they made their faces go blank. Then Skywalker turned away, showing only a hard-edged profile as he addressed me in a rather caustic manner.

"There has been no change in his condition. He's still sleeping. As that's probably for the best, I'm keeping everyone out."

Eyes flared wide with surprise, I pointed to my chest. "This includes me?"

"Yes it does."

"But I'm his doctor."

"Were," Owl Man said flatly. "You've already done all your form of healing can do."

I didn't agree. "He is still in danger," I replied vigorously. "If rot gets started in the wound—"

"I know what to do." The quiver in his voice betrayed his great effort in maintaining control. "I strongly suggest you go along home. That is all I have to say."

Skywalker turned so far to the side that I could no longer see even the outline of his face. I looked from my friend to Owl Man as the three of us stood together in an uncomfortable silence. Then, clearing my throat, I managed, "Yes, well, if there is nothing more you feel I ought to do, I might as well leave Big Tree to help with the guarding."

Skywalker whirled at the waist and looked steadily at me. "White Bear ordered him to stay close to you."

I exhaled slowly. "That was before I made up with my wife. Now that I have, I'd prefer Big Tree be . . . elsewhere."

Owl Man cackled, but Skywalker's mouth didn't even offer a smile as his gaze bore into mine, a sure sign that he was about to worm his way inside my head. To thwart

162

the attempt, I immediately did what I'd learned to be the best way to protect myself. Looking down, I intentionally watched my toes wiggling just under the soft covering of my shoes as I counted slowly to fifty.

Skywalker must have heard the counting and understood that I was blocking him, for he angrily cried, "Do as you like! But if you end up dead, you'll have no one to blame but yourself!" With that he stormed toward the lodge doorway.

I looked up at Owl Man. His eyes touched mine, then scurried away. And he, too, made for the door, disappearing inside without so much as a backward glance. My mouth was crunched in a deep frown as I reexamined the actions of the two men. Owl Doctors can be spooky, but I've never known them to act without reason. Something had prompted those two to snub me. My bet was that they were protecting someone. I had an even bigger bet that I knew just who that someone was.

Her little son was learning to walk, but White Otter was still a nursing mother. She would be for another year. When I called at her home, she was feeding her baby. She wasn't alone. Her mother, Beloved, and her grandmother Duck were with her. I wasn't happy about intruding this late at night—or that the one name that came to me during the seconds my mind cast about for just who Skywalker and Owl Man might be eager to protect had been White Otter's. I had a good idea why they felt they needed to protect her. Just as I knew that protecting her had everything to do with the baby at her breast. As long as The Cheyenne Robber seemed to be recovering, she was safe. Safe only because the child needed her more than the people needed vengeance against her. But if he died . . .

For modesty she sat off to the side and with her back to the door as she suckled her child. Even though he was an infant, that little boy was as masculine as his father, and what I could see of him—one bare leg bent at the knee, the little foot resting on his mother's hip while the other leg waved languidly in the air—he was a thoroughly contented baby.

"I beg your pardon for the intrusion," I said softly. Beloved's scrutiny was swift. In an instant she took in the meaning of my pinched expression, the significance of my half-mumbled apology. She quickly stood to her feet, barring any further view of her daughter.

"We should talk elsewhere," she said, her voice hollow.

I followed her outside.

Beloved would not look at me. It hardly mattered, for I could barely see anything more than her outline. In the near-total darkness I would not be able to judge the truth of her words by her expressions. For that I would have to rely solely on the timbre of her voice. So with her head down, her hands holding tightly to each other, fingers entwined, she drew in a deep breath.

"I need not tell you that my daughter's marriage is not all that she hoped it would be." Beloved paused, considered carefully, then began again in a strong but calm voice. "She loves him too much. From the very beginning I've tried to tell her this, but from the moment he smiled at her, she has been lost to good advice." She looked at me now. I couldn't see her eyes, only the dark hollows of her face, but I could feel her studious gaze. Her voice remained low, but a certain energy came into the flow of her words. "He keeps her confused! One day he's devoted; the next, he's totally indifferent. And he's been this way since the baby was born. Sometimes I think he's jealous of his own son."

"That could very well be," I said guardedly. "Someone like The Cheyenne Robber does not take well to being supplanted." I hesitated, then gravely forced myself to ask, "Will you now tell me about the other women?"

She sounded a half laugh, not because she was surprised by the question, simply embittered by it. Shaking her head, she turned and began walking. I hastened after her and, when we were again side by side, matched my stride to hers. We had no destination in mind; we were just moving together in the darkness like a pair of restless spirits.

"His seeing other women began long before White Otter delivered. My fool of a son-in-law can't do without his comfort, and when he couldn't have it from her, he went elsewhere. But the thing that makes me hate him is the night I held out his newly born son to him. He was happy about his baby, happy his wife was doing well. He told me to tell her that he loved her—that he loved her and was very proud of her. I was not touched by his words. If you must know, it was all I could do not to slap him. Because I knew the instant he handed me back the baby that he was going off to meet another woman. I knew it as sure as I was breathing. So I told my daughter only that her husband was pleased by the child. I said nothing of his love or his pride. And I was right because weeks after that night, the stories confirming his secret dalliance grew worse. Duck and I did all we could to protect White Otter, but the ugly gossip man-

165

aged to slither past our best defenses. Because of him, I've had to watch my lovely daughter cry. Then, when she ran out of tears, I watched her slowly shrivel up inside. I begged her to divorce him. Even her father begged her. But that man has a hold on her that nothing can break. Not while he's alive, anyway."

Looking up at the starry sky she inhaled deeply, then let the breath go. After a second or two of reflective silence, she said with a certain lightness, "And now you know why I stabbed him."

ELEVEN

"You did not!"

I know how infantile that sounds, but I was just so appalled that Beloved would admit to something she clearly had not done that the words blurted out without my thinking. As surprised as I most certainly was, Beloved burst out laughing. Before I could continue on, I had to wait for a lull.

"Well, for one thing," I said as the worst of her laughter began to fade, "while I might possibly believe The Cheyenne Robber would stand still long enough for you to stab him half to death, there is the matter of what I know about you."

Laughter immediately ceased. Her tone hard, she asked, "And that is?"

Now she was just taunting me. Bringing my face closer

to hers, I said each word purposely. "That you are the gentlest of women." Beloved did not back away even though she well knew that, none too subtly, I was talking about her first husband.

Duck's son, Beloved's first husband, had been called Runs The Bulls. The man had been an impressive sight. In my mind I hold the image of him striding through his village, doing his chiefly duty, making certain that all was well. But that image is deceptive, for the man was a thoroughgoing bully and doubly dangerous because he was not the brightest star to shine in the night. But he had been intelligent enough to know that he did not deserve the woman who was his first wife. That her heart was not with him. And so he had sealed her to him with fear, making her life a terror. Duck had tried to protect her from the worst of it, but when men and women are alone, a woman has no protection beyond the love in a man's heart. I don't know everything she went through. I do not want to know, for what I can imagine is more than sufficient. And if she could not raise a knife against *him*, then she could not raise a knife against anyone else. Certainly not The Cheyenne Robber.

Her tone was soft, her breath warm on my skin as she dared, "I will watch with interest as you strive to prove me a liar."

So there it was. A mother's challenge. She was letting me know that she would do anything, say anything, to protect her daughter. Straightening to my full height, I let the silence hang between us for a moment, then in a clipped tone said, "At least give me the reassurance that you will say nothing to White Bear for another day."

168

I heard what passed for a whispery laugh as she reached out, touched my hand with the feathery gentleness of a butterfly's caress. Then she turned, walking away with slow, heavy strides, the radical opposite of the quick-striding willowy woman I knew so well. Watching her go, I felt my heart beginning to break and I knew that I could not allow her do what she planned. Running after her, I caught her by the arm, forced her to stop, and, because I was desperate, commenced to yell at her to listen to reason. I have no idea of everything I said, but I do know that she remained indifferent to my appeals. Her passiveness was infuriating, so I yelled louder. We both suffered a start when there came a sudden shrill screeching and then the blur of a bulky thing coming fast out of the blackness.

I dimly recognized the bulky blur as Duck just before the old woman—screaming and windmilling her arms—was all over me. Before I could defend myself, the harridan was pelting me with her fists, calling me everything she could think of. Now, our language does not have specific curse words, and the ones you know in English do not transpose into Kiowa. But we do have descriptive terms, and the terms Duck used meant that my father had an unnatural love of, shall we say, nature. None of this did my self-esteem any good whatsoever. Plus, that little old woman could hit really hard.

Beloved stood out of the way of her mother-in-law's flying fists and kicking feet, leaving me to battle Duck all by myself. I had another problem other than simply dodging kicks and blows. Physically stopping her wasn't as easy as it should have been because Duck was hard to grab onto. It wasn't that there wasn't enough of her to grab. Quite the contrary—there was too much. And most all of it in front. Grabbing her there not being an option, I tried for her flailing arms, which made the painful tussle go on a bit longer than I cared for. I thought I'd managed to put an end to our unseemly scuffle when I grabbed her from behind, locking my arms around hers and lifting her off her feet. A move that put a considerable strain on my back because she was . . . well, all right, fat—and a thrashing fat woman can crack a man's spine. But at least I had her arms pinned, and for that small mercy I heaved a sigh of relief.

Which possibly could have been a mistake because no sooner had the sigh escaped my throat when the back of her head crashed against my face. The next thing I knew I was seeing bright streaking stars that were not in the night sky but everywhere I chanced to look. When pain finally registered I let her go, my hands quickly covering my injured nose. A second or two later I was bent over and wheeling around, my nose gushing blood. Not to put too fine a point on it, but during this moment of weakness I was literally at Duck's mercy. If she'd wanted to shoot, stab, or beat me to death with a rock, I wouldn't have been able to stop her. Fortunately, Beloved decided to save me.

My next memories—except for the ones concerning the vain effort to staunch the prodigious flow of blood from my broken nose—are hazy. But I do know that I walked with my head tipped back and between the two women as they guided me along. I heard them squabbling back and forth, but the hard truth of the matter is that I was more concerned for my condition than whatever either of them was saying. The next hurdle came when we reached The Cheyenne Robber's lodge. Now, it was a big, big lodge, twice the size of mine, but the entry hole was exactly the same size. Meaning that it was round, wide enough for one person to pass through, and what served as a threshold was about a foot high off the ground. Ordinarily entering a lodge was something I did without ever thinking much about it, but now that my head was tipped back against my shoulders and I was gargling blood in the depths of my strained throat, lifting a leg and hunching at the same time was a dexterity I wasn't able to master. Beloved and Duck fought about the best way to get me inside. I believe they were keeping their voices low, but my pulse beat was loud in my ears, so I can't be certain. All I know is that they were loud enough to attract White Otter's attention because an instant later she was in the doorway, the upper portion of her body leaning through it, imploring her mother and grandmother to hush because she'd just gotten the baby to sleep.

Then White Otter noticed me and squawked, "What's happened to Tay-bodal?!"

Beloved was explaining when White Otter impatiently cut her off, saying that they had to get me inside and quickly before all of her neighbors began to gather. Pretty soon all three women were pulling and pushing. Dutifully, I stepped when told to step, and I'm not sure exactly which way they bent me but I do remember seeing the top of the opening as I was hauled through it. Once we were all safely inside, I tried not to wake the baby with my bleeding.

White Otter sat beside me with a rag on my face to catch the worst of the blood. Breathing through the pulp that had once been my nose was unthinkable. I had to catch a ragged breath through my mouth whenever I wasn't swallowing coppery-tasting fluid. Duck was not one bit sorry for my pitiable condition. To her way of thinking, everything was my fault. She also insisted that all that was needed was an old remedy to make me right enough to be sent on my way. I disagreed, and with a lot of noise, which all three exasperated women tried to ignore, but I kept it up. Mainly because I knew that the old treatment of putting a drop of oil in my ear would do nothing for a broken nose. What would help could only be found in my medical bag. Despising my stubbornness, White Otter made a disgusted sound in the back of her throat and then scooted out, running for my home and my wife. While we waited, I kept my head tipped back and applied pressure on either side of my flattened nose.

Crying Wind came bustling in, carrying a large, heavy bag. It seemed that she'd been so concerned about my injury that she grabbed every medicine in my extensive stockpile. The bleeding from my nose had lessened, but the swelling was still going on. I was pleased that I couldn't see myself, for I must have made a horrific sight. This impression was enhanced when my wife looked at me and screamed. Of course, her cry woke the baby, sending Beloved hurrying to her wailing grandson while Crying Wind drew evil looks from White Otter and Duck. But because my injury was caused by these women, Crying Wind could have cared less that her involuntary reaction irritated them. She set the bag down and knelt before me. Sucking air through her teeth, her expression strained, she began—as carefully as she was able—to peel the blood-soaked rag from my face. When she saw the damage underneath, she cried out again, frightening the baby even more. Well, that made White Otter really angry, and she let Crying Wind know it. My wife, just as combative as the younger woman, let fly one or two of her own convictions, and then all three women were yelling at each other over the wails of the baby. In the meantime, I rooted around in the bag until I found exactly what I needed: a small jar containing a white powder.

It comes from a plant that looks like a lily, the flower growing along streams and rivers in northern Kansas and beyond. I collected the root of this plant, dried it thoroughly, then pounded it into a powder. Other Indian doctors use this medicine for all sorts of things, but I preferred to use it on bleeding wounds because just a pinch of it was enough to cause blood to clot. Now, even though I was tempted, I didn't think I ought to sniff the stuff up because I had no idea what it would do once it got inside my lungs. What I did—and this was really painful because my nose was so tender to the touch—was I put a bit of the powder on the tip of my little finger and pushed it up one nostril. I then repeated the process with the other. Almost immediately the bleeding stopped. But I'm afraid there was nothing in that bag that would improve my appearance. A broken nose produces blackened eyes and swelling that only time can heal. And for however long it took for my poor nose to heal itself, I was doomed to look like a very bad dream.

It takes a lot to startle Duck, but startled she was when over the din Beloved announced that she didn't have time to continue the fuss because she had to turn herself over to White Bear. This declaration not only stopped Duck mid-yell, it also abruptly silenced my wife and White Otter. The next thing I knew, I had my arms full of squalling baby as the three women turned their attentions on Beloved.

"Mother!" White Otter shouted. "What are you saying?"

"I'm saying," she asserted in as calm a voice as she could manage, "that I am responsible for all the trouble. I cannot allow my crimes to cause an innocent man to fear for his life and White Bear to go to war against a brother chief."

White Otter visibly paled. Except for the baby, silence ensued. After a tension-filled moment, Duck collected herself. In a ragged voice that I had to strain to hear over the bawling baby, she said to White Otter, "Your mother is a wonderful woman, but I'm afraid she's a liar. She's lying to protect me. I'm the person that one over there"—a quick toss of her head in my direction indicated me—"has been looking for. And I am the one who must go to White Bear."

White Otter tried to withdraw from the old woman's embrace, but Duck tightened her hold. "You?" Tears formed and fell down her cheeks as she stared, appalled, at her grandmother. "You tried to kill my husband?"

Duck slowly nodded.

"Why?!" White Otter screeched. "Why would you do that to him? To me?"

The old woman's arms fell away, hanging limply by her sides as she lowered her head and commenced to sob. I stood, thrusting the baby into my shocked wife's arms. Placing my hands on Duck's quaking shoulders, I said, "Those are very good questions. I would like to hear the answers myself."

Duck rallied, lifting her head to look at me—and with such loathing that I withered. "I will not answer," she seethed. "Not here. I will make my talk only with White Bear."

Amazingly, while I had suspected White Otter but totally refused to entertain Beloved, I eagerly leaped to accept Duck as the culprit. You see, I had known the old woman for quite awhile. I knew a lot about her. Most of it unpleasant.

She wasn't actually White Otter's grandmother any more than she was now Beloved's mother-in-law. I think she always knew that her son had not fathered White Otter, but she would have killed anyone who voiced this opinion out loud. As I told you before, she was terribly protective of Beloved, but she was her son's mother, meaning that both suffered an attitude of ownership over the young woman known then as Sits Beside Him. I have also always suspected that she knew who the true father was and that it was by her doing, more than her simple-minded son, that two people terribly in love were kept separated for a decade and a half. So while I could admire Duck for her love of Beloved, I could not help but dislike her on account of Hears The Wolf, for that man, my good friend, had suffered an intolerable agony every single day of those long years. And Duck would have taken that secret to her grave, White Otter would have never known the father who could only love and protect her from afar, if fate hadn't intervened and brought me into all of their lives.

At that time I'd been deeply embroiled in another mystery, and that puzzle had inadvertently led me first to Duck. Within a short amount of time, I realized just how brutal that old woman could be. My solving the mystery had cost

Duck her son—a hard blow, considering that she was a widow. On account of me she found herself reduced to the cruelest poverty, having to beg scraps and live on the fringe of any camp that showed her mercy. To anyone with ears she blamed me, never her son or herself. And I have to confess, I kept a clear ground between us because that old woman was half crazy and more than a little scary.

For Hears The Wolf, life was as it should have been all along. He now had his wife, changing her name to Beloved, and his rightful daughter. As Duck was not a blood relative to any of them, he was not in any way required to show the slightest consideration to his wife's former mother-in-law. But being the type of man he is, he eventually went after her, bringing her into his home, addressing her as Mother. After a while, softening up under Hears The Wolf's undying patience and an unconditional love for an old woman who'd done nothing—as far as I could see—to deserve any of it, Duck straightened up behaved in a saner fashion. And because I was friends with her new protector, she'd even managed to be polite to me. But now her renowned instability again glittered in those beady little eyes. So could I believe that she had it in her to raise a knife against two men, one of them White Otter's husband?

Oh, yes. I could believe it without the slightest qualm or hesitation. And believe it also solved the puzzle of Owl Man's and Skywalker's odd behavior. Being mystics, those two had most probably discerned the old woman's guilt, which is why Owl Man couldn't trust her or anyone close to her—meaning Beloved—around The Cheyenne Robber. He and Skywalker could easily send the women away, but that left them in a quandary about what to do with their perceptions. I deduced that this was what they had been busily discussing when I'd come upon them. Their insight was one thing; proof, very much another. For that proof, they still needed me. But they couldn't sway any outcome by pointing me in Duck's direction. I had to find her out entirely on my own.

I had.

Blocking from my mind the keening being produced by three mournful women and one confused baby, I marched Duck off to face White Bear's rough form of justice.

Answering my announcing shout, White Bear threw back the door flap, and a hairsbreath later there he was, wide-eyed with surprise. I couldn't fault him for that because the sight of a beaten-up me with a surly old woman in tow was more than enough to surprise anyone. It was a painful effort to speak, and, listening to me, White Bear experienced an equally painful effort trying to hold in a belly laugh. Even to my own ears I sounded extremely nasal, but the instant he understood that I was presenting him with the confessed killer of Three Elks and The Cheyenne Robber's attacker, all merriment vanished from his face in the space of a blink. So serious now that his very demeanor was threatening, White Bear motioned for us to come inside.

Two of his counselors, Hunting Eagle and Brave Horse, were sitting by the fire. Having heard everything, their ex-pressions were duly stern. And from there things proceeded badly. Duck could be the most irritating, the most fractious human being imaginable. For his part, even though he needn't have been, White Bear tried to be courtly, offering the old woman a good place to sit, any type of refreshment she might wish. Duck refused it all, standing stubbornly while White Bear, his two counselors, and I made ourselves entirely comfortable.

"I just want to get this finished," she said waspishly. From her tone, one would have thought that we were awaiting her judgment, not the reverse. But that was Duck. That, was how she was. She was the defendant, yet she was more than capable of making four forbidding men feel thoroughly defensive. White Bear did not like feeling defensive.

"Very well, then," he responded curtly. "It will be as you wish. Get on with your telling."

Now while his clipped message was enough to chill me to the marrow, it wholly satisfied Duck. She drew in a deep breath, then launched into what she had to say. And typical of her, she began with a stinging insult.

Looking White Bear unashamedly in the eye, she said boldly, "I have never liked you. You are an idiot. Worse, you surround yourself with idiots. I am glad I am old. Glad that I am about to die because I do not want to go on watching you and yours ruin our great Nation."

If Duck's primary aim was to destroy herself, those statements alone certainly worked a treat, for as soon as she finished her contemptuous declarations, every man present—and this included me—promptly decided her unequivocal guilt. From that point on, and this was purely in the guise of fairness, we heard her out with not one of us actually listening. We were simply waiting for her to finish, waiting for the ax of White Bear's retribution to fall.

"I know you"—meaning White Bear because she still held a deep an unwavering eye contact with him—"thought a lot of that one who died, and that just shows how easily

178

fooled you are. He was a rascal, bad to women. And then there was that family of his." She spat these last words as if they were foul on her tongue. "That father and that . . . mother.

"Turned The Horses has always been lauded as a hero, but the fact of the matter has always been that he only did what anyone would have expected him to do. He has since made a lifelong occupation of that single moment of common sense. From there he proceeded to marry any woman that no other man would care to have simply because he didn't have to pay too much to have them. His last wife, Red Flowers, is a woman he didn't have to pay anything to have because by the time she was only fourteen summers, she was so brazen that her then husband was about to cut off her nose on account of his shame. That's when Turned The Horses offered to have her. Giving her to a mean old man seemed like a better punishment than cutting her nose, so the first husband agreed. Motherhood did little to slow down his youngest wife's night-crawling ways. If anything, she became worse."

White Bear was growing impatient. A sneer in his tone, he said, "I knew better than anyone the dead man you're speaking of. You claim that he was bad to women, but I know that he never raised his hand against a woman."

"Abuse comes in many forms!" Duck shouted, showing her exasperation. "Fists are only ever used by the dull witted. The one we're talking about was not stupid. He was like his mother. He was sly. He damaged women with charm and sympathy."

Now, this created a spark of interest, especially in me on account of my remembering the incident of the previous summer, when The Cheyenne Robber had shot Three Elks in the haunch and declared it an accident. Even then my own wife had insisted that the shooting hadn't been an accident, that The Cheyenne Robber had done it to warn Three Elks he was being much too helpful toward White Otter.

"He used kindness to try to lure women away from their husbands," Duck continued. "He only succeeded once, and that woman fell to ruin. I'm sure you all remember her. Her name was Many Robes Woman."

This created a bit of a stir. Yes, we all certainly knew her, but the only thing we knew was that she'd had run off with a white-man trapper. We saw her now and again. She was a good wife and a mother to a brood of children. None of us understood what this had to do with Three Elks. I offered this question to Duck, causing her to focus her entire attention now on me.

"She was about to be married," she said crisply, "to a good man of our Nation. But she would have been that man's fourth wife. The one I killed began his sweet talk, telling her that she was too young, too pretty, to be a lower wife. So she rebelled against her father's wishes, shamed the man who had offered for her. She was disgraced among her own and so she took up with that white man. We women knew who was to blame for that, although we couldn't prove it, and you men wouldn't listen. The only thing we could do was talk among ourselves. Unfortunately, time has a way of dulling the memory, especially among younger women. When he started coming after my granddaughter, I knew he had to be stopped."

"The Cheyenne Robber stopped him," Hunting Eagle

said, his disdain with her long-winded confession evident.

"That's what all of you *thought*." she cried. "But The Cheyenne Robber couldn't stop him because that one knew too much about what The Cheyenne Robber was getting up to. If anything, shooting that man only made everything worse because the one I killed, to get even with him, came to White Otter, telling her things he hoped would end her marriage and publicly shame The Cheyenne Robber. When I heard him telling her these hurtful things and knew he didn't care about her feelings, only that he was trying to use her as a weapon against a man he couldn't fight fairly, I knew I had to kill him. So I did."

We were all a bit nonplussed, and a heavy silence descended. Duck waited while our gazes wandered, none of us caring to look directly at her.

White Bear, looking up at the ceiling as if answers of how to respond to her charges hovered there, took a long time considering. "I want to know," he eventually prompted, "what could be said that would be so dangerous as to cost a man his life and warrant an attack on my nephew."

"I don't have to tell you that!" Duck yelped. "All you have to know is that I did it, and I'm glad."

"Yes," I interjected, "but you haven't told us how you were able to draw him out and slit his throat. From behind. For that was the pattern of the wound. He was cut from behind."

"How would you know?" she scoffed.

"I know," I said patiently, my voice sounding ridiculous even to my own ears, my nostrils now closed solid, "because Wolf Blanket demonstrated the two ways to cut a man's throat. From the front, a knife would be pulled straight

181

across in a slashing movement. From behind, the wound curves. I was able to examine the body. The wound was definitely curved. Which means that you had to have held him by the hair, pulling the head back to fully expose the neck."

Duck had a ready answer. "He turned his back on an old woman, someone he didn't consider a threat. Which was too bad for him. I've skinned a lot of buffalo in my life. Cutting him up felt like nothing."

The anger radiating from Brave Horse almost scalded my skin. Chancing a glimpse at the remaining faces, I read White Bear's and Hunting Eagle's blatant loathing. I knew that more than anything she'd previously said, that this last thoroughly unrepentant statement had absolutely damned her.

TWELVE

Still in the throes of fairness—which I suspect White Bear demonstrated purely as a means to negate any future doubts that might arise—he ordered Hunting Eagle to remain as a guard on the old woman while he, Brave Horse, and I took ourselves off to Owl Man. In spite of everything Duck had had to say, I still wasn't persuaded that she was as guilty as she insisted she was. Something was missing from her confession. Something vital. But White Bear wasn't interested in listening to my doubts. As a matter of fact, he ordered me to shut up, saying that my grating voice was doing his ears a grievous mischief. So none of us said another word. After a while, keeping quiet was all right because I really was in a lot of pain, each step sending a shock throughout my entire body that ended with a sharp stab inside my head. Then, too, the brisk pace White Bear determinedly set quickened my heart beat, and each speedy thump compelled my nose to throb just as speedily. We finally arrived to find Owl Man's lodge well lit by a surround of bonfires plus torches that had been added. Only a few yards from the doorway the guards crouched before one of the fires, actively engaged in a game of dice. When Big Tree, one of the players, caught sight of me, his eyes widened with dismay. Then those baleful eyes pierced mine as his mouth plunged down at the corners, forming a severe frown. He had trusted me to be on my own, and I'd insulted his trust by managing to run into mischief. Shaking a discouraged head, he returned his concentration to the game.

The first words out of Skywalker's mouth were, "Taybodal, what have you done to yourself?"

For a professional mystic he really could ask the most inane questions.

White Bear, with a disgruntled wave of his hand, passed the matter off as utterly immaterial. "Oh, he just battled with another woman. As usual, the woman won. Now, I want to talk to my nephew, and don't try telling me he's asleep because I can see his eyelids moving."

With a groan and a cautious shifting of his body, The Cheyenne Robber opened his eyes. Dodging around Hunting Eagle, I went to my patient. When I was kneeling beside the bed, The Cheyenne Robber exclaimed, "You look terrible!"

Peeling back the bandage to have a peek at his wound, I said in a thick, nasally tone, "Yes, but I suspect I'll live." After checking that there was no fresh beading between the stitches, I pressed the bandage back down. "As will you. Have you been drinking a good amount of broth?"

He was still staring at me with an unwavering interest as he answered with a nod. Then his attention was diverted by White Bear jostling Skywalker out of the way, his wider posterior filling the cushion Skywalker had rapidly vacated. Making himself comfortable, White Bear crossed his legs. "I'm want to ask you a question," he said sharply. "And you will answer honestly."

The Cheyenne Robber appeared to be quite calm, but as I was still in an attentive mode, measuring the beat of his heart by pressing two of my fingers against his inner wrist, I felt his pulse increase.

"The old woman known as Duck has confessed her attempt at killing you."

The Cheyenne Robber's pulse jumped another notch.

"She refuses to say why," White Bear continued. "Only that she did it and that she isn't sorry. She also claims to be the one who killed the youngest son of Turned The Horses. Do you happen to know anything about that?"

His pulse rate was now so rapid that I feared his heart would beat its way out of his ribs. Amazingly, none of this internal agitation showed on his face. If anything, his lids looked heavy, as if he were on the brink of a badly needed doze. I admired his control. My heart only ever beat that fast when fleeing, without dignity, from whatever life-threatening thing was chasing me.

"What I know," he said indolently, "is that my wife's grandmother is crazy. We've all known it for some time. My father-in-law, Hears The Wolf, calls her crazy times 'Duck's scrappy spells.' When she's having one of her . . . spells, he does his best to protect her. But no one can control her when wild ideas come into her head." He coughed weakly, leaned his head farther back into the slightly raised pillows, and closed his eyes. In a voice barely above a whisper, he finished, "I think maybe that is all I care to say about my wife's family."

White Bear, his lips pressed together in a thoughtful line, nodded with his entire body. In that moment, Duck's fate was irrevocably decided.

White Bear just could not wait to tell Wolf Blanket that he was free. He was so delighted that he practically danced as we strode out of the light of the circling torches, entering again the darkness. I suppose, viewing everything entirely from White Bear's perspective, things had worked out remarkably well. A valued member of his inner counsel had been spared. Now all he stood to lose was one old crazy woman.

For a man who was absolutely besotted with women, losing one—no matter her age or his particular hankering of her rarely, if ever, affected him. That was because White Bear was purely a man's man. It was only his brother warriors that he loved forever. And as much as it galled the pure fire out of me, I grimly forced myself to concede that Wolf Blanket was one of his beloved brothers. Warriors of the same society trusted each other with their very lives, making their relationships stronger than their marriages, stronger than the blood ties of their own families. I had no place within this select brotherhood, and that meant that White Bear would always love and admire Wolf Blanket more than he would ever love or admire me.

Suddenly seething with jealousy, I also wanted no part in delivering to Wolf Blanket the joyous news of his rather timely acquittal. Pleading exhaustion and a headache, I stalked off in the opposite direction. None of the three proceeding merrily on offered a parting word.

That hurt me a lot more than my broken nose.

My son and our girl-woman guest were both soundly asleep. Crying Wind was awake. No sooner had I entered than she was on her feet, advancing rapidly, stopping me just as I cleared the doorway.

"I want you to get her out of here," she whisper shouted. "Now!"

"But—"

"I don't want questions or excuses," she said in an angry hiss. "What I want is her gone."

I really was feeling tired now, the exhaustion I'd formerly pleaded, washing over me in waves. Heaving a burdensome sigh, I responded hollowly, "What happened?"

My wife folded her arms beneath her breasts and gave me a flinty stare. I couldn't see her feet on account of her long skirt, but I easily imagined one of them tapping impatiently. All of these movements were indicators that whatever it was she'd waited up to spew could not be good.

Once we were several yards from our home, she launched into a tirade. "To begin with, that girl confided a few confidences I wish I'd never heard. Plus, she seems to suffer the delusion that your saving her from Raven's Wing means that she is now my sister-wife."

We were still walking but sort of going nowhere and in a circular pattern while keeping our voices low so as not disturb any of our neighbors. But with this last startling statement, my wife had begun waving her hands around as she spoke in a rush.

"I can take a lot of things but not that. You're going to have to choose between us because I refuse to stay with you if that girl is someone you intend to marry. And before you answer, let me remind you that her baby will never belong to you. The child belongs to Raven's Wing, and I know he is going to claim it because it's the only one he has."

I don't know just what triggered it—exhaustion, bewilderment of what I'd just heard, lingering shock that Duck was more of a lunatic than I'd ever imagined her to be, or the effects of a swollen and throbbing face maybe, but I got pretty mad. So I stopped walking and started—even though I sounded a whole lot like a honking goose—shouting.

"Before you scamper to divorce me *again*, let me remind you that I cannot be held accountable for the delusions of a foolish young woman. My only interest in her has been merely as a concerned doctor. I have not, nor will I ever, consider her for a second wife."

I was breathing hard through my mouth. Crying Wind had pursed hers as she mulled what I'd forcibly said. Following this lengthy ponder, she responded in an even tone, "Then take her straight back to her rightful husband, and I will forget this entire incident."

Sometimes Onde women were the most exasperating creatures ever to draw a breath.

"I cannot do that," I fired back. "I took her out of there because Raven's Wing was abusing her."

"She has parents," Crying Wind quickly reminded me. "A mother and a father who would happily take her in."

"Yes," I sighed miserably. "And that mother and father

live on the far side of the encampment, and I'm too tired and my head hurts too much to walk her all the way over there."

"Then I'll go get two horses from the field."

You know, it's really hard to steer a balking pregnant woman. Especially in the dark. But because of my desperation and my rapidly failing physical condition, I would brook no hesitation on Always Happy's part. Blocking her whiny, pleading voice from my mind, I helped her climb onto the mare Crying Wind held steadily by the bridle, and after I was seated on my own horse, I took the mare's reins from my wife's offering hand. Thumping my heels against my horse's ribs, we set off.

Always Happy and I were not the only ones paying a late-night call on her parents. Raven's Wing was there, standing just outside the lodge, embroiled in a heated argument with the girl's father, the latter holding him off by threat of a raised club near Raven's Wing's face. Always Happy's mother was weeping and cowering fearfully behind her husband, who was either White Bear's older brother by birth or society adoption, I don't really remember on account of I didn't ever really know this man that well. What I do recall, however, is that they were both big—and certainly both were hot tempered. It was immediately apparent to me that White Bear had wasted no time in not only releasing Wolf Blanket, but calling off the guard he'd placed on Raven's Wing. Then the very first thing that man did was go hunting his wife, beginning with the most logical place. So, as it was working out, it was a good thing my wife had been stubborn about getting rid of our guest because the instant Raven's Wing became convinced that his wife was not where he'd assumed she'd be, he would have come straight for me. Then I would have had to face him purely on my own and probably been beaten up more badly than I already was.

"I'm telling you for the final time!" the older man hollered. "I don't know where she is. I wouldn't tell you even if I did know. I'm *glad* my daughter ran off."

"She didn't run away from me!" Raven's Wing shouted. "She was taken by that interfering Tay-bodal. And I know he brought her here, so give her back."

Neighbors standing off in several clumps were riveted by the highly vocal dispute. Only one person seemed to hear the two approaching horses, and when the girl's mother quickly glanced our way, saw her daughter, she gasped raggedly. Raven's Wing, with a quick turn of his head, saw exactly what his mother-in-law did. In that same second his father-in-law chose to strike, the war club he'd been shaking in Raven's Wing's face coming down hard. In the next second Raven's Wing was sprawled out on the ground.

I had to give that old man credit. He was still able to wield a lot of strength behind that club. Raven's Wing was knocked cold as anything I'd ever known. But I was the only one concerned about his condition. The parents and a horde of neighbors all went for the now-sobbing Always Happy, helping her down from Crying Wind's mare, then escorting her to the safety of her parents' home. In the process, all of them stepped over the splayed-out aggrieved husband and indifferently knocked me about in the bargain. Within minutes the lodge was packed with people, all of them anxious to hear Always Happy's version of the events. I was alone with Raven's Wing, carefully examining the side of his head with what little of the ocher light managed to spill out of the opened doorway. Then that inadequate light vanished completely as the girl's father filled the doorway.

"Is he still alive?"

"Yes."

"Well," he said, his gruff tone becoming hesitant, "I guess that's all right. I wasn't really trying to kill him, you know."

"I know."

The old man's voice took on a worrying edge. "You tell White Bear that. You tell him that a father's duty is to protect his daughter. And be sure you remind my younger brother that he is the father of many daughters. He would have done the same himself. You tell him that I'm not about to loose my place on account of this squabble."

His sudden worry about his seat at White Bear's council fire caused me to remember the day from the beginning, concentrating on the arguing that had gone on when White Bear let it be known that he was rearranging his assembly. His doing this meant that some of his men would be elevated while others faced being taken down a notch or even evicted. Rank is the most important thing in the lives of some men. It hadn't surprised me that there had been angry protests. At the time White Bear hadn't completely made up his mind about just who would be what. And now I believed I understood why I'd found Raven's Wing physically battling with his wife.

He hadn't been trying to hurt her as much as he'd been trying to hold on to her. If he'd heard the rumors my wife had heard, rumors his own brother had confided to Crying Wind, then he also knew that Always Happy wanted out of their marriage. Raven's Wing's actions had been that of man desperate to keep the bond of marriage between himself and his chosen chief. Too much had happened to lose him his rank. His brother's death wouldn't have affected it, but his father's tirades, the threat of war between the bands, certainly had. Blood ties always being stronger than sworn oaths of loyalty, White Bear could no longer afford to trust Raven's Wing. But if the man would persist on staying with the Rattle Band, then he could stay . . . but under close guard until the turmoil between the two bands was settled. The only means that Raven's Wing had to assure White Bear of his continuing support, even against his own father, was his marriage to Always Happy. And when I took her away, I'd taken not only his wife and unborn child but whatever frail hope remained of him retaining his status.

It clawed my spirit to realized that I'd unintentionally helped to destroy another human being. My throat so tight that breath barely squeaked down into my lungs, I managed to say to White Bear's worrying older bother, "I give you my word, you will have nothing to fear from White Bear."

That old man immediately began to credit me with more influence than I ever had, for he said in a near-grateful tone, "You're a good man, Tay-bodal. I've always said so. Even to those who make jokes about you."

"There is one favor I do ask," I said wearily. "I would like some help with him."

Many hands assisted in first lifting and then the belly-down placement of Raven's Wing across the spine of my wife's mare. Mindful of him slipping off and cracking his head again, I walked both horses, gently leading one of the proudest, most politically ambitious men in my memory into the fullness of his defeat.

Upon reaching his darkened home, there came the troublesome problem of getting him down off the horse all by myself. For a good deal of time I simply stood there, one half of my tired, maltreated brain trying to convince me that he would be just fine where he was. Well, knowing what I did about blood flow, I knew that wasn't right, so there I was back at the beginning, trying to figure out how to manage on my own when a lanky figure came sloping out of the darkness.

"I had a feeling you needed me," Skywalker said softly. He came to stand beside me, so then there were two of us gazing up at the unconscious man doubled over and dangling off a horse's back. Skywalker drew in a deep breath, let it go, then took hold of one of Raven's Wing's arms. "Grab his other arm," he quietly ordered, and we hauled him down and between us managed to drag-carry him inside his lodge.

I didn't bother asking just how he knew that I needed help or where to find me in order to give it. With Skywalker there were just some things better left unasked. We got the injured man into his bed, propping him up against a backrest. Then Skywalker went about building up the fire so that we would have light and I began searching for the household water supply. I found it in a stoppered jug, though there wasn't very much. As my arms, legs, and hands were shaking, I knew I didn't have the spare strength to take the jug to the creek, fill it up, then bring it all way back again. What there was would simply have to do. Pouring a sparse amount of it into my cupped hand, I transferred it to the side of Raven's Wing's skull. The man had been blessed with a wealth of hair. I really could have used all of the water to wet it back in order to get a good look at his head, but then I wouldn't have had any to give him to drink. Restoppering the container, I set it aside and focused on the far wall, using the tips of my fingers as my eyes, feeling around on his dampened head. I knew what to feel for because I know how heads are put together. I've known for most of my life that a man's head is not just one big round bone. I learned this at a very young age by studying a lot of bare skulls.

There was a nation of Indians, the Tonkawas, who ritually cooked and ate parts of their dead enemies. Now, a war chief I never really got along with all that well, a strapping fellow by the name of Big Bow, led a raid against the Tonkawas one time, and he brought back over a hundred human skulls that he had rescued from the village he'd destroyed. We didn't know who the heads belonged to because they had been reduced to pure bone, but worried that some of them might be relatives, the Owl Doctors decided that what ought to be done was have a big blessing ceremony and then bury all the skulls. It took three days to get everything just right, and before the blessing ceremony could begin, followed abruptly by the skulls being consigned forever into the ground, I went inside the tiny lodge where they were all sitting on a blanket in a well-ordered row. Holding each of them in my hands, I examined them from every angle, amazed to discover that all of the skulls were made the same: by a series of separate plates that seemed knitted together. As I said, I was quite young back then and still considered to be a bit strange. I suppose any youth daring to sneak into a death lodge just to handle a lot of bald skulls was a bit strange, but I've never regretted the experience, for it afforded me a better-than-working knowledge of the way our heads are formed, where the weakest and the strongest places are located.

"Is he badly injured?"

I glanced to where Skywalker squatted near the awakening fire, the first fragile flames doing their feeble best to lessen the interior's gloom. "It's hard to tell," I answered gravely. "I don't feel a break in the skull, and there's no sign of bleeding on the outside. But he might be bleeding on the inside, and that, I'm afraid, is beyond my skills."

Skywalker shifted himself, half rising and walking in a crouch to the bed. Squatting again, his shoulder touched mine as he murmured, "This is the type of medicine I'm fairly good at."

Recognized doctors always took precedence over me, and when one decided to intervene, there was nothing for me to do but to sit back on my heels and watch. Skywalker was the one Owl Doctor I never really minded displacing me. He didn't bother examining the steadily swelling knot on the top of Raven's Wing's head. What he did instead was brush curled fingers across the man's forehead as three times he blew air against the still face. After that he proceeded to chant, in a voice so low and soothing that it set me to thinking about a velvety, purling river. As I listened, my eyelids began to grow heavier and heavier, and it was with effort that I pried them open after each blink. After a little while I couldn't even do that, and I remember thinking that that was all right. That I'd just listen with them closed. The rest is a blank.

My next recollection is waking to a ceaseless low buzz of voices. I was startled fully awake when I realized that I was stretched out on the floor, a stiff blanket covering me from head to toe. Peering out from behind a corner of the blanket, I saw shapes. Knuckling my eyes, peering again, the shapes came into focus. Six men—White Bear, Lame Crow, White Horse, Big Tree, Dangerous Eagle, and the irksome Wolf Blanket—were seated around a lively fire, conversing in whispers with Skywalker. All of them were drinking coffee. I knew because I could smell it. The wonderful bouquet, more than any muted discussion, was most probably the very thing that woke me. I had no idea where they had gotten that coffee. Quite frankly, I didn't care. All I knew was that some of it had better been left for me. Then an awful thought occurred. Something bad had to have happened during my exceptionally heavy sleep to attract this type of crowd. Fearing the worst, I turned my head, searching for a sight of Raven's Wing. Every part of my body relaxed when I saw him very much alive and sitting up in his bed, quietly sipping from a metal cup. His eyes slowly found mine. Then he looked quickly away, fixing his complete attention on the cup he brought to his lips.

The lodge doorway was closed, so in order to get a fix on the time of day I looked up to the smoke hole. Behind the rising curls of smoke, pale stars were dwindling in a gray-black sky. It was morning, but not by much. I began to kick off the blanket.

"Well," White Bear drawled, "the dead returns to life."

196

The others turned their heads, smirks greeting me as I pulled myself up into a sitting position. "I smell coffee," I said.

Skywalker extended the cup in his hand to me. "Here," he grunted. "Have mine."

I opened my mouth to protest, but he insisted with a stony look. I took the cup. It was almost full. I took a greedy drink and—"Where did you get sugar?!"

"From the same place we got the coffee," White Bear chortled. "From Turned The Horses." He turned his face back toward the fire. The others followed suit. "He didn't want to give me anything," White Bear continued dismally. "But good manners, especially as I came with the news he'd been waiting to hear, won out. That old man has been hording. If I had known about it during this past cold season, I would have robbed him."

This statement was greeted by a round of "Ho's," the other men, even Skywalker, heartily agreeing that anyone, most especially a chief, who did not share with those in need deserved to be robbed. Being stingy was an intolerable offense. White Bear would not allow Turned The Horses's begrudging nature go unpunished. Everyone in that lodge knew it. I glanced uneasily at Raven's Wing. He continued sipping from his cup, offering not a word of comment.

There was a too-lengthy awkward moment; then White Bear went on, "I told him that we found out who killed his youngest son." He turned his head again, looking past me to Raven's Wing. "And I blessed him with the news that his other son would be returning, this very day, to his true home."

Cold dread passed through me as I heard from his own

197

lips White Bear's decision. It wasn't as if I had any deep affection for Raven's Wing. I barely knew the man. But hearing his banishment from the Rattle Band did affect me. I repeatedly assured myself that none of the fault was mine, but I was finding it difficult to look again at the person who, only days before, had enjoyed lofty prestige. Now he was to be a warrior of a poor band belonging to an ancient chief with only one heroic deed to his credit: While a young herder, he'd managed to turn a few stampeding horses.

I think what disturbed me most was the knowledge that even if Raven's Wing managed to escape his father a second time, he was far too old to start again his climb toward his burning ambition: of one day wearing an Onde's hat. Because of White Bear's punishment, Raven's Wing would live out his days as a Kaan . . . someone no better than me.

With a bit of a shock, I found myself suddenly looking straight into Raven's Wing's steely gaze as he muttered words that only I heard: "I will hate you for the rest of my life."

THIRTEEN

Up until I'd heard him say that, I truly had felt bad for Raven's Wing. But hearing him say those words proved to me beyond all doubt that he was indeed his father's son. Each in his own way was mean and miserly. One chose to horde all manner of goods while the other grasped after honors and prestige. Raven's Wing blaming me for his downfall galled me all the way to my soul, and so I stood, remorse for any small part I'd played in his undoing sliding away like water droplets off my skin, and walked the small distance away from him, sitting myself down in White Bear's chosen circle, not minding at all that facing me across the circle was Wolf Blanket. I breathed a small sigh of contentment knowing that, warrior or not, I held a place in White Bear's regard. And that place was firmly fixed in the minds of everyone present when, with barely a thought to what he was doing, White Bear picked up his battered old coffee pot and casually poured more coffee into my nearly drained cup.

"Deer Trail says the old woman has been making her prayers all night."

I knew he meant Duck. As she was for all intents and purposes dead to him now, he could no longer speak her name. I began mourning her as I drank deeply the refreshed coffee, swallowing with it, my sorrow. Funny isn't it how when someone dies or goes away, the bad things you knew about that person go, too, leaving only the good things to remember. That's what was in my mind as I forced hot coffee down my gullet. I saw Duck, all right being scrappy, but somehow managing to be funny at the same time. I saw her boundless energy as she worked side by side with Beloved, always being quick to take on the harder tasks so that Beloved wouldn't spoil her hands. And when Beloved protested, I remembered the way Duck would chastise, "You have more time to be old than you do to be young. And while I live, you will enjoy being young."

"But I'm a grandmother."

"Yes, but you're not really old until you're a great-grandmother. Like me."

I think what hurt the most was the too-vivid memory of Duck caring for her great-grandchild. Many times I played witness to the loving way she held him or carried him on her ample hip. She would die today, and that little boy would grow up without one shred of remembrance of her. And because she died disgracefully, he would never know about the old woman who had loved him beyond measure. It tore at my heart as I began to feel that child's loss.

If there had been anything, any small little thing, that I could have done to save her, I would not have hesitated. But she had condemned herself, and The Cheyenne Robber had fully confirmed her confession. There was nothing I could do.

Nothing.

Somehow I managed to swallow another slug of the too-sweet coffee sloshing around in the cup that shook uncontrollably as I held it against my mouth. Then I felt a hand come down on my shoulder. Because my eyes were swimming with fresh tears, it required several blinks to clear them enough to recognize my comforter to be Big Tree. He didn't look at me. Didn't acknowledge the fact that he was touching me, but his warming hand remained during the time needed for me to harden my heart against what was to come.

For a very long time no one spoke. The only sounds that came to my ears were the snap and pop of the fire, the steady chirping of crickets, and the dim, deadened singing of frogs way off in the distant creek.

Finally, the last of the precious coffee consumed, White Bear poured the dregs from the pot into the fire, which hissed its appreciation and threw back the crisp aroma of roasting grounds.

"Everyone go home," he said in a brooding, low-voiced tone. "Put on your finest clothing. Choose your best horse. A woman we have known all of our lives dies this day."

In the bleary darkness of predawn, we filed out and set off in different directions.

A little knot of something sat just outside the doorway of my home. As I neared, the knot moved. My little son raised his head. Even from a distance I could see that his expression was pinched from weariness. I sent him a wave as I increased my horse's stride, pulling along my wife's sluggish mare. As I covered the distance between us, I couldn't help but think that perhaps he'd been worried that his mother and I had fought again, and I had gone off once more, this time possibly never coming back. The dread of living with women and babies again must have tormented him, that had to be the reason he'd spent the night waiting for me. But he was a proud little fellow. He said none of this as he shrugged out of the horse blanket he'd used as a cover. Just as I reached him and climbed down, he stood, extending his arms. Obeying the unspoken request, I picked him up. His legs twined around my waist as he lay his careworn small head against my shoulder.

Rubbing a circle on his bare back, I said tenderly, "You are a doctor's son. You have to get used to my being with patients for long periods of time. While I'm doing that, your job is to guard over your mother."

"Yes, Father," he muffled sleepily. And then he proceeded to snore.

There was no fire going; the only light to see by came from the steadily brightening sky filtering down the smoke hole. But it was enough to see Crying Wind spread out all over the bed. She was doing some fine snoring herself, but she woke with a start as I entered carrying our sound-asleep little boy. She sat up, knuckling her eyes as I laid him in his bed and covered him with a blanket.

"We were worried," she whispered.

"I know." Standing by the small bed, indicating the boy with a lift of my chin, I whispered, "I found him outside."

"Outside!" she yelped. I quickly waved my hand, and she, just as quickly, lowered her voice. "He was in his bed when I finally gave up waiting for you."

"It would seem he took your going to sleep as being his turn to keep watch."

Crying Wind heaved a huge sigh. Then she shook her head. "It's a good thing you look so awful. Otherwise I'd think you'd been with another woman."

I laughed soundlessly, appreciating, with a sharp twinge of sadness, that while everything good with my life was beginning all over again, another life was about to end.

I had expected my getting dressed would involve a lot of to-ing and fro-ing between our and my humble little medicine lodge, but I'd underestimated my wife's confidence in our reconciliation. In my prolonged absence during the night, she'd busily packed me up and moved me home. So it was with appreciative ease that I cleaned and groomed myself while she returned the two horses to the field and chose another. I was waiting outside when she came back, my eyes flaring wide the instant I saw her choice.

"That's one of Skywalker's best horses!"

Crying Wind was not in the mood to argue the point. "He won't say anything," she grumbled, handing me the reins. I petted the beautiful roan's muzzle as she took up the blanket our son had slept in, gave it a good shake, then flung it over the roan's back. Mounting up, I sat proudly. I was clean, dressed well, and astride a powerful horse. All of this necessary, I realized as depression settled over me like a heavy burden, just to be party to the killing of one old woman.

. . .

The sun was just peeking up over the vast horizon when we gathered at White Bear's enormous red lodge. Turning his horse's head, White Bear lead the way to the Grandmother's lodge. My attempt to straggle behind was thwarted by Skywalker. Walking his horse beside mine and, as my wife had predicted, saying nothing of the fact that my horse was actually his—if a smirk can be counted as saying nothing—he made certain I kept up. I no longer wanted to be any part of this. Then again, neither did he. But if Duck's last moments among us were to have any dignity, she would need the presence of two sympathetic members of the expulsion party. So I took in a deep breath, hoping that in doing so I was also taking in a bit of Skywalker's inner strength.

The encampment was unusually quiet, only a few curious dogs watching the somber parade. The doors of the homes we passed remained firmly shut. Death was close, its presence more pervasive than the dew-heavy morning air. People sheltered against it as they listened to the plodding hooves passing by. The silence, the utter stillness, triggered a memory. It was streaky at first. Little more than a vague recognition of a memory, and in my mind's eye colors swarmed without form, the dominant color, white. But then the darker colors sharpened, and the white began to drape itself over . . .

A chill went through me. A chill as sharp and as bitter as the light freezing wind that had once stung my cheeks, had done its best to invade the layers of my winter clothing as I followed a solemn procession through a frozen valley.

Where hundreds of trees bowed down before us. That day had foretold this one.

I silently cursed myself for a fool. The signs had been plainly there. If I hadn't willed the premonition away, I could have prevented everything. I could have—

"No," Skywalker said flatly. "Throw that thought away. No one has that kind of power."

Startled, I turned toward him as our two horses carried us along in their slow, methodical gait. I don't know how long I returned his stare, but it was long enough to vividly recall that he'd been in that valley, too. That he'd been riding farther up ahead. If I'd felt the portent of that place, then he—

"You knew," I accused in a hissing whisper.

"Yes," he replied, "I did." He turned to face me, his eyes capturing and holding mine. "Just as I know something else."

"What?"

"That whatever comes into view in my inner eye is not for me to approve or prevent. I am only a man. The Creator has given us all the freedom to chose the direction of our own lives. I might sense, might even know for certain, how a thing will end, but I do not have the right to interfere. And neither do you."

I could not have disagreed more, but just as I was about to argue, he brought his horse closer to mine and spoke low but harshly. "You've only had a taste of what I live with every day. You know nothing of the burden, the responsibility."

"Then what good is your power?" I half cried.

"It tells me how to pray," he said firmly. "And when I come to know that despite my prayers a thing will most certainly happen and I become lost to despair, Owl Man then knows what to pray in order to save my sanity." Thumping his heels against his horse's ribs, he cantered away, leaving me to trail the procession entirely alone.

Deer Trail stood just outside the Grandmother's lodge, obviously waiting our approach. The instant he spotted White Bear leading the procession, he turned, bent at the waist, and called through the door. I saw Skywalker's spine tense and quickly looked in the direction he stared, catching sight of what he was seeing: a large black-and-white speckled horse shifting its weight from one back hoof to the other as the luxuriant tail swished.

Hears The Wolf's favorite war horse.

Everyone else recognized it, too, and as I was following up the rear, I saw the hands of those riding forward nervously grasping the hilts of scabbard knives. Hears The Wolf was formidable. If he intended to make trouble, he could be counted on to make a lot of it. Even if doing so meant his going up alone against seven men. Or, more correctly, six because I had no intention of fighting him.

Hears The Wolf came out first, stooping through the doorway, then standing to his full, impressive height. He was dressed in his finest clothing: white leggings with matching vest and shoes and a black breechcloth. His hair was brushed out and oiled. Small sliver discs hung like chains on either side of a face that was contorted with fury as he stared at White Bear with malevolent intent. Duck tried to come out, but her way was blocked by her rooted

son-in-law. Typical of her, she shrieked something unintelligible while striking a fist against the small of his back. He
quickly turned, placing his hands on her shoulders, and tried
to shove her back inside. She began to scream at the top of
her lungs, and we couldn't help but hear what she said then.

"Get out of my way you thick head!"

"But Mother—"

"Don't you argue with me! This is my die day, and
you're not going to spoil it."

Hears The Wolf tried to wrestle with her, and I was
pleased that he wasn't able to battle her any better than I.
If he wasn't careful, he'd end up with a broken nose, too.
Yet unlike me, Hears The Wolf knew when to quit. Gasping
not because of the tussle but because his valiant heart was
breaking, he turned his head to the side, but not before I
saw the tears streaming down his face. He was trying to
stop their flow, choking down gulps of air as we came to a
stop and White Bear dismounted, then strode forward, stopping before Deer Trail.

"We have come for the one the Grandmother shelters.
I ask you, the Grandmother's custodian, to give the woman
over for punishment."

"And her punishment will be . . . ?" Deer Trail grimly
asked. The old man already knew. So did his lady wife,
which was why she'd chosen not to be present. She and
Duck were the same age, had more than likely been girlhood
playmates, then brides, then mothers. Now, as old women,
they were the keepers of one another's memories, an obli-
gation so precious it beggars description. It clearly pained
Deer Trail to ask the damning question, but he'd been required to do so as a matter of formal record.

"Banishment," came White Bear's somber answer.

Deer Trail looked over his shoulder at Duck, who was busily straightening her best dress, smoothing it down, making certain that she looked just right. She did look nice. That touched me in a new and deeper place inside my heart. I suppose because I'd never seen her all dressed up before. Normally she went about in a disheveled work dress, gray hair carelessly fashioned into two sloppy braids. Now she was wearing a decent dress with long fringes at the sleeves and base, the bodice decorated with painted-on designs of pale blue. The Creator's favorite color. Her hair was untied and combed smooth. On her feet were a pair of brand-new shoes. She looked ready for burial. Adding to this illusion was the sobering fact that she wore no jewelry.

A person facing banishment was regarded as someone already dead. Everything they had of value was duly given away. With women, jewelry went first, followed by treasured household items. I was dimly wondering to whom she'd given her knife—the knife she'd said she'd used to kill one man, severely injure another. Then I saw it, still in its battered sheath, tied just above Hears The Wolf's right knee and left to hang against the side of his leg like an ugly brown stain flawing the otherwise perfect whiteness of his legging.

Deer Trail's quaking voice sounded. "It is with deep regret that I release this person." His voice caught, then trembled out the few remaining words. "And in releasing her to you, I say the name, She Makes Him Duck for the last time."

Hears The Wolf was unashamedly weeping now. We all

were. Even White Bear. The only one not crying was the old woman in question.

"Ha!" she laughed hollowly, the barking sound startling us all. "I remember when my husband gave me that name. It's because I used to throw things at him. Never hit him, though. He thought it was because he was too fast. What an idiot. I never hit him because I wasn't really trying. It was more fun just to watch him dodge and dance like a panicky fool. Come to think of it, that was the best part of being married to him."

I heard a snorting noise and with shock realized that Skywalker, leaning forward in his saddle, was giving in to shaky laughter. But he stopped laughing and sat smartly up when Hears The Wolf began hollering.

"*No!*" His shout made our horses jittery. Mine was nodding its head repeatedly and doing a side step as Hears The Wolf jumped to place himself between Duck and White Bear. Shielding his mother-in-law with his body, he vented his fury on White Bear. "You will not tie her arms and drag her behind your horses. I will knock you down if you dare try."

White Bear, the tying rope in his hands, hesitated. Then said, his tone half reasoning, half pleading, "The drag is part of it, and you well know it."

"Not this time," Hears The Wolf seethed. "Not with . . . her. She will leave the Rattle Band the same way she came to live among us. With dignity. And riding behind me." He turned to a now ashen-faced and unnaturally sedate Duck, offering her his hand. She took it, and standing almost at arm's length they regarded each other for a long moment.

Finally, in a voice so low that we strained to hear, he said, "Mother, will you again honor an unworthy son?"

"Yes," she breathed.

Every member of Turned The Horses's band had turned out to witness the expulsion of Three Elks's murderer, treating the event like a celebration. The sun was in its slow rise in the east when we arrived, hanging like a huge red ball just above the horizon. Catching sight of Duck sitting behind Hears The Wolf, the latter riding beside White Bear, the happy attitude of the waiting people faded. Turned The Horses's aspect darkened with fury. Signaling those standing around him to help him, he rose from his pallet and began tottering forward. We were still mounted, Hears The Wolf's striking horse standing well apart from ours. With the aid of his sons, Turned The Horses was trundled passed the lone horse bearing the two riders. In good time he reached us, and, standing before White Bear's great black horse, the elder chief tilted his head back and as best as he was able, he shouted, "What disgrace is this?"

"There is no disgrace here," White Bear replied languidly.

With raised eyebrows and a puff of his cheeks, he looked over his shoulder at those of us ready to back him up. Satisfied that he had men of courage with him, he sat forward, the shifting of his weight in the saddle sending a squeak of disturbed leather into the morning's stillness. Taking a deep breath, White Bear addressed his brother chief.

"You demanded a life for a life. If the way this life is being presented is not acceptable, we will leave, taking the woman home to safely live out her days in my band." He leaned forward, driving his gaze like a lance against that deplorable old man. "But know this, Turned The Horses, you and I will be even."

The very suggestion sent the old man reeling, his two sons struggling to keep him upright. White Bear and his lieutenants began to snicker, mocking the old man's display of weakness. I wasn't laughing, mainly because I was too caught up by the sight of him. In the strengthening light of the day I was being afforded a better look at the man unwilling to pay for an experienced doctor. Which was too bad for him because in the fullness of mellow sunshine, I could now tell that his haggard face with its waxen, orange-ish hue and the whites of his eyes just as yellow as a daisy flower, all meant that the man's liver was bad. I knew, too, that Burned Hand could carry on bleeding him daily, but the disease attacking that vital organ would merrily continue its destruction. For what ailed that old man—indeed, nearly every man in his family—had to do with an illness only then making an insidious inroad into our Nation. And that illness was caused by too much love for the white man's whiskey. I could have told him all of this, and my doing so would have spared him the unnecessary pain of Burned Hand's medicine knife. But I knew I wouldn't tell him anything of the kind as I directed my gaze to the person Turned The Horses was bound and determined to show no pity whatsoever.

Duck.

I clamped down hard on my back teeth when Turned The Horses shouted up again to White Bear. "I accept the life you've brought to me. I accept it, and I cast it out." Skywalker tried to be helpful, but Hears The Wolf, so distraught that he was close to raving, roughly shoved him back. The rest of us had all dismounted, our small number quickly swallowed up in the horde of the now near-jubilant, hooting members of Turned The Horses's band. You have to understand that ridicule played a hard part of banishment. Derision is nothing more than vocalized rejection, and that, I'm afraid, is what banishment was all about. Sending someone out, alone, unarmed, and with the unquestionable knowledge that the normally protective group would do nothing to save the condemned from certain death.

What with all the ribald caterwauling going on, it was impossible to hear any of the words Duck had to say to Hears The Wolf as they stood together, his head bowed, her two work-roughened hands holding the sides of his weeping face. But I knew that whatever she was saying wasn't intended to be overheard. That her parting words were supremely private. Then she let go of him and turned to Skywalker, who was standing only a few paces away. Somehow she managed to outshout all of those voices deriding her.

"Keep him close!"

"Always!" Skywalker hollered back.

"Your word?"

"You have it."

She gave him a satisfied nod; then she turned.

The scene of that lone dark figure walking into the full blaze of the morning sun was a sight that became burned into my mind. It was a sight so powerful, so fraught with emotion, that I couldn't breathe. Then the people around me began to surge, the combined noise of their voices hitting my ears in a physical assault. I had to clamp my hands against the sides of my head as yelling people bumped by me, chasing after Duck and throwing rocks at her back. As one woman darted by, I recognized her, and as quick as a flash, I grabbed hold of her raised arm and yanked her back just as hard as I could.

Red Flowers still clutched a rock, but because of my solid grip on her wrist, she couldn't throw it. Remembering what Duck had said about this woman, that she wasn't a decent wife, had never been a fit mother to Three Elks, and knowing, too, that I'd never actually known Duck to lie, my lips curled back in disgust as I said viciously, "Not you. You are not worthy."

My free hand forcibly removed the rock from her grasp, and with a jerk she wrenched herself loose. Backing away, briskly rubbing the wrist I'd held as if desperate to erase the warmth of my hold, she commenced to scream.

"You don't know anything! You don't!"

Then she ran off. Not after the tormenting mob hurling stones at the vanishing specter of Duck, but back toward the encampment.

I never saw either woman again.

The ride back to our own camp was indeed quite grim. Skywalker rode off to the side near Hears The Wolf. The breezes coming from the east carried the sound of his lowered voice my way, but his words were made chaotic by the wind, coming to me only in scattered snatches. I couldn't hear enough to piece together exactly what he said. I could only discern that he was attempting to be a source of comfort. Then, too, I wasn't being allowed to be much of an eavesdropper because Wolf Blanket was, in a gloomy way, unusually chatty.

Pacing his horse to mine, he said tonelessly, "That was bad business."

Bearing firmly in mind that if Duck hadn't confessed, in all probability it would be him not her taking that long walk toward death and feeling rocks pelting his back, it was difficult to judge the level of his sincerity.

In spite of my lack of reply, he continued on, the pitch of his voice becoming a degree lighter. "I want to thank you for all you did for me. I know, given the circumstances, it couldn't have been easy for you." A long awkward moment of silence ensued. Seemingly undaunted, the man tried yet again. "So it's going all right for you, then? The make up between you and Crying Wind?"

I turned a stony face toward him. "Yes. Everything between us is just as it should be."

He emitted a sigh. "Well, I can't say I'm glad. As you know, I held another hope."

"I'm fully aware of your hopes," I returned icily. Then I had nothing more to say for several moments. Not until my accursed curiosity got the better of me, and I heard myself blurt, "There's is one little something I still don't understand. You said you were leaving my wife and walking to your own lodge when you happened on the dying man."

He nodded.

"That was a lie." My mouth pressed in a stern line, I waited for him to deny the accusation. He didn't bother to try.

"Yes, it was."

"You were going to meet him, weren't you."

214

He looked off toward Skywalker and Hears The Wolf. Several minutes passed before he turned his face back to me. "He asked me to," he said flatly. "He said he had information that I would find extremely useful. I took it to mean that he meant something about you."

"Me?" I barked. "Why would you think that?"

Wolf Blanket shrugged deeply. "Well, the two of you were fairly friendly. And to be perfectly honest, if he knew anything I could use to sway . . ." His words trailed off as a shadow of guilt swept across his face. With the shadow's passing, his voice changed again, this time becoming loud. "You are not an appropriate husband for a woman like Crying Wind. I've said this from the beginning, I'll go to my death saying it."

He really shouted this last part, the veins in his neck distended. I glanced away from him and saw the heads of the lead riders swiveling to look back over their shoulders, every one of them blatantly listening as Wolf Blanket ranted on, thumping his chest with his fist for further emphasis.

"I was preparing myself, doing everything I knew to do to attract White Bear's notice. I placed my life at his feet, was always the first to accept the war pipe when he offered it. I did all that to prove I was the man worthy of his widowed cousin. And then what does he do?" Foam was beginning to fleck the man lips. Alarmed, I began to wonder rapidly just how fast the horse my wife had borrowed from Skywalker was able to gallop. "He threw her away on you! So, yes, I went out to meet Turned The Horses's dead son. And I went hoping with everything inside me that he knew something terrible about you. Something I could use to disgrace you before White Bear. But more importantly, I prayed he would tell me something that would turn Crying Wind's heart away from you and toward me."

"But you found him dying," I said—and, I am pleased to say, without a fearful tremor in my voice.

"Yes!" he hollered. "And I knew that he was dying. I knew there was nothing anyone could do to save him."

"You weren't taking him to help as you formerly claimed," I reiterated for the advantage of those busily listening. "You were concerned only with finding a witness."

"Are you completely dull witted?" He bellowed rhetorically. He was so caught up with his denigration of me that he was beyond noticing that our seemingly private chat was far from private. "He was all but dead. It was too late to hope he could speak before a witness. All I wanted to do with him then was take him to die among his society brothers. But Raven's Wing came out of nowhere, and before I could explain, he attacked me."

"He didn't give you a chance," I finished for him. "He attacked when you weren't ready to defend yourself."

"That's exactly right," Wolf Blanket said, a shade calmer. "It wasn't a fair fight. If it had been, he wouldn't have beaten me. He knew that because we've wrestled many times, and I always won. So he hit me when I wasn't expecting it; then he had me down."

"Did you notice any blood on Raven's Wing?"

"What?" Wolf Blanket yelped, his eyebrows shooting all the way to his scalp line.

"Blood," I asked again. "Did you see any blood anywhere on him."

All the wind went out of his hysterics as he pondered the question. Then, stammering, he said, "N-no . . ."

"Are you sure?"

"Of course I'm sure!" he scoffed.

"How?" My tone may have sounded even, with maybe just a mild twinge of curiosity, but inside I was a screaming wreck. If this idiot answered the way I prayed he would, we had more than enough time to dash to Duck's rescue. I tried to be helpful, lead him like a balky mule toward the longed for conclusion. "Now, remember, as you once expertly demonstrated, the dead man was cut from behind and across both large neck veins. Which means blood would spray—"

"To the front and both sides!" His agitation growing he squirmed in the saddle. "Blood would have been on the knife hand and it would come back onto the killer's face and hair."

"All right," I wet my lips, tried to remain as patient as possible, "picture in your mind Raven's Wing advancing toward you."

Like an obedient child, Wolf Blanket scrunched his eyes closed, doing his best to force the remembered image.

"Do you see him?"

"Yes," he drawled.

"And is he—"

"No," he said definitely, his eyes flashing open. And realizing what I had been hoping to hear, his eyes softened, and his posture slumped. "I'm sorry," he said, and I believed that this time he actually meant it. "There was no blood at all on Raven's Wing."

White Bear violently reined up his horse. When I looked his way, our gazes colliding, he was breathing hard through his nose, nostrils flaring. "And now we will speak of this thing no more. Do you understand me, Tay-bodal? It's finished."

FOURTEEN

White Bear's final words were echoing in my mind when I experienced a violent shove that sent me backward, rocking me on my heels. Frantically grabbing hold of the edges of the high bureau, I steadied myself on my feet as I tried to fight off this, the first stage of withdrawal. But the fight was useless, and try as I might to hold on, the separation of me and the young man in the mirror continued, his image rapidly fading. Too soon, there was only a rheumy-eyed old me in the glass. Hesitantly, my gaze drifted to the clock on the far wall. The clock's small pendulum was swinging its normal measured beat. The clock face told me that five minutes had passed. Only five. Which made a grand total of one minute for each decade that I'd lived since the time that young man and I had been one in the same. I looked back to the mirror, hating the sight of the wizened old man, blinking back tears.

My reflection and I turned from each other as I shuffled away from the bureau. Leaving it meant that my mirrored reflection had disappeared completely. One day, I will disappear, too. But not yet. Not today. My awake dream had been sent for a purpose. And I knew just who'd sent it.

Skywalker.

Since his death he has been pestering me. You'd think he'd be happy in wherever it is he is in the Forever. But, no. Not him. He's as annoying dead as he was when he was alive. Which means he's always finding little tasks for me to do. Especially in these final years of my life. I don't mind as much as I did a decade ago, when the visions first began. Back then, the daydreams sent me scurrying to a healer in the hope that he could make them stop. But modern-day Owl Doctors don't have the right power. When the old ways were shunted off to the side, the good things that had been so much a part of those ways just shriveled up and disappeared. So now when I hear young men profess to be "Traditional Doctors," I think, Ha . . . the last Traditional Doctor was put on a prison train and taken off to Florida.

And he died there.

Yet death did not stop him being a pest. Bluntly put, for a long time he was making me crazy. Then somewhere along the way I gave in to him. Doing that, I gradually lost all fear of his sometimes baffling images. The fear may have gone away, but I couldn't stop being just a little mad and, all right, rebellious. I wanted a quiet life. I felt I'd earned it. But he wouldn't even consider that maybe now I was a bit too old, a bit too stiff in the joints, to just jump whenever he sent me a prod, urged me to tie up whatever loose end needed tying before making my journey to where he is. Now he was on to me about Three Elks. A young man I hadn't thought about in fifty years.

I was thinking about him again as I went to the stove, got a good fire going in its belly, and set the pot on to heat up the leftovers of last night's coffee. While the coffee was warming, I removed the clothing from the peg—the same clothing that had frightened the liver out of me on waking, mistaking my own clothes for an intruder. Once I was fully dressed, I poured myself a cup of the badly needed coffee and carried it to the door, pausing just before stepping over the threshold to slap on my old black hat. I still love hats. Some things about me have stubbornly refused to change.

The sun was on its way up now, its warming rays making a bright yellow carpet across the warped flooring of my cabin's covered porch. As I stood there appreciating the morning, knowing by its warmth that it was going to be a hot day, my cats came meowing, rubbing their arched bodies against the rough fabric of my trousered legs.

I have three cats. I can say their names out loud only because I changed them slightly from the names of the dead men my cats so strongly remind me of. The big white one with the ringed tail is Little Bear. The orange fellow with the knowing look in its blue eyes I call Sky Eyes. The slinky black that habitually darts about with absolutely no purpose in mind is The Cheyenne Stalker. Taking a sip of my coffee, I began thinking of those of us who made it through all the bad times. The ones still very much alive. It's a good list. And I thank the Creator every day, especially today, that

I'm not completely alone. That there are still some of us around.

Being careful about my cats, I wandered in the direction of my favorite of the two porch chairs. The one that doesn't move. It can't because I knocked off the rockers. Both chairs were gifts from Hawwy. He's old, too. And as deaf as a post. So it was no good arguing with him when he turned up a couple of years back hollering, "Tay! I brought you something."

Hawwy always hollers. Has to. Can't even hear his own voice if he doesn't. After he left the army, he became a rancher. Did that for forty-odd years. Now his sons do the ranching, and he keeps busy with making them crazy. Around these parts Hawwy's known as an Indian Man. Not because anyone mistakes him for being an Indian but because he's had himself two Kiowa wives. The first one was Cherish, The Cheyenne Robber's younger sister. The second, and the last, White Otter, The Cheyenne Robber's widow. Of course she's been called Betsy for about thirty years or more, but to me she'll always be White Otter. It was she who dressed out my much-loved wife in a beautiful buckskin dress. And her doing so sure put that preaching man's nose in a twist.

Before she passed, my wife had been a Bible-toting woman for twenty years. As a matter of fact, Crying Wind was one of the very first converts Big Tree made after he worked himself up to being a deacon over there at the Rainy Mountain Baptist Church. Well, the preaching man took one look at my wife after she was all laid out and said in a peeved tone that she should be dressed to meet the Lord like a Christian lady. Betsy—White Otter—said Crying

221

Wind was going to heaven as a Kiowa, and the Lord would like her just fine. To make her point, she went on to fix little feathers in my wife's brushed out hair.

For that whole day, before they covered her over with the coffin lid, it did me good just to sit real close to Crying Wind's sleeping box and look in at her. Because, you see, for that small amount of time, I was able to seal up inside my heart the picture of the way Crying Wind used to be. Before she took to wearing calico and bonnets and ugly old boots that clobbered the dusty road leading her to church meetings. Looking as though she was merely sleeping, Crying Wind was again my beautiful prairie woman. The illusion was so wonderful, so precious, that I really didn't give a toss if my wife's being *dressed savage* hairlipped the pure hell out of that preaching man. For this was the part of her that was completely mine. The part that even with all his sounds of fury when he laid in to preaching, he knew, deep down, he could never touch.

And I believe that's all I care to say about that.

Now, where was I? Oh, yes. Hawwy's chairs. Well, the old coot loves rocking chairs. Loves to sit in them and rock grooves into his porch boards while hollering at his boys. I really didn't care how he passed his time until he got it into his deluded mind that I'd love rocking all my days away, too. It just seems to me that the older Hawwy grows, the stupider he gets because it took five of his grandsons to help him load the things into the wagon. Then he goes and insists on driving the wagon all way over to me right by his fool self. Which meant that once he pulled up in my yard, our two frail old bodies were all there was to struggle with getting those heavy rocking chairs out.

Well, it was a scorcher of a day, and we both almost liked to have died. Which is exactly what I told him, yelling just as loud as my old lungs could, "Haw-we-sun, you're still a soldier trying to kill an Indian!"

Then he reared back and hollered, "Tay! I believe we're gonna be all right if you've got some cool sweet tea."

Mercifully, I always keep a bucket of tea cooling in the well, which he knew, and it's a good thing I do that or right now he and I would be a pair of sun-baked skeletons spread out all over my yard, pitiful relics of one last Blue Jacket–Kiowa battle. And the only victors left standing on the dusty field of iffy honor: two stupid chairs.

But I digress.

Not long after he left, I took a hammer to the rockers on one of the chairs, leaving the other intact for when Hawwy deigned to pay me more visits. The only trouble I have anymore about my favorite chair is that my cats prefer it, too, and so whenever I want to sit, we four have a little fight, The Cheyenne Stalker hissing and spitting at me, much like his namesake used to do, Little Bear glowering and growling in the back of his throat, and Sky Eyes sedately perched on the armrest, ready to take up residence in my lap just as soon as I've seen the other two off and am able to sit myself down. I went through the usual dance with the first two cats, Little Bear only giving up his seat when my nearing and determined posterior threatened, scooting out of the chair in the last seconds and flying through the pickets of the porch railing, diving headlong into the azalea bushes Crying Wind had planted as little sprigs and had fussed over, dejected right up until the day she died by their lackluster growth. It was about a week after her funeral that I took to dumping out used coffee grounds and dirty dishwater over the railing, a thing that if she'd been alive to see it, would have had her chasing me around and threatening me with the business end of a broom. But her being gone was still so fresh and painful that I was mad at her. For years she'd promised that I could be the one to die first on account of us both knowing just how useless I was on my own. Oh, and I was. Everything I tried to cook burned up in the pan, and because I couldn't get the hang of washing with a scrub board, all of my clothes were gamey. Nothing was going right, and my heart was so thoroughly broken that I began to perceive her death as an act of betrayal. That's when I decided that if she wanted to be dead so bad, then she should just go on ahead and take her damn bushes with her. So yes, I dumped everything on those azaleas. Even potato peelings.

The bushes loved it.

And the cats came to love the garbage littering the ground beneath the overgrown bushes because the garbage attracted mice, and the thick bushes afforded a perfect cover from which they could pounce. I very much doubt my wife would have approved of all of this, but she would have delighted in the profusion of pink flowers brightening the foreground of our home's drab, weather-beaten wood. Which proves that even during the worst times of our lives, beauty has a way of shining through, offering the promise that with a bit of patience and endurance, things will eventually sort themselves out. In a roundabout way, my dwelling on this took me full circle, got me back to thinking of the things I'd seen in my vision. Sky Eyes circled twice before settling himself in my lap as I sipped at my coffee and stared into the middle distance. As I absently stroked along Sky Eyes's spine, his deep purr sent a comforting thrum through my bones.

So very long ago I'd been given one day to solve a puzzle. I'd done my best, worked as feverishly as I could, yet I hadn't solved it. Only Duck's confession, a bit too neatly, had. I hadn't been entirely convinced back then on account of too many unanswered questions. Fifty-odd years hence, those questions still lingered. But my previous suspicions, by wont of ensuing circumstance, had to be pushed as far back into my mind as they would go. For you see, the summer of that same year began what would become a fifteen-year war between the Kiowa Nation and the United States. The turbulence, the sheer chaos of those dangerous years took every ounce of energy I had to survive, protect my family. Then came all the hell that attends the type of *peace* that is brought to bear against a conquered people. We lost as many good men, maybe more, to peace than we ever lost to war. Somehow my little family and I managed to survive, even grow, adding two daughters to our number. Our two girls, Rachel and Esther, are married with grown children of their own. One daughter lives in Cache Creek; the other, over in Lawton. Favorite Son has been called Fred Buffalo ever since they took him off to that school in Kansas, and he used to be a teacher up in Oklahoma City. He's a retired grandpa now. My kids come back to this old house when they can, but mostly it's just me and the cats. And quiet mornings like this one, to sit and remember. Really remember.

Annuity day was the very same day Duck was banished. An hour after her expulsion, Ft. Larned was under a somewhat orderly siege—if you can imagine a swarm as any-thing approaching orderly. Later that day the other two bands upped stakes; the Rattle Band left the next morning. The Cheyenne Robber was forced to travel by travois, as he was still much too weak to sit a horse. But he wasn't too weak to fight with his wife, and White Otter, no longer overly worried about his health, didn't hold back. White Bear put himself in the middle of their bickering but only to protect his ailing nephew. Hears The Wolf, just as pro-tective of White Otter, jumped in, too. And that was bad because their taking sides in the on-going marital war caused a riff between Hears The Wolf and White Bear. Three days out of Kansas, Hears The Wolf packed up and went over to Lone Wolf.

Lone Wolf was glad to get such a distinguished warrior. As memory serves, he was glad to get anybody. He may have been principal chief, but the Nation was becoming split down the middle between White Bear who wanted only war and Kicking Bird who wanted peace at any cost. Lone Wolf did everything he possibly could to hold together a Nation determined to divide itself, and so for over ten years after annuity day at Ft. Larned, the Kiowa were at war with everybody—but most especially with ourselves. The subject, as well as any memory of Three Elks and Duck, simply got lost in the chaos.

Until now.

Hawwy was sitting on the lower porch, rocking his fool brains loose as I steered my one-mule buckboard up the long tree-line graveled drive leading into a spacious, circular area fronting his house. It's a pretty fancy place for a rancher.

A white two-story with floor-to-ceiling windows and two wraparound galleries. On the upper gallery he can walk right out the French doors of his bedroom and have breakfast coffee in the full sunshine if he's of a mind to. But mostly it's Betsy—White Otter—who does the walking out of those elegant doors because she's still Kiowa enough to pitch the bedding. That's what the women from the old times used to call it: pitching the bedding—taking the sleeping blankets and hanging them off tree limbs or bushes to sun and air all day long. Any woman who didn't do that was considered a dirty person. So that's what Betsy uses the upstairs railings for. I have never known her to take the time to sit down at the little table on the upper gallery. Betsy's too busy a person to sit.

The roof of the house has always been funny to me. It's pitched like a normal house until it gets to the very top. That part's flat and with more railing all around it. Hawwy calls that bit of oddity a widow's walk. Said that all the houses back East have them on account of the women needing to watch for boats floating around on the big water, looking for their men to return home. When he first told me this, I looked out over the rolling countryside and piped, "Hawwy, you see any big water around here?"

"No," he said, and this was during the days he didn't have to holler every word, "but I see cows. And from up there I can count every head."

Well, that would have made perfect sense if I didn't already know that part of his being so fancy about his house was his way of trying to outdo Quannah Parker. Once those two stopped fighting bloody wars against each other, they commenced trying to out do each other on just about everything else. Quannah was the first person ever to get a telephone in his big white house, known as the Star House on account of him having the builders form big white stars on his red-shingled roof. He wanted those stars to show that as the last Comanche war chief and the present principal chief of the entire Comanche Nation, he was on equal footing with each and every army general. Plus he knew that his stars would annoy the hellfire out of Haw-we-sun.

They did.

Hawwy had only been a captain when he left the army, but he had won a big medal when he was riding with Col. Randal Mackenzie, for escaping the trap Quannah had laid for him. Not only did Hawwy get away, he managed to save nearly every man under his command. According to Betsy, those two old coots refought that same battle every day . . . but over the telephone—Hawwy was the second to have one of the gadgets, and there being only two telephones in the whole county at that time meant that those jokers had no one to telephone but each other.

Quannah may have beaten Hawwy at having the first telephone, but Hawwy was the first to have a horseless carriage. Had the contraption delivered by train. Then he didn't know what the hell to do with it. For weeks after it was delivered all it did was sit there under the breezeway. Then what do you know but here comes Quannah wanting to see it and maybe have a ride. Now, Quannah Parker never went anywhere without his eight wives or his army of personal guards, and then there was his bevy of children ranging from every age imaginable. When Hawwy saw all those wagons crammed with people coming up the drive and immediately understood that they were all coming just to get a look at his automobile, the man knew he was stuck. Mainly because he would have gladly dug his own grave and then shot himself in the head before he would admit to Quannah Parker that he still hadn't figured out how to drive it. So with all the pomp at his ex-soldierly command, he escorted Quannah to the passenger side, and then he clambered up behind the steering wheel yelling for Sonny to crank her up.

Now, Sonny is The Cheyenne Robber's firstborn. He was only a little fella when his real daddy died, and his mother married Hawwy. He remembers some of the old times but not a lot. The only man he knows as his daddy is Hawwy, and to my old friend's credit, he's never treated Sonny as anything other than his very own. And Sonny, who calls Hawwy *Paw*, worships the ground Hawwy walks on. Which was why Sonny—he was only still a kid back then, and even though he looked exactly like his real father, he'd been blessed with his mother's good sense—wasn't too sold on the idea of Paw trying to drive that automobile anywhere. But he also knew that Hawwy's pride was on the line, and so after a few good cranks that thing sprang to rickety life.

I was told—by Sonny who couldn't stop laughing during the telling—that while that thing was bouncing like it was doing a dance, and Hawwy looked as if the thing was scaring the pure whey out of him, he still wouldn't quit. After doing a lot of fiddling with levers, the thing bolted off, panicking hot fire out of the horses that were still harnessed to the heavy wagons. The horses began rearing and making that throaty sound that only truly terrified horses are able to make while that noisy automobile zigged all over the place, barely missing the horses and the wagons. A wide-eyed, fear-whitened Hawwy at the wheel and a holding-on-to-his-hat-with-both-hands Quannah eventually sped off into the horizon.

All the people standing on the lower balcony got sprayed pretty good with dust and gravel, and when the plumes of grit settled a bit, they were able to see the car heading out over the pasturelands like a scalded hare. Then the land dipped, as it does here abouts, and automobile and occupants disappeared. Betsy used this lull to shoo her horde of guests inside the house to eat the big lunch she'd prepared. Then she quickly sent two of her sons to ride out to look for their father. Lunch was over when the horseless carriage reentered the yard, being pulled by the two horses carrying Sonny and his half-brother Elliott. Hawwy and Quannah were still in the open-top automobile. Quannah's hat was gone, and the two of them looked a mite shook up, but otherwise they were no worse for wear.

After the automobile came to a perfectly safe stop, Quannah was heard to say, "Hawwy, I believe this thing of yours works better with horses."

Hawwy turned a beet-red face toward his old nemesis. "But you still want one, don't you!"

"Yes."

"Good. You can have *this* one!"

Quannah arched a brow as he looked at Hawwy and gathered his thoughts. Proving beyond a modicum of doubt that he would forever be Comanche, Quannah hedged, "And what about horses to pull it?"

A thoroughly galled Hawwy looked at Quannah's bare head, knowing that if he didn't give in to the wily chief, it would later be said that his visit had cost him his best hat and that Hawwy had done nothing to make amends for the loss.

"Sonny! Elliott!" Hawwy bayed. "You boys take your saddles off Chief Quannah's horses."

A little bit after that, Hawwy was standing alone in the graveled yard watching his black and shiny-brass automobile, as well as two of his best range horses, heading down the shaded drive. From his seat behind the steering wheel Quannah turned and waved good-bye.

My whole point of telling you this story is to emphasize my old friend's nature. That he is generous. That he knows what he ought to do when it comes to Indians. And when comparing Haw-we-sun to other white men I've come to know, I have realized over these long years that this ingrained quality of his is nothing less than an inestimable gift. So what else would I expect him to do when Betsy's father, Hears The Wolf, became so old that he could no longer live by himself but take that responsibility onto himself? Which is exactly what Hawwy did, building his father-in-law his own little house and hiring a male nurse to live with him.

Hawwy was rocking in his chair as I reined my mule to a stop and pushed my foot against the wagon's brake handle. Without altering his rocking pace, Hawwy yelled out the traditional Kiowa greeting: "Get down, friend." A greeting from the old days inviting a guest to climb down from his horse.

Kiowas don't have many horses these days. Mostly, folks do a whole lot of walking, but the greeting—even for those traveling by way of shank's mare—has remained. In

231

this case, I could climb down from a wagon bench, and I did. Then I climbed the flight of six brick-made steps to the porch. Languidly waving a smoldering cigar toward the chair beside him, Hawwy wordlessly invited me to sit. I took the offer but sat very still so as not to encourage the chair into unnecessary motion.

"I've come to ask a favor," I said loudly and bluntly.

Hawwy nodded as he belted, "Whatever I have is yours." This was yet another traditional response. The older the man grew, the more traditional Kiowa he became— never mind that he was an almost stone-deaf full-blood Irish person.

Leaning forward, resting my forearms on my knees, dangling my hat between my parted legs, I hesitated for a spell, trying for the best way to put forward my request. For years I'd come asking this particular favor. And for years, I'd been fobbed off with one excuse after another. But today was different. Today Hawwy had to understand how important this was for me. So I just gave up and bellowed the thing straight out. "I need to speak to Hears The Wolf."

His eyes never left mine as that single eyebrow of his furrowed over the bridge of his nose, and he slowly rolled the butt end of the smoking cigar between puckered lips. I did not dare blink as I returned his fixed stare. Finally, realizing that this time my asking was not a casual wish but the actual favor he'd so indifferently consented to bestow, Hawwy frowned; then the chair became perfectly still, and he slumped in defeat.

•   •   •

The little house was about a quarter of a mile behind Haw-wy's big house. The hot sun was beating down on our heads and shoulders, as Hawwy and I walked the well-worn dirt path leading to it. With every step he tried to prepare me for his father-in-law's present physical condition.

"Now, Tay," he blared in what passed as a reluctant drawl, "he's got to be at least a hundred years old. I know you haven't seen him for about five years, but that's all been his doing. He hasn't wanted anyone to see him. Especially you. I don't know why, but I strongly suspect that the old fellow managing to outlive so many of his warrior brothers has unhinged him. He keeps yelling, 'Now is my die day,' and then wrapping himself up in a blanket, he sits on his porch—and in all weathers, I might add—all the day long, waiting for death. At sunset when he realizes that he's still alive, he allows his nurse to move him back inside to feed him his supper. Comes the new dawn, the whole she-bang starts all over again." Hawwy cast me a sideways glance. "He can't walk anymore. Hasn't walked since you last saw him at . . ." His voice trailed off.

"At my wife's funeral."

Hawwy sighed robustly. "That's right. And he was wob-bly on his legs even then. Somehow he managed to get through the funeral, but the next day, he couldn't get out of bed. Me and Bets hurried him to the hospital, and they kept him for weeks while I was making arrangements about a special wheelchair. That and build him the house he's in now because me and Bets thought it would be better for him to be closer to us," he added almost as a throwaway statement. "But I have to say, for such an old codger, his

233

arms are amazingly strong. When he gets mad at Darryl—that's his nurse—he can get the wheels on that chair really moving. And that's exactly the way he used to run away from the hospital."

I heard myself chuckle. I heard Hawwy chuckle, too, and some of the tension in his too-loud voice, eased. Looking at me, his face brightened by a small smile, he decided to continue. What with the shouting tone of the conversation, I couldn't help but listen attentively as we held a steady stride.

"I sent all the way to Chicago for that chair. And because he's such a tall man, it had to be custom-made to fit him. Bets and I thought his having the chair right away would do him good because while he was in the hospital having to wait for the house to be finished, all he was able to do there was sit in his bed and stare out the window. Well, the day the chair arrived we hauled it over to him, and he was so happy you would have thought it was Christmas. The man was totally enthralled that a chair could work as good as legs. Bets and I stayed until we were sure he would be able to handle it by himself, and then we left. We weren't home but about an hour when the telephone commenced to ring, and the doctor on the other end of the wire was yelling that no one could find Henry Wolf. That's the name the hospital insisted he have," Hawwy added his tone peeved. "So Bets and I climb into the surrey again and off we go straight back to the hospital.

"Now, the trouble with the staff searching high and low for him was that they hadn't figured on an invalid old man being able to go much farther than the hospital building or the immediate outside grounds. Figured they'd confine their search first to all the inside hidey-holes, then later expanding the hunt outside the building's bushes. So this is where my years of riding with Randy"—Randall Mackenzie—"paid off. While the doctor in charge was telling Bets that he and his nurses couldn't be held responsible, I used old tracking skills, noticing that at the end of the corridor outside his room there was a service door. I went there, opened it, and sure enough I saw wheel marks in the dust. I followed them, and a couple of miles down the road, there he was, just sitting there, facing west and chanting to the setting sun."

"Did you manage to hear and understand the words he sang?"

"Oh, yes," Hawwy holler-chirped. "I've heard enough death songs to know exactly what he was singing, and the words of his song were hardly complicated." He glanced uncertainly at me. "Is it permitted to repeat them?"

I took a deep breath, let it go slowly, measuring the exhale to the tramp of my booted feet. "In this case," I answered gravely, "I think it would be all right."

"Well, then, here goes." Hawwy sucked in a lung load of air, then howled, " 'Dear ones of my youth, pity me. Brothers who still say my name, come for me. I am here.' "

Intense pain took hold of my heart. Unable to speak because of it, Hawwy and I finished our short journey in blessed silence.

Even though I had been warned of his condition and thought Hawwy's warning more than abundant, my first sight of my old friend hit me with the force of a physical blow to the chest. Hears The Wolf had less than a decade's seniority over me, but the shell he had become could have easily been mistaken for twenty or thirty years. Looking more like a skeleton with dried skin glued over bones, he was wrapped in a blanket, sitting in his chair on wheels. A breeze ruffled hair as white as the shirt his attendant—a young blond man, sitting on a bench in front of the window and reading a newspaper—wore with a pair of dark-blue jeans. Noticing our approach, Darryl, the attendant, folded the newspaper, set it to the side on the bench, rose, and walked to the edge of the covered porch. He paused just long enough to lift his arm in a wave; then he quickly descended the steps, coming to meet us as we came up the path that neatly bisected the front yard.

Hawwy and I stopped just as the male nurse neared. I took a look around as the nurse and Hawwy exchanged shouted greetings. The yard consisted of two wide stretches of vivid green, clipped short, sturdy buffalo grass and rose bushes—every one of them in full riotous bloom—fencing in both halves of the lawn. Hawwy, looking away from the nurse, noticed me gawking at the bushes.

"Darryl's got quite the green thumb," he chortled. "And tending roses gives him something to do during my father-in-law's frequent naps."

I glanced at the male nurse who was beaming with pride on account of his flowers. I smiled the lie that I thought his roses were very nice. The whole while my lips were stretched painfully, I couldn't shake the feeling that Hears The Wolf hated his flower-fiddling companion. I guess I felt that way because if our positions were reversed, if it was me imprisoned in that chair having to watch a grown man play with flowering bushes, I would most certainly hate him. The words that the young man shouted to a near-deaf Hawwy as he turned away from me confirmed the notion.

"I don't know if he's up to having a guest today, Mister Harry. He's having one of his testy days. The kind where I can't let him near the kitchen."

Hawwy grunted, having understood completely, leaving me a tad baffled. Happily, he chose to enlighten me. "Some mornings he wakes up wanting to make a try for Darryl's golden hair. But first he has to get in the kitchen where all the knives are."

"Ahh," I replied, fully understanding now. Hears The Wolf was still warrior enough to want to take one last scalp, a gift he could present to his brothers as a way of apologizing for having outlived them. "I still need to speak to him. It's very important."

Hawwy looked to Darryl for the deciding opinion. The young man shrugged, his arms slapping against his blue-jeaned thighs as if to say he didn't mind if Mister Harry didn't. I didn't wait for Hawwy to mull it. I took off for the porch. And my old friend.

"You're going to have to yell." That was Darryl, hovering right behind me as my hands gripped the armrests of the rolling chair, and I gazed through the tears swimming before my eyes at the ruin time had wrought against a well-remembered face. "He can't hear if you don't yell."

His having to shout to Hears The Wolf as well as Hawwy made me worry that Darryl's throat was continually blood raw. Turning away from the chair and speaking softly so that only Darryl could hear me, I said, "Teach me how to move this chair."

237

FIFTEEN

It took some doing, the three of us working in tandem, and during the effort, Hawwy's bull roar continually bombarded mine and Darryl's eardrums, but nevertheless we managed to carry the chair down off the porch. During our struggles, I thought I saw a trace of a smile tugging at the corners of Hears The Wolf's lips. But with muscles straining beyond my old body's limits and my spine about to snap like a dried twig, it was hard to judge for certain, so I dismissed the notion, concentrating instead on not killing myself during this unusual form of activity. Once the chair was settled on the dirt path, Darryl made a great display of teaching me just how to push the chair and then how to set the hand brake. Minutes later Darryl and Hawwy went inside the house to make a pitcher of lemonade while I pushed the rolling chair, taking Hears The Wolf off for a little wander.

I continued pushing until the house was lost from sight. Then I aimed the chair for the tree-shaded bank of the creek that cuts through Hawwy's sizeable ranch. In this part of the country, that creek runs so narrow that a man could, and with precious little effort, jump across to the other side. There are thousands of little creeks just like it around here, which makes this country so good for raising cattle. Mostly these other creeks have no names, but this one does, for this little bit is only the tail end of it. Up around the edges of Fort Sill, this same creek is wide, deep, and fast moving. It's that upper edge that earned it the name Sitting Bear's Creek, for it was there that that great old man, the last chief of our highest warrior society, The Ten Bravest, had been propped up against a tree and left to die by the army soldiers who'd gunned him down. There's a lot of history in this big, wide country. And every square mile, every inch, every little hint of a moccasin-worn footpath lingering in its rust-red soil, is invaluable to those of us who lived that history.

I managed to propel the bulky chair into the shade, to a spot where we were we able to hear the creek gurgle and hopefully be refreshed by a cooling breeze rattling through the upper branches of the trees. Bending my legs in preparation to sit, I received a shock.

"Tay-bodal," Hears The Wolf said in low, rumbling tone, "if you're not too tired from all that pushing, I would like you to help me out of this thing. I want to sit on the ground, too."

For a moment I was too stunned to react. Oh, I expected

the man to still have some sense. I guess since I still had some, and I needed him to have some, too. It was his talking to me in such a reasonable way that threw me in a bit of a tizzy. His tone was too mild, too . . . normal. Well, normal for a nearly hundred-year-old man. He didn't speak at all the way a deaf person ought to. He began edging forward in the chair, and that caused me to recover and hurriedly move to his aid. After some strenuous tugging and then a precarious balancing act, we were finally sitting side by side. And just like in the old days, we were again two friends simply enjoying the day, the sounds of life, the pulsing warmth of Earth Mother beneath us.

"That young man believes you can't hear," I finally said.

Hears The Wolf closed his eyes for a moment. Opening them again, looking up at the tree canopy, at the blue of sky peeking through the leafy branches, he rasped, "He believes it because he wants to."

"Haw-we-sun believes you are deaf, too."

Hears The Wolf barked a laugh. "Hawwy believes everyone is deaf—my daughter, their children, their grandchildren. But mostly he believes it of you."

"Me?" I cried. "How do you know?"

"He told me. When I was being held prisoner in that hospital. I was asking my daughter to have you come pay me a visit, and somehow that idiot managed to hear me. Then he started yelling about you being as hard of hearing as a suck-egg mule." He emitted a long, weary sigh. "That was the last time I asked."

"You didn't want me if I couldn't hear you." It wasn't a question. It was a saddened statement. A lengthy silence ensued. So lengthy that I got used to it and had a bit of a start when he spoke again.

"For a very long time I've wanted to talk to you about my dead wife's former mother." I knew he meant Duck. "She told me not to grieve for her, but I did. Oh, I knew she wasn't anything more than a bad-tempered, crazy old woman. Time has not dimmed my memory of her tantrums. Nor has it lessened my knowledge that she truly loved my wife and she, her. When we were first reunited, my wife told me some of the things she went through during her first marriage, how if it hadn't been for her mother-in-law, she would not have had the strength to survive, not even for the sake of our child. That's the reason I went out and found her among the Dapone and brought her home to live with us. And even though she could be the most difficult woman under the sun, the truth is, Tay-bodal, if it hadn't been for that old woman, I would have had none of the happiness I enjoyed." He turned his head toward me, his craggy features churning with mild disgust. "It wasn't right the way she died. I'm afraid I blamed you. I blamed you even more for avoiding me, especially during the last years."

"Well," I replied meekly, "I was busy in other directions."

He made a noise in the back of his throat as he pulled the blanket more tightly around his shoulders. "Weren't we all," he grunted. "Those were some pretty bad times all right." He looked at me again, teeth scraping the corner of his lip. "Do you remember when they had hundreds of us corralled behind walls over there at the fort? Hawwy came in there only one time, and I got down on my knees and begged him to bring you to me. You see, by then we all knew about the prison train. I didn't want to go without first mending our broken friendship. I told him to tell you how important this was to me, but you didn't come."

I briefly mulled those terrible days, then said with a shake of my head, "He never mentioned your request. I would have found a way to see you if he had."

Hears The Wolf snorted. "Well, I should have realized he forgot."

"I don't think that's the reason," I said, defending the gallant soldier Hawwy had been way back then. Placing my hand on my old friend's shoulder, I urged him toward a more reasonable direction. "After the choosing was finished, and you were not one of those having to go, he probably kept quiet because he knows you to be a man of great pride and, well, you were free to see me any time you wanted to."

Hears The Wolf furrowed his bony brow and pursed his lips, obviously remembering back over those years of turmoil. He put those memories to voice. "Many bad things have been said about him since that day, but I was there." I knew his mind was again fixed on the prison train and that now he was talking about Kicking Bird. "I was in the line of men he had to walk before when he did the choosing, had to place his hand on the shoulders of those who had to go off. I am a witness that he saved as many of us as he could. But there were those—" His voice caught. And then he couldn't continue.

We both wept as we thought of Skywalker and The Cheyenne Robber, but that was all right. Tears always come into my eyes as I remember standing inside the crush of wailing people, watching as my best friend and his younger brother were led away in chains. That was the last day we ever saw them. And three days later Kicking Bird was dead. Killed, it is still claimed, by Skywalker's curse.

With the back of my hand I flung tears away from my cheeks as I willed myself to remain in the present. Hears The Wolf quickly shook off the painful recollection, too, for in a tone bordering on nettled, he said, "It was after that day that Hawwy became busy courting my girl. Then he was busy getting himself out of the army and running around claiming all the land that was left. So no matter what you say to defend him, I still say that idiot forgot. And because he forgot, you and I wasted too many years not talking to each other."

Well, that wasn't true. Those years were hardly wasted. We of the older generation had used every minute of that time buffeting the ill winds of peace. With all that buffeting, old friends scarcely had the time to sit and visit with each other. Irked that he chose to forget how it really was, chose instead to blame Hawwy for something Hears The Wolf could have settled on his own, I tossed my hands in surrender.

"Fine, think whatever you like. You're the most stubborn man I have ever known, so just go on ahead and be as stubborn as you want because I'm too old to care anymore."

Hears The Wolf rumbled chesty laughter and turned his weathered face toward me. A face that was deeply creased by a smile as we made and held intense eye contact. "I am so pleased that my final day is being spent in this peaceful place . . . with you."

We went quiet again. It was my turn to ponder. I didn't

want this to be his last day. I'd only just now regained a valued friend who'd been lost for so very long. I didn't know if I had it in me to lose him all over again. That was extremely selfish because I knew he would be better off in that other place. There he wouldn't be old or confined to a rolling chair. There he would be with brothers happy to see him. But his going would leave me with an emptiness. As I stared off, that emptiness yawned before me. It was dark and bigger than all the years he'd avoided me plus the years I'd been prevented from seeing him. Which I now understood hadn't really upset me all that much because just knowing he was still in this world with me had seemed enough. But tomorrow he would be gone, and I would still be here.

I squeezed my eyes shut as the hurtful thought went all the way to my soul. With one more friend gone, how lonely indeed this new wilderness would be. I hadn't realized that I was holding my breath until my screaming lungs urged my burdened brain to induce my mouth to fly open. Even I was surprised by my sudden, loud gasp for air. Hears The Wolf, realizing that I was all right, that I'd simply forgotten to breathe, looked askance.

"You're still strange, Tay-bodal. You do know that."

"Yes," I admitted. "But isn't it good some things never change." Sighing deeply, I took his cold hand in mine. "Now that we're talking again, I think maybe it's time you told me why, so long ago, you killed that young man."

His head turned with an audible snap. His lower jaw slightly hanging, he stared at me for well over a minute. Then he commenced to yell, "Do you mean to tell me that after all the years you've had to think everything through, that's the best you could come up with? That *I* killed that person?"

"Well," I replied, uncertain now of the things I'd just this morning pieced together from the frayed cloth of deteriorated recollection, "you did, didn't you?"

He was staring again. I began talking faster. "I figured you did it on account of your son-in-law. Because you knew he was fooling around with other women, and one of the women found herself with child, which forced her to marry someone she didn't want, and because that marriage wasn't working out and the younger brother, the one you killed—"

Hears The Wolf raised a silencing hand. "Tay-bodal," he croaked, "some of the people you want to talk about are still alive. As for the ones who are dead, you and I are so close to lying down in our own graves that I can't see that it would do either of us much harm if you just went on ahead and said all of their names out loud. I know your doing that would certainly help me keep most of what you're babbling straight in my mind."

"Fine," I snorted. I began all over again, this time in a more adamant fashion. "You knew The Cheyenne Robber was going to be a father by Always Happy and that Three Elks found out about it and planned to use what he knew to ruin The Cheyenne Robber's marriage to your daughter. That man couldn't wait to do this on account of the feud between them but mostly on account of The Cheyenne Robber shooting him in the backside, making Three Elks the subject of jokes. But because Raven's Wing was his older brother and his telling the tale might be passed off as his making up a lie just to get even with The Cheyenne Robber, he thought it was best to get someone else to do the telling.

245

The person Three Elks chose was Wolf Blanket because, being a grasping person, Three Elks knew that all he had to do was give him this information, and Wolf Blanket would do the rest. Wolf Blanket would also be handy to suffer all the blame when White Bear lashed out at the one who caused his favorite nephew's disgrace.

"Three Elk's plan would have worked perfectly if you hadn't gotten to him first. You probably went after him just to talk, convince him not to cause your daughter more heartache. But he wouldn't listen, so you killed him. Then as the day wore on and an innocent man was being held for your crime, the guilt and rage of what you'd done began to fester, and you exploded against the person you held in blame: The Cheyenne Robber.

"Duck knew you stabbed him, which was why she was so eager to tend him alone. She needed to convince him to say nothing, knowing what would happen if her daughter, Beloved, and her granddaughter, White Otter, were suddenly left without a strong man to provide for them. A woman's world back then could sometimes be a very cruel place, but it was most cruel toward unmarried women past their prime, which Beloved most certainly was. Duck knew firsthand how terrible, how mean that life could be. To save Beloved from a life as a Dapone, to save White Otter from any forced marriage she would have had to endure, she chose to take the blame in your place."

For well over a minute he continued to stare. After a overlong silence, I bayed, "Are you going to deny it?"

"Only every last word," he mildly responded. Squinting his eyes, he looked off. Then in that same calm voice, he said, "Tay-bodal, I give you my word, I did not kill Three

Elks." When he looked again at me, his eyes were fully open, completely honest. "I had no reason to kill him. Yes, I knew he was intent on ruining my daughter's first marriage, but I also knew that The Cheyenne Robber was a poor husband. I knew all about his other women, but I didn't hate him. Quite the contrary. In spite of the heartache his wandering ways gave my girl, I loved him. Because you see, I understood him. Understood that his being married to anyone, even to a woman he truly adored, simply went against his nature. But I'm a man. I could understand what my daughter never could. And I could forgive what she could not."

He took a moment to rest, then proceeded on. "It was around about the time you're talking about that my girl was beginning to hate the very air The Cheyenne Robber breathed. Knowing this, I was anticipating her divorce. I was also more than eager to welcome her into my home. You must remember, I had missed all of her growing-up years, and then when her mother and I were at last joined in marriage, our daughter was already herself a married woman. So I'd never had the pleasure of living with her, providing for her. Having her and her baby come to me, place themselves under my protection, was something I dearly wanted. The idea that The Cheyenne Robber being disgraced by any of this is, I'm afraid, equally hard to believe. Oh, he would have been mad at my daughter for leaving him, and there would have been that other woman to sort out, but that would have been about the extent of it. Primarily because White Bear would have never stood for anyone thinking that his precious nephew was a disgrace. Most especially because of a dispute over or about a woman." He squirmed around to face me squarely. "Now, let's talk about your idea of me working myself up into a murderous frenzy. And let's begin with my asking you this: In all the time we've known each other, when did you ever know me to act in mindless haste?"

Well, he had me there. But I wasn't quite ready to stop making a fool of myself. "All right, but bear with me a moment longer. The Cheyenne Robber was stabbed directly in the chest. There were no defense wounds on his arms or hands, meaning that his assailant was someone he knew, someone he wasn't afraid of. If that wasn't you, then who?"

"Duck," he answered with a laugh. My eyes must have been as big as fists, for he laughed again. "She really did stab him. I should know because I had to pull her off before she could stab him a second time." Becoming serious again, heaving a leaden sigh, he went on, "She was in one of her crazy spells. Completely out of her head. He said he was all right enough to go for help on his own, that I should take her and keep guard over her until he decided what he would do in the matter of her attack on him. I pleaded with him to consider that she was a crazy old woman who didn't know what she was doing. He waved me off, telling me to just get her away from him. He was bleeding pretty bad, and I should have been more concerned about that, but Duck was an armful and so I made the wrong choice. I took her one way, and he staggered off in another. Duck was fighting so much that I didn't look back. I didn't see that he'd fainted. If he hadn't been found, he really would have died, and that *would* have been all my fault."

Now it was my turn to stare at length. "D-do you recall what set her off?"

248

"Oh, yes. You see, she'd heard all the rumors, too, the ones about him making a baby with another woman. But she didn't know which woman. None of us did. Then again, Beloved and I were more concerned about protecting our daughter from gossip than we were with trying to figure out just which girl was carrying his child. Duck, on the other hand, was bound and determined to know. She took to following him, and when she saw him talking to a pretty girl, she figured that was the one. When she accused him, he made the mistake of laughing in her face. And that's when she knifed him."

I hunched forward, my upper body bowing over splayed-out legs as I thought out loud, "Then that was what Skywalker and Owl Man sensed when the women were tending The Cheyenne Robber."

Hears The Wolf barked another short laugh. "Those two didn't have to sense anything on account of our having a big old family fight right there in front of them. They knew Duck was responsible for the attack on The Cheyenne Robber, not by Owl Doctor magic but because I couldn't shut her up."

"And she wouldn't shut up about Three Elks?"

"Now, that's the funny part," he said, his creaky tone carrying the lilt of half surprise. "She got real stubborn on the subject of Three Elks. Skywalker made a move to get close enough to touch her, and she got all hysterical, knowing full well that touch was one of the ways Owl Doctors had of understanding the things hidden deep in hearts. When she pulled her knife on him, my wife and I got her out of there. Once we had her home, I left all the women on their own because frankly I needed a drink of whiskey, and White Bear had some. The next thing I was told was that you had shown up not long after I'd left. And that really upset me for during my drink with White Bear, I thought I'd come up with a workable plan to save Duck from herself. I took a long walk to think the plan through, and by the time I was finished thinking, you were already presenting her to White Bear. But the thing that stunned me most was hearing about how she'd confessed about Three Elks because I swear to you, Tay-bodal, not once during her tirades did she admit to having anything to do with the killing of him. In fact, the morning she died, she asked the Creator's forgiveness for harming The Cheyenne Robber but not a word did she say about Three Elks. That's when I knew she didn't do it. And that's when I begged her to let me fight for her. The only thing she had to say in reply was, 'You must live to fight for your grandson. He's worth ten of his father.' "

That was a pretty long speech for a desiccated old man who hadn't spoken much in over five years. The effort winded him. I waited while he noisily wheezed, working to catch his breath.

Once he'd settled down, I said bluntly, "She thought she was protecting you."

"Yes," he agreed miserably. "Over the next wearying years, I figured that out. Which means she died for nothing because I didn't do it."

"Then who does that leave?"

"I don't know," he answered. "It's still a puzzle."

Well, I'd had just about all of this puzzle I could stand. "My dear friend," I said with finality, "I'm afraid you can't die today."

He grinned at me. "That's all right. I don't think I want to go just yet, anyway."

Our next exercise was getting him back in the chair and then me pushing the thing so fast that I feared my little walnut-sized heart would crack wide open. Hawwy and Darryl were sitting on the porch enjoying glasses of lemonade when we came freewheeling up the path, Hears The Wolf hanging on for dear life and cackling. Even before I could get that chair to slow down a bit, I was yelling to the pair on the porch.

"Haw-we-sun! I need to use your telephone!"

Thankfully, Darryl took over the chair pushing during the run for Hawwy's house.

Betsy was in a flap about her father, but she calmed down some when she saw the blush of life radiating on his high, age-pronounced cheekbones and the the sheer joy shining in his sunken eyes. Whatever was going on had given him back his spark. But as happy as she might be about that, she continued to fuss over him. Hawwy and I went into the large room that served as his office, and he began working the little crank on the side of the wall telephone.

During the passing years more telephones have come into private homes, and on account of that, a special book had to be printed listing every telephone owner and their allotted number of rings. Which is why I refuse to have one. Telephone bells blare all the live long day, and each household has to stop whatever is going on to listen and count the rings in order to figure out if the call is meant for them or a neighbor farther down the wires. Personally,

I have more to do with my life than count the number of jarring bells—never mind that the most I'm ever doing is sitting and petting one of my cats. But just then that silly invention was a blessing, so I looked through the book for the names, and Hawwy made the calls. It's a good thing the man has a big house because a little less than an hour later, a whole lot of people started turning up.

The very first to arrive was Raven's Wing. He still carried himself proudly. I imagine he was mighty proud that he'd managed to outlive every one of his father's sons and that he was still able to get about on his own, even if he did so with the aid of two canes. Hawwy and I met him and his only son, Jefferson, as they came into the grand foyer. Raven's Wing spoke to Hawwy but pointedly refused to deign so much as a glance in my direction. After all this time the man still hated me. He'd promised that he would until the day he died, and Raven's Wing was nothing if not a man of his word. Hawwy directed them to the main sitting room, and with Jefferson following him, Raven's Wing traveled like a spindle-legged land crab in that direction.

Minutes behind them came Big Tree, who bounced on in as if time hadn't touched him one little bit. Then there was Sarah Blanket—née Always Happy—accompanied by the two very round and jolly daughters she'd had by Wolf Blanket. On entering the main sitting room, all three women blatantly snubbed Raven's Wing, who sat leaning forward on his canes, glowering at his former wife. As for Wolf Blanket, he could not be present because he had been one of the warriors sent off to the prison in Florida, where he died. The three women headed first for Hears The Wolf, expressing delight in finding him alive. But what their gushing actually implied was that they were genuinely surprised. I guess because despite the fact that he was still breathing, was still relatively warm to their touch, he looked like death. Betsy, knowing an insinuation when she heard one, went on the defensive, flitting around her father like a hummingbird, removing the women, aiming them for a couch. Then she commenced serving her guests cups of punch set on plates containing little sandwiches. Hawwy and I were still in the foyer waiting for the last guest, Lame Crow. Finally he arrived with his grandson Peter.

Even though Lame Crow and Big Tree were about the same age, Lame Crow wasn't anywhere near as bouncy. But he did make it into the house on his own steam, without the aid of anything and slapping away Peter's hand as his grandson walked protectively beside him. The living room was already full up when Hawwy's sons and daughters and their wives and husbands and children—apparently none of them wanting to miss out on the afternoon tea party—came pouring through the big front door in waves. Naturally, the first person they aimed for was Grandpa Wolf, a move that caused Betsy to flit herself half to death in order to protect him from them.

As the afternoon social got under way, over the ordinary noise of chatting people and clinking glass and china, the organ recital commenced. No, not music. Nothing quite that pleasant. *Organ recital* is simply my term for whenever the doddering gather in one place and activate the ailment list. While drinking punch and chewing sandwiches, everyone wanted to know how so-and-so's liver was doing. This was followed quickly by someone's complaint about kidney troubles. Then there were comparisons on the degrees of severity of heart palpitations. Sarah and her well-rounded daughters offered several levels of fear on "the die-a-bee-tees," all the while eyeing the three-layer chocolate cake sitting pride of place on the gateleg serving table.

Being old is a mess. I can't say as I'd ever recommend longevity to the timid.

A large chatty crowd was not at all what I had in mind when I had Hawwy do the telephoning. Then, too, there were some pesky questions needing to be asked that I didn't much want Betsy to have to hear. I love that little girl like she's my own. I wouldn't upset her for the world, and my calling to everyone's memory the subject of The Cheyenne Robber's known infidelities would most certainly upset her. Nor could I imagine that form of auld lang syne sending a rush of pride into his two sons. Added to this was a deaf-beyond-all-the-hope-of-prayer Hawwy's persistent belting of "What? What?" every other minute. I'm sure a professional policeman could have coped with all of this, but I am not a professional policeman. I'm just an impatient, nosey old man. Besides, despite Hears The Wolf's steady reassurances that he was all right, that he was having a good time, his color was going off, and his eyes were sinking farther back into their sockets. If he was going to live through all of this with me, I had to move a tad quicker.

"Betsy," I said gravely, gaining not only her attention but everyone else's, "there is a subject your father and I wish to discuss with our old friends." Nodding toward Hears The Wolf, I finished, "He and I would appreciate total privacy."

"What? What?" Hawwy piped.

Betsy leaned toward her husband, placing her hand over

his. Yelling against his ear, she said, "We're moving to the garden, dear."

"What for? It's hot enough to boil lizards out there." To add emphasis to his statement, he looked up longingly at the two paddle fans suspended from the high ceiling, both turning silently and diligently, the mechanical breezes refreshing the large room.

Betsy would not be deterred. Nor would she bother trying to give him a shouted reason for their needing to abandon the coolness of the living room for the blistering heat of the gardens. She stood, encouraging her balking husband to stand, as well. Then with the practiced ease of a gracious hostess, she herded all and sundry out of the house. Hearing the front door firmly shut behind them, I glanced at those remaining.

Sarah Blanket, Raven's Wing, Hears The Wolf, Big Tree, and Lame Crow.

All eyes were on me as I walked to the center of the room. They were so quiet that Hears The Wolf's breathy wheezes sounded loud.

"I asked all of you here today to help clear up an old puzzle. And as Hears The Wolf reminded me, since we're too ancient"—and with a quick nod to Deacon Big Tree—"or too Christian to worry about stirring up ghosts, I will go ahead and speak the names of those who have gone on. Because the person I want to talk about is the one once known as Three Elks."

The old religion is a hard thing to shake. Even though what we all once fervently believed is today considered to be mostly superstition, everyone, save for myself and Hears The Wolf, gasped. (And that everyone one included Southern Baptist Deacon Big Tree.) I allowed a moment for their collective shock to ease, then gamely ventured on.

"This morning, my old pestering friend sent me a vision."

Heads began to nod; Big Tree and Hears The Wolf muttered, "Ho." Everyone knew I meant Skywalker. There was no need for his name to be said. "The vision was so real, so clear," I continued, "that I was a young man again, reliving a near-forgotten time. He sent it to let me know that the matter of Three Elks must finally be resolved. I brought this thorny problem to my friend Hears The Wolf, and together we decided to call this talk, lay before all of you the things we know, ask that you share—honestly and without fear—everything you know."

Lame Crow raised a questioning hand. Giving him my full attention, he slowly lowered his hand as he hesitantly asked, "And whatever is said, it remains . . . with us? It goes no further?"

"You have my word," I replied. "When we all leave this room, nothing said here leaves with us. The past will be buried one last time."

"Good," Raven's Wing blurted, rocking himself, even though he was seated on a stationary wing chair. "I approve of this. I want this talk. I never believed my brother was killed by that old woman. No. Not once did I believe it."

I looked that embittered old man straight in the eye. "I have given *my* word that the talk begins and ends here. Do I have *your* word?"

Raven's Wing needed a moment to consider, for he was a vengeful old soul. And he was crafty. I had heard of an incident a few years past where his complaints about his neighbor's dogs had gone unnoticed and then somehow those dogs were released from their holding pen. Being dogs, they of course found their way onto his property where he'd shot every last one of them. His being that spiteful meant that if he didn't made his vow out loud, if his consent was little more than a nod, he might keep quiet . . . or he might not.

I decided to push him. "Unless you speak your promise, no talk will take place. The mystery of your brother's death will always be that: a mystery. And his restless spirit will blame you."

And, ooooh, the look he gave me. His face all screwed up as tight as a bull's hind end going uphill, he sneered, "You have always been a scoundrel Tay-bodal. All right, I give everyone here my word, but I also say that I don't believe in yours."

Sarah snorted disdainfully. "That's because you don't believe in anything."

He shot her a look of utter loathing. "I once believed in you. Until you played me for a fool."

"You played yourself," she spat.

"Stop it!" Big Tree shouted. "The whole world is weary of the fighting between the two of you." He looked to me to carry on. I did.

"Raven's Wing is absolutely right. Duck did not kill Three Elks. But she did try to kill The Cheyenne Robber on account of her knowing that he'd fathered a child outside his marriage." I turned, looking meaningfully at Sarah.

"Ha!" Raven's Wing crowed. Glaring smugly at his ex-wife, he jeered, "You've been found out at last."

"You silly old madman!" she hollered. "You still have that in your head."

My eyes flared as I hurriedly asked, "You mean, your firstborn, Jefferson . . . isn't—"

"No," she said hotly. "He is not. And I would think that anyone with any sense could just look at him and know."

"Th-then," I stammered, feeling my face glowing with embarrassment, "who is his father?"

She jerked a thumb in Raven's Wing direction. "He is. Always has been."

"B-but I heard . . ." I cleared my throat. "I mean, we all did . . . that when you married Raven's Wing, you were already—"

"I was," she declared unashamedly. "But the whole thing with him happened so fast that even I wasn't sure we'd had sex until three months went by without my woman's time. That's when I knew I had to marry him the way he kept begging me to do."

"I never begged you!" he hollered.

"You did, too!" she hollered right back. "And on your knees. I knew you only wanted me on account of my uncle. That was why you raped me."

"I didn't rape you!"

She turned her ample body and stared a hole straight through his forehead. "If sneaking up on a young girl while she's berry picking and lifting her skirt and putting yourself inside her without asking permission isn't rape, what else is it?"

Raven's Wing remained silent but thoroughly chagrined; his color deepened, his piercing eyes glowed like a pair of candles as he stared at her. With a snort of disgust, she looked away from him.

Clearing my throat, I ventured to say to her, "But during the time that you were married to Raven's Wing, it was being said that you were meeting someone else. And that someone was The Cheyenne Robber."

Sara commenced to shout. "I was never *ever* with The Cheyenne Robber! But I was meeting someone else." Raising her arm and pointing her hand, she finished, "I was meeting him! The Cheyenne Robber's bashful best friend."

All eyes turned to Lame Crow.

If the world suddenly opened up a bottomless hole, Lame Crow looked as if he would gladly drop straight down into it. Then he recovered, speaking rapidly. "It's true. I once loved her. I didn't even mind that she was going to have a baby. But I was young. I was stupid. And she smiled at me."

"She smiled at everybody," Big Tree chortled.

"Yes, I did," she said shrilly. "In those days I was a very happy girl. Happy girls smile."

"You were a shameless flirt, you mean," Raven's Wing blasted. Satisfied with having gotten back at her, he was smug.

Lame Crow sent him a frown; then he looked up at me. "The Cheyenne Robber found my slight crush to be useful. He said he wouldn't tell anyone about it if I would help him. I did. What I would do, after meeting with her, was leave her where he wanted me to. After that, I don't know what happened." Using a handkerchief to wipe sweat from his brow, he concluded. "That's all I have to say."

I turned back to Sarah. "Yes," she said smugly. "It happened just like that. Except that all we ever did when we met was kiss. Then he would take me to my sister's home, where he would shake my hand just before he ran away. Now, I may be old and have forgotten a lot, but even I remember that it takes more than a few kisses and a handshake to make a baby. Therefore, you can all exclude Lame Crow as being the father of my firstborn child. As for The Cheyenne Robber, I never even saw him. After Lame Crow left me at my sister's, she told her husband that she had to see me safely back to my home. We would only ever get halfway there when she would disappear, leaving me to walk alone."

For what felt an eternity, the air in the room—even though it was being turned by the ceiling paddle fans—felt totally still as we each drew our own conclusions as to what had become of her sister. But while I was fully appreciating the cunning of the long-ago deception, I was also recalling that at one time Sarah had three older sisters, all of them married. So which sister was she meaning?

The question was answered when Sarah vehemently said, "For all my life I have suffered on account of everyone believing that my child was The Cheyenne Robber's. The worse abuse came from this one over here." With a jerk of her thumb, she indicated her former husband.

"That wasn't our trouble!" Raven's Wing thundered. "You knew I didn't care who the father was."

"And I know *why* you didn't care!" she shouted back. "You were afraid for the child to be yours. Afraid your family's sickness would be passed on. You were happy to think The Cheyenne Robber fathered my child. But you also believed that I continued to go off with him."

"But you did!"

"I did not! You old fool, will you never listen? I just said it was Lame Crow."

"About your family's sickness," I quickly interjected, speaking to Raven's Wing, "that had to do with whiskey. A thing you avoided. A thing you continued to avoid all of your life and your son with you. The wisdom of that choice is the reason neither of you have ever been troubled. But even so, throughout his life, you held on to the belief that your son's good health was more to do with his not being your blood son."

"That's right," he grimly conceded. "I was afraid for him to be mine. I wanted his life to have been started by The Cheyenne Robber. I knew I would always be proud of a child that came from him." He raised his face, tears shining in his eyes. "It was on account of The Cheyenne Robber being so . . ." He made several attempts to choke down his emotions, but finally gave up, unable to say more.

That was all right. Everyone in the room understood the things he couldn't bring himself to say. That The Cheyenne Robber was the most virile man any of us had ever known. That any son produced by him would be a child of wonder. And they were. Sonny and his younger brother, Chaser, were exceptionally handsome, robust men. In brief, they were their father all over again.

Raven's Wing turned his grizzled head toward his ex-wife. "Old woman, I've hated you for a long time, but now that you've given me the truth about my son, I'm finished hating you." Lifting his head, he looked at me, his eyes now completely dry. "Tay-bodal, I think maybe I'm finished with hating you, too. But I don't know about that part yet."

As touching as that was, there were still one or two niggling details that needed clearing up. I put those questions to Raven's Wing. "If it's true you didn't care about the child's paternity, why was it I found you being so rough with your then heavily pregnant wife? You seemed to me to be a man tormented by jealousy."

"I was!" he yelped. "But only because she was such a terrible wife. She was always out, running who knew where. The day my brother died, she disappeared again. I asked some women if they'd seen her and they said yes, and pointed out of the camp. I was looking for her when I found Wolf Blanket carrying my brother's body. When White Bear ordered me to remain in my lodge, I had all that hate for Wolf Blanket, all that grief over my brother, building up inside me when she came home late—late even for her. She looked as if she'd been out rolling around in the grass. I guessed that she'd been rolling with The Cheyenne Robber and that neither of them had cared at all about the death of my brother or the helpless baby sleeping inside her. Thinking that, I went crazy."

I rounded quickly on Sarah. "Why did you never tell him the truth about his son?"

She rolled her eyes. "I tried to. Over and over again. But truth was wasted on him. He only believed what he wanted to. He wouldn't listen. He wanted The Cheyenne Robber to be the father. His dead brother wanted the same thing. And he wanted my baby, too. But not for the same reason Raven's Wing wanted it. Three Elks wasn't interested in being a good father. He only wanted to use my child to torment The Cheyenne Robber. But I couldn't get this fool to hear me about that or about his brother being a danger to my unborn child.

"I'm telling all of you, that man was tricky. And he was mean. I didn't dare try telling him the truth because the truth would have put him on to my sister. She was married to a very jealous man. He would have killed her and The Cheyenne Robber's child—the man now known as Sammy Thunder."

For a long moment I could only gape. I wasn't alone. The other men were gaping right along with me, for now we all knew that Sarah was talking about her middle sister, the one known as Keeps The Fire. I remembered her as being shy. Painfully so. She'd also been stunningly pretty. And Sarah was right about Keeps The Fire being married to a jealous man. Wildly possessive, he'd made his bashful wife walk with her head down so that no other man could look on her face. He was also known to challenge any man who dared try. Between his domination of Keeps The Fire and his brawls with men he suspected of trying to speak to her, I couldn't help but wonder where she had found the courage to meet with another man.

But then, I thought, she hadn't been meeting just any man. She'd shared stolen moments with The Cheyenne Robber. Suddenly, everything fit. The Cheyenne Robber was a legendary seducer. The harder a woman was to get, the more he wanted her. A profoundly shy, extraordinarily pretty, and extremely married woman must have driven him half crazy with desire. On Keeps The Fire's part, the fact that her lover was none other than The Cheyenne Robber had to have made her confident that he was the one man able to defend her against her husband's fury. Until she came up pregnant, and then the woman he truly loved, White Otter, began threatening him with divorce. Not wanting to loose his rightful family, he'd left Keeps The Fire carrying his child, frightened and confused over why his passion for her had abruptly vanished.

An image of Sammy Thunder rose up in my mind. Then, from the murky recesses, I dredged up the image of The Cheyenne Robber and overlapped Sammy's face with his. One looked nothing much like the other, Sammy's features being almost as delicate as his mother's. But the eyes . . . the eyes were identical. How could I have missed not knowing—for all of these years?

A trickle of sweat ran down my backbone as I said almost breathlessly to Sarah, "She had no one to turn to but you. She was your older sister, but you were stronger in spirit. She knew you would protect her. And that's what you were doing when you killed Three Elks."

She swallowed hard, one corner of her mouth nervously ticking. "Yes," she murmured. "I did what I had to."

She'd fallen back against the couch and was staring upward, seemingly engrossed by the shadows of the slow-turning fans playing across the ceiling's painted surface as the rest of us, absorbed in the moment stared at her, no one speaking, no one even twitching. But I think that each man present was also remembering her as she had once been: a very young girl named Always Happy. A girl frightened about Three Elks's designs on her child but, even above that, frightened for what might happen to her pretty, gentle sister should Three Elks discover the truth about her. It needn't be said that in his lust for vengeance against The Cheyenne Robber, Three Elks would have thoughtlessly destroyed Keeps The Fire.

"I planned just how to do it," Sarah said tiredly. Then she was looking solely at me, gratitude shining from her eyes that at last she was finally free to let go of her long-held secret. "My plan began with getting him off somewhere alone. That was the hard part. He was such a showoff, always strutting around acting big. Then that day I saw him walking out of the camp. I knew my time had come. He was very upset that I'd followed him until I told him that I was ready to do what he wanted—leave his brother and marry him. He didn't seem pleased. He confirmed this saying he didn't want to run off with me anymore. I asked him where was the love he'd been swearing for me, and he laughed. He said I was nothing to him. That he had a better way of getting even with not only The Cheyenne Robber but with Raven's Wing." She looked at her former husband. "He hated you. Hated you for trying to make him into as hard a man as you. He wanted to get even for all the times you tried to kick the softness and the laziness out of him. Making you look like a fool suited him perfectly, and he told me that the one who was coming was the one person who could do it."

She looked intensely back to me. "Hearing him say all of this made me scared. I didn't know who was coming, and I didn't know how much time I had. The only thing I knew was that this was my only opportunity because he would never meet me alone again. So I kept him talking, asked him who it was that could be so powerful to stand against Raven's Wing and The Cheyenne Robber. He wouldn't tell me. All he would say was that the one who was coming would do anything to have the great favor he was about to give.

"I asked what favor. He said, a favor that would benefit everyone involved. Except for"—she eyed me warily—"you," she finished in a breathy whisper. Then the pace of her speech picked up. "He said the one who was coming was only interested in one thing, and that was Crying Wind. I still didn't understand, so just to get rid of me he said that He Goes had agreed to say that you hated Crying Wind's little boy. That since you were still her recognized husband, you were planning to punish her by handing her boy over to He Goes. He said that once the one who was coming heard all of this and took these words to Crying Wind, he would then take her to He Goes to confirm everything. He said once that happened, He Goes would have his revenge against you, and Crying Wind would never speak your name again. He said that then the one who was coming would be able to make her his wife, and he would be so grateful that he would be willing to help him against The Cheyenne Robber and his brother. He laughed again and said, 'And all of this means I escape being burdened with you and my enemy's whelp.' "

My knees buckled; I landed hard in the chair directly behind me. So *that* had been Three Elks's game! And what floored me the most was that it would have worked. He Goes had hated me so much, he would have sworn to anything as long as he was assured that whatever he put his pledge to destroyed me completely. Losing Crying Wind forever would have done exactly that. No matter how I looked at it, the biggest mercy of my life had been Three

Elks's death. I swallowed down a lump of air as I listened again to the woman who was sitting just a few paces across from me, but now, because I was swimming in a daze, that short distance felt as wide as a canyon.

"He was going on and on about his big plan when he sat down. His sitting made it all so easy." Her voice carried a note of wonder. "He was still talking when I grabbed his hair and . . . The next thing I knew, he was rolling around in the grass, his hands on his throat, blood pouring through his fingers. I was scared. I started to scream. Scream for him to die. And then a hand came over my mouth, blocking the sound."

"Wolf Blanket's," I said just above a whisper.

Tears beginning to well in her eyes, she nodded. "He had a hold of me the whole time Three Elks was thrashing around. I thought I was finished. But then, he—" she choked—"he said, 'I heard all of it. Do you hear me, woman? I heard. I was hiding in the grass, listening. If you hadn't cut his throat, I would have.' When he released my mouth, I asked, 'What about your wanting Crying Wind?' And he said, 'She is a great lady. How could I have her with this one holding my honor in his fist?'

"I understood he meant that he'd heard enough to know that if someone as conniving as Three Elks had him, he wouldn't let go. That Three Elks would always be there to threaten any joy he might know. Then he did something wonderful. He shook me to my senses, told me to run, hide down in the grass, and not to come out until it was safe. Then he picked up Three Elks and carried him off.

"I did exactly what he said, and from where I hid, I saw this old coot over here"—meaning Raven's Wing—"beat up a truly good man. He took that beating on account of me. And all the while he was being accused, his own life in peril, he said nothing. While he was being held in the Grandmother's lodge, I went to him, begged his forgiveness. He told me to go, not to come back, not to do or say anything foolish because my first responsibility was the safety of my child."

Hearing this, I vividly recalled the look Wolf Blanket had tried to press on Deer Trail when that old man carelessly divulged the fact that a visitor had come to the Grandmother's lodge. Wolf Blanket hadn't wanted the old man to reveal the visitor's identity. He'd been right not to want any name mentioned because hearing who his visitor had been would have set me on to her.

"Once I was in my father's home," Sarah continued, "I wanted to tell everything, but I couldn't think how to do it without naming my sister. Then, too, my father was already worried enough that White Bear might hold a grudge against him for hitting Raven's Wing on the head. I thought if I could just have a little rest, I would find the right words to say. So I went to sleep. Unfortunately, my family allowed me to sleep almost the entire day away, and when I woke up, I heard about that poor old woman being sent out. I was too late to save her, so I did the only thing I could do. I wept for her." She said this to Hears The Wolf, who nodded slowly but said nothing. Sarah clasped a hand against her mouth as tears welled, then flowed. After a moment, she cleared her throat.

"Barely a week later, I had my baby—only to have my child snatched from my breasts, claimed by the man who didn't even believe it was his true son he was taking away from me. I was in such despair that I wanted to kill myself when . . . there was Wolf Blanket again. He began courting me. He knew my terrible crime, he ached with me for the loss of my son, and together we did our best to put all of it behind us. The day I married him, I went to him with a heart filled with all the love I had, even though I knew he was only marrying me because he couldn't have—"

"Crying Wind," I rasped.

"Yes," she sobbed brokenly. "He loved her. For all of his life, he loved only her. But he treated me the way he would have treated her. Like the virtuous born-to Onde lady that only she was. And for that I was grateful."

A long spell of silence ended when Big Tree emitted a low-toned whistle.

The tea party was definitely over. But the secrets shared remained in that room as we filed out to join the others sweltering in the garden. Then making his excuses for him, waving off Darryl's offer of assistance, I wheeled Hears The Wolf away.

"I'm certainly glad I didn't die today," he said as I struggled to guide the chair along the rutted path.

"I'm glad, too," I grunted.

"We had one last good fight, didn't we, my old friend."

"We certainly did." The chair shuddered and recoiled, flatly refusing to roll over a small stone. I had no choice but to maneuver the thing around it.

"Maybe I'll go ahead and die tomorrow."

Panting now because maneuvering that rolling chair

around a rock wasn't easy, I barked, "Or maybe I'll just find something else to keep you interested in living! It would serve you right."

Hears The Wolf threw his head back, cackling laughter at the endless sky.